ROCKET'S RED GLARE

A list of titles by James Patterson appears
at the back of this book

JAMES PATTERSON
THE WORLD'S BESTSELLING THRILLER WRITER
& MATT EVERSMANN

ROCKET'S RED GLARE

CENTURY

UK | USA | Canada | Ireland | Australia
India | New Zealand | South Africa

Century is part of the Penguin Random House group of companies
whose addresses can be found at global.penguinrandomhouse.com

Penguin Random House UK,
One Embassy Gardens, 8 Viaduct Gardens, London SW11 7BW

penguin.co.uk

First published 2026
001

Copyright © James Patterson, 2026

The moral right of the author has been asserted

Penguin Random House values and supports copyright. Copyright fuels creativity, encourages diverse voices, promotes freedom of expression and supports a vibrant culture. Thank you for purchasing an authorised edition of this book and for respecting intellectual property laws by not reproducing, scanning or distributing any part of it by any means without permission. You are supporting authors and enabling Penguin Random House to continue to publish books for everyone. No part of this book may be used or reproduced in any manner for the purpose of training artificial intelligence technologies or systems. In accordance with Article 4(3) of the DSM Directive 2019/790, Penguin Random House expressly reserves this work from the text and data mining exception.

Printed and bound in Great Britain by Clays Ltd, Elcograf S.p.A.

The authorised representative in the EEA is Penguin Random House Ireland,
Morrison Chambers, 32 Nassau Street, Dublin D02 YH68

A CIP catalogue record for this book is available from the British Library

ISBN: 978–1–529–97831–5 (hardback)
ISBN: 978–1–529–97832–2 (trade paperback)

Penguin Random House is committed to a sustainable future for our business, our readers and our planet. This book is made from Forest Stewardship Council® certified paper.

ROCKET'S
RED GLARE

PROLOGUE

Yusufiyah, south of Baghdad

Sergeant Jeff Carnes sat paralyzed in the passenger seat of the smoldering Humvee, slowly regaining consciousness after the concussion of the RPG.

As small-arms fire ricocheted off the Humvee's armored doors, Carnes tried to figure out how badly he was wounded. Garbled chatter was coming over the radio, but he couldn't shake his mental fog enough to answer.

The daze extended to everyone else in the vehicle. "I'm okay," someone said.

For how long? Carnes asked himself.

Despite mounting pain, he turned his head to glance out his window and saw two angry Iraqis looking back at him from about twenty feet away. He watched one of the bandits hand a grenade launcher to the other, as if in slow motion.

Carnes tried to muster the strength to make a last-ditch call for help on his radio, but his hands wouldn't work. All he could do was brace for the impact of the round and hope the inevitable—death—was instant and painless.

In even slower motion, he watched the black-and-white-checked shemagh worn on the head of his executioner ruffle in a nonexistent breeze. As the material seemed to lift off the Iraqi bandit's head, a ripple of dark red liquid erupted from underneath the headdress. The RPG fell to the ground and the man collapsed.

Sergeant Carnes had seen people die before, but never so suddenly or so violently. One second the terrorist was lifting an RPG; the next he was a corpse.

"Holy shit," he mumbled as he witnessed the accomplice also fold.

As his senses began returning, Carnes heard the muffled sound of allied gunfire coming from the driver's side of their vehicle, then saw a group of people in civilian clothes and body armor running at full sprint toward the enemy. A moment later he saw a small American flag held against his window by a tall man with Oakley sunglasses and a rhinoceros silhouette on his helmet.

Carnes read the man's lips: "We're the good guys. You're gonna be okay."

THREE DAYS LATER

CHAPTER 1

Nantucket County Jail
Nantucket, Massachusetts

My latest deployment in Iraq had ended in a blazing firefight.

Team Rhino and I had fought our way out of an ambush south of Baghdad, and Al-Qaeda had put a bounty on my head for greasing one of their suicide bombers.

Now I was standing in the middle of a holding cell on the tiny island of Nantucket in Massachusetts.

I'd made it back to the island via the last ferry, parked my car and grabbed my gear. *It's good to be home,* I'd thought as I walked to my house.

Actually, I hadn't exactly walked to my house—it was more like I sneaked in. And to be clear, the gear I'd grabbed was a Sig Sauer pistol, a Colt .45, an AR-15, and an HK MP5 submachine gun with all the fixings.

I get why that might've seemed suspicious.

Moments later, I was laid out on my kitchen floor, forcibly arrested by the seven legitimately deputized agents of the federal government who'd been waiting inside.

My overseas heroics didn't seem to matter much to the guys who'd thrown me in jail last night. I've been shot at on many occasions and made it out without a scratch. But this was my first time in jail. Not exactly Rikers or Sing Sing, I know—not much violent crime on this island since Nantucket's days as the whaling capital of the world—but a pain in the ass all the same.

So here I was, my pesky ego starting to hurt as much as the ass kicking I'd gotten from the feds earlier. I could see the local boys in blue and the other agents glancing over their shoulders at me in the cage. *Fuck them.* I just stared back. I didn't hide my contempt.

I shook my head, gathered my thoughts, and took stock of my surroundings, though I sure as shit wasn't planning on staying here long.

I had a cellmate. He was about eighteen—twenty, max—and not going to pose much of a threat. As soon as we made eye contact, he shifted nervously and looked at the floor. It must have been his first time in jail, too.

"Nice watch," I said.

"Uh, thanks," he replied, nervously trying to pull the sleeve of his sweater down over the glistening silver band. He was a tall, good-looking kid with a lanky runner's body that stretched to just over six feet. The few days of summer growth on his face didn't amount to much. He was dressed like a typical summer resident; shorts, sandals, an old fishing sweater—and a $6,000 Rolex, the Submariner with the green bezel.

I had an old stainless Submariner, which had cost me a little over three grand about fifteen years ago. No way this kid had spent a dime of hard-earned cash on his watch. Doubtful he'd ever worked hard enough even to get a blister.

"Is that the fiftieth-anniversary model?" I asked.

He seemed resistant to my line of questioning about the Rolex, so I figured I'd go in a different direction to boost his ego just a tad.

"So, what are *you* in for?"

"I wrecked a car," he said curtly. Then, echoing my emphasis: "What did *you* do?"

Touché, asshole.

"Well, I got into a fight with a state trooper. Or maybe a local cop—not quite sure. Apparently, because of those love taps, I got flagged as a threat to someone important—a senator, I think. Some asshole who's staying in the house next to mine. What are the odds?" I shrugged my shoulders and raised an eyebrow.

"Senator Harrison?" The kid was pretty astute.

"Yeah, that sounds right. You know him?"

"He and his wife have a house up here," he said sullenly.

Switching gears, I asked, "The wreck—anyone get hurt?"

"No," he sighed. "And I didn't really wreck it, either." He placed his head between his hands, rubbed his temples, and breathed deeply, as if deliberating how much he wanted to share with me.

"Well, what's the issue, then?"

He lifted his head from his hands and stammered, "Okay—Jesus—alright, I took my mom's car out for a ride with some friends."

"Then what happened?"

"We went to Madaket to see some girls. We had a few beers and then drove out on the beach. I got it stuck in the sand, and the tide came in. It's ruined."

The scene was getting more dramatic by the second.

"I hate it when that happens. What kind of car?"

He scowled and shook his head mournfully. "It was a fucking Porsche, okay? A Cayenne." He hung his head back down in shame.

I took a moment to consider the disconnect. This kid with the $6,000 watch had just ruined his mom's $100,000 car, while I'd gotten my ass kicked by a bunch of cops just for walking into my own house. *Classic Nantucket.*

I straightened up a little and tried to sound serious. In my best older-brother voice, I said, "Well, listen, man, seriously, no one's dead. Trust me, that's always a good start. And second, no one is shooting at you. A car is a car; your mom will have to get another one, right? Sure, I bet she's pissed right now, but deep down she's pretty psyched that you're still alive, I swear. Where do you live, anyway?"

"Summer or winter?"

It was the ultimate gentrified *Fuck you*. But this pretentious little asshole clearly had a wiseass streak, meaning the kid had potential. I decided to play along.

"I'll take WHERE YOU WINTER for $200, Alex."

"Palm Beach, Florida. We come up here in the summer. Our place is over on Cliff Road."

Of course it was. Cliff Road is probably the most expensive real estate on the island. People who live there don't worry about sunken Porsches. It's budget dust. They'll laugh about it at the yacht club or at the next commodore's ball or cotillion or whatever these people do for fun.

"Phillips?" said the desk sergeant at the cell door.

"Nathan R., that's me," I said, standing up.

Time for me to make my phone call. I gave my new buddy a knowing nod, stood, and walked toward the door.

The group of officers and curious onlookers had grown to half a dozen, including a pair dressed in business suits. Federal types, I assumed. I was about a foot taller than any of them and in far better shape than the entire group. While everyone watched me for signs of dementia or some other category of lunacy, I politely held out my wrists for the officer to cuff.

"Thank you, sir. May I have another?" I said to no one as I stepped to the telephone.

"One call," the desk sergeant said curtly.

I smiled my kindest smile and picked up the receiver. I dialed a phone number I knew by heart, a number known to only a handful of people in the world. If ever there was a man who could fix anything, Tristan Dent was that guy. He had always taken care of me.

The phone on the other end rang, as it always did, exactly three times.

"Nat, my man," the familiar voice bellowed down the line. "How's it feel to be the most wanted man in America?"

"Brother, I need a little favor."

CHAPTER 2

Harrison Campaign War Room
Baxter Road, Nantucket

Senator Coleman R. Harrison of Pennsylvania took a sip of whiskey and tried to concentrate on the heat sliding down his throat. Usually by his third drink he felt warm and loose, but not today. Today he felt nothing but fear and regret.

He should have felt on top of the world. He had a beautiful wife, a house in Bryn Mawr, and a summer place in Nantucket. He had access to a private plane and could walk into any Michelin-rated restaurant without a reservation. Hell, he'd been welcomed to palaces from Paris to Tokyo and had played polo with William, Harry, and even Charles himself.

And as a rising political star, he was closing in on the coup de grâce, the political Stanley Cup, the absolute cherry on top: winning the next primary on the way to accepting his party's nomination for President of the United States.

Senator Harrison's numbers were as solid as a front-runner's could get. He was an easy twelve points ahead of Theresa Larson, Governor of Colorado, and favored for the party nomination this August. And the pundits were already projecting a landslide victory over Harrison's presumed opponent, a former professional wrestler.

He was in political nirvana—and personal purgatory.

Harrison tried to focus on all the goodness in his life, yet try as he might, he could picture only the disappearing act. And he was the star of that one-man show.

He knew his wife, Elise Courville, had married him with dreams of becoming his first lady, politically and personally. Their home life was civil enough, but it had been loveless almost from Day One. Harrison's fidelity had lasted a year into their five-year marriage. They now slept in separate bedrooms, leaving him to rationalize that she had basically forced him into having affairs.

Of course, when Elise had abruptly kicked him out of the Cliff Road house they'd shared until a month ago, all his theories about her began to unravel—along with the advantages she'd provided.

The money was hers. The Gulfstream was hers. The house on the Main Line was hers. And she was taking it all away. "No more restaurants, no more polo matches, no more trips to Paris, and certainly no *Time* magazine cover or *Washington Post* headlines," she'd told him. "At least not the ones you want."

His wife made no mention of divorce, but she'd dropped a far worse threat: "I am going to tell my father."

Her words stung. As did the political reality that his father-in-law, Charles Courville, French ambassador to the United States, was not someone to have as an enemy.

Thankfully, Harrison could still count on his staunchest ally: his campaign director, Walter Fitzgerald. Fitzgerald called in a favor from a loyal donor and got them set up in a house on Baxter Road, on the other side of the island.

Fitzgerald also made sure to leak the fact that this location was Harrison's new campaign war room, a necessity for planning the grand strategy that would propel them from Pennsylvania Senator to Pennsylvania Avenue. "Publicizing it," Fitzgerald told Harrison, "will keep you from fucking this thing up even more."

Tonight's fundraising event at the house had gone smoothly, but Harrison had been acting on autopilot, barely holding it together beneath the surface as he glad-handed donors. The last ones hadn't left until well past one in the morning.

The senator looked out the window of the Nantucket summer home into the darkness, where the Atlantic waves rolled onto the eroding beaches of Siasconset. *Just like my luck,* he thought, *the waves keep crashing and crashing.* Nantucket was on the western edge of a nor'easter that would leave everything from New York to Maine socked in for the rest of the night.

Coleman Harrison was close to becoming the leader of the free world, but he wasn't in charge. What Walt Fitzgerald didn't know was that Elise Courville was not the only woman who'd given Harrison an ultimatum.

Aimee Sullivan—Harrison's twenty-eight-year-old redheaded press secretary/mistress, equally gifted at manipulating the media and her boss—was about to make him pay dearly for his sins. The night before last, after staffers had vacated the campaign war room, Sullivan was scheduled to prepare Harrison for the upcoming debate. But within minutes, they'd abandoned the office for the bedroom. The debate prep morphed into an unusually rough session featuring some of Sullivan's more sinister talents.

Afterward, Sullivan proceeded to explain her priorities. Despite her relative youth and her inexperience in military matters, what she wanted was a seat at the table of the National Security Council.

Harrison didn't know if he could resist Aimee Sullivan's unrelenting demands. *Give me what I want, Coleman, or you'll never fuck me in the Lincoln bedroom.*

CHAPTER 3

Nantucket County Jail

My conversation with Tristan Dent lasted less than ninety seconds. I hung up the receiver and was ushered back to my cell.

I sat down, crossed my legs, looked at my cellmate, and tried to make nice.

"My name's Nat Phillips." I put my hand out for a shake.

The kid straightened up immediately and had a surprisingly firm grip. "Josiah Wilson, sir, good to meet you. Everyone calls me Si."

He looked me in the eye. "Man, I really fucked myself this time. This is way worse than when I got bounced out of school." He muttered woefully, "My father wanted to teach me a lesson, so he called the cops. What do you think they'll do to me?"

"Who, these dudes?" I pointed with my thumb at the local cops outside the cell. "Take a look at that fat bastard, Si. Are you kidding me?"

"They told me my father's not coming for hours; he's so pissed at me." Si looked seriously distressed about being here in jail.

"It'll be alright," I told him. "Clearly your dad is not planning on having you face charges. I'd put money on him just wanting to make you sweat over your expensive joy ride for a little while longer."

I folded my hands around my crossed knee. "Look, it could be worse. Last week Al-Qaeda tried to teach *me* a lesson. After I killed one of their suicide bombers, they put a bounty on my head. I mean, seriously? The guy was on his way to die anyway, right?"

It was true. But the bounty was a risk the State Department wasn't going to take, especially after the ambush. That's what got me and my team sent home from Iraq less than two days ago.

Si and I had a few hours to kill before Tristan could get me out of here, so I told the kid why I'd been in Iraq, and sketched my work with Chesapeake Security and Training Company—CSTC for short.

Si was all ears, hanging on my description of life with an outfit I liked to call "Disney for gunslingers," where we routinely trained Delta and SEAL teams. I had the kid on the hook. How often does anyone get to spend the night in jail with a special operator?

I ran down CSTC's three operating groups: "Land, Sea, and Air. Each group consists of three teams, a who's who of special operators and security specialists. I lead Team Rhino in the Land Group. We also have Bear and Bull. Mako, Tiger, and Hammerhead are our Sea Teams, and Eagle, Hawk, and Falcon are Air."

I said, "If you've got to do a dangerous mission, at least do it with good people, a smile on your face, and try to have fun. That's what we do."

I continued the play-by-play, talking about the events in Iraq. "Anyway, if you ever meet my teammate Meg Fuller, don't believe a single word she says, 'cause I shot the guy first. Of course, after the lead injection, his thumb released the detonator and he went kerflooey and blew himself to smithereens. Hey, happy martyrdom to him. All I did was help the guy on his merry way without taking any of us with him, the fucker. The nerve of them getting all worked up over a dead suicide bomber. You see the irony, Si?"

He couldn't help smiling at my little routine, but seemed suitably impressed. Si showed some humility as he detailed his own situation. He was twenty years old, an only child, "in-between" colleges, hoping to begin a new slate at Dartmouth in the January term as a government major with a minor in computer science. Until then, he was dividing his time between Nantucket and Palm Beach, living at home with his parents, Alan and Constance Wilson.

Tough life.

Alan Wilson was chairman of the Wilson Group, one of the most successful hedge funds, rivaled only by BlackRock Capital. Old Al was a big hitter and definitely wasn't going to end up at the soup kitchen over his wife Connie's Porsche currently being parked in Davy Jones's locker.

Si and I bullshitted for a while and I had to admit, I really liked the younger Wilson. He seemed like a good kid. I suspected he just needed a bit more purpose and direction—and probably an ass kicking too, for good measure. Everybody needs one from time to time. I couldn't fault the old man for trying to get his only child energized by something other than girls and beer. Successful dynasties aren't normally run by delinquents.

I had some money saved from my last trip to Iraq and desperately needed some work done around my place—starting with repairing the doors the feds had just kicked off their hinges—and the kid obviously needed something useful to do with his time, so I suggested I talk to his dad about having Si come help me out. It seemed like a good fit for both of us.

At 6:00 a.m., I had just finished laying out the plans when the front door of the county jail opened to a man on a mission. The gray-haired sixty-something, dressed in a dark suit and carrying a briefcase in one hand and an umbrella in the other, walked directly to the duty officer's desk. He put his leather briefcase down, adjusted his tortoiseshell glasses, and went to work.

This must be Tristan's guy.

I couldn't hear the exchange, but the finger-pointing between the suit and the duty officer was heated. Then the officer picked up the phone and started dialing.

The duty officer practically stood at attention as he listened to whoever was on the other end, then motioned to another cop to unlock the door to our cell.

I told Si to call me later, and walked out to meet my liberator.

CHAPTER 4

"Samuel Starnes," the man in the suit said to me, holding out his card without taking his eyes off the duty officer.

The flustered sergeant finally hung up and flashed an apologetic smile at me.

"Mr. Phillips, I apologize for the inconvenience and the unfortunate events of last evening."

The officer paused as he searched his memory for the words he had just been told over the phone:

"The attorney general thanks you for your service to the country," he recited. "You are free to go, sir."

Holy shit—the attorney general? Say what you want about Tristan Dent, but don't ever say he isn't resourceful.

Without speaking another word, Starnes waved at me to follow him. We exited the building. A shiny black Mercedes sedan was parked in front, its engine running. There had been a storm earlier, but now the rain had just about stopped.

"I'm sorry I can't escort you home this morning, Mr. Phillips," Starnes said. "A Coast Guard chopper is waiting to take me back to Boston before the storm picks back up. Call me direct if anyone gets pissy with you."

He opened the sedan's back door, jumped in, and sped away.

I fished his card from my pocket and learned that the Honorable Samuel Starnes was a retired federal judge with senior status who, according to his card, worked on *Special Projects*. I had to laugh. Starnes would be a good friend to have on speed dial if Chesapeake Security and Training Company and Team Rhino were going to rise to their next great challenge: Rocket's Red Glare.

Sometimes I had to remind Tristan that the whole concept of CSTC had been my idea. What started out as me sharing war stories from Iraq had turned into a place for former military to shoot our guns and play with Army toys.

I remember that day vividly. Sipping bourbon and smoking cigars, Tristan and I—fast friends since our days together at Fort Benning—had been watching sailboats tack their way across the Choptank River. Since 9/11, the military's elite units had been searching desperately for offsite training areas, and I asked him about his farm. Tristan and his wife, Alison, owned 2,500 acres on the Eastern Shore of Maryland, perfectly wedged between two environmental preserves and the Chesapeake Bay.

We envisioned using all that land to make some dough from Uncle Sam.

Not that Tristan needed the money. Tristan Dent was not only the first millionaire I ever met—a few years later he became the first billionaire too.

His father, Henry Dent, had come home from Europe after fighting in the Hurtgen Forest and threw himself into work, by day selling real estate to returning veterans and by night tinkering in his garage building collapsible stretchers. Over the following decades, Henry had expanded his empire from affordable veteran housing to commercial real estate, and he now held a lucrative patent on a product highly sought after by the Department of Defense.

By the time Tristan entered the world, the Dent family fortune was worth a healthy $50 million. Thirty years later, it was worth a little over half a billion. Shortly after that, Tristan's then-girlfriend urged him to consider investing in an online bookstore, and that Christmas Tristan pulled the trigger twice — first buying a sizable chunk of Amazon.com, then buying Alison West a five-carat diamond ring at Tiffany.

Well before that, however, Tristan's father had mandated that his only child serve at least one enlistment in the Army before taking the reins of the Dent family business. Otherwise, control would go to a distant cousin.

Tristan didn't see the condition as an obstacle. He embraced it as a great adventure. Not only did he challenge himself to try out for the hardest unit at Fort Benning, Georgia (home of the Infantry), but he made the cut — and thrived. Had it not been for a broken back after a parachute malfunction, Tristan could have ended up a career Army Ranger.

That's where we'd met, and when I mustered out, the two of us built CSTC at a record pace. Within a year we were routinely getting asked to support missions downrange. Tristan worked the contracts and I found the people, building Team Rhino for the first overseas deployment in CSTC's young history.

The expert men and women I recruited didn't need individual training. Boston's finest son Jimmy Teagan was a friend to us both from our time with the Rangers. Oliver Smith and John

Paul Kennedy were 5th Special Forces Group guys I'd worked with in Baghdad. Oliver knew Wolf Kerr from the SF Combat Diver School in Key West. Tristan's wife, Alison, knew our commo guy, Stu Arden, from her ski-bum days in Jackson Hole. Rudy Martin, our first medic, was former Air Force; he'd been first on the scene when Tristan broke his back. They'd stayed in touch.

I'd personally recruited Meg Fuller from a graduate program at the University of Virginia, where I had once studied. One of my professors had given me a heads-up about a talented student in his National Security course.

"I wish she had been with me in Vietnam," he said of the young woman who was already fluent in French, Russian, and Spanish and learning more languages. "She's an analyst and an operator—the total package. An asset like her needs to be roaming the national security space, not studying it," the professor said. "Give Meg Fuller a few years and she'll be running either Langley or the NSA. Guarantee it."

★ ★ ★

Now I was wondering how the hell I was going to get back to the other side of the island.

I definitely wasn't going back inside to ask the cops for a lift, so I started to walk in the general direction of Siasconset. It was not yet 7 a.m., and except for a few trucks making morning deliveries the streets were still empty. Not even the damn coffee shops were open yet.

I spotted a hunter-green Range Rover pull into the spot in front of the county jail vacated by my new friend Starnes, and a fifty-something man dressed in the running shoes and shorts of a marathoner or triathlete jumped out from behind the wheel and headed inside. The second "man on a mission" I'd seen in the last hour. Had to be Si's dad. I debated sticking around, then decided against adding any more drama to young Josiah Wilson's life.

I pulled out my cell phone and left Tristan a message, thanking him for springing me from the hoosegow and letting him know I'd been doing some serious thinking about his new plans.

The concept—as Tristan had explained it to me after exfiltrating Team Rhino from Iraq—was to establish a team of US-based operators who could, if needed, augment the existing paramilitary and law-enforcement organizations within the United States during times of national crisis.

"A lawful, in-extremis operations network. We're calling it *Rocket's Red Glare*," Tristan had said. "I've been working on this for a while, Nat, and I think it's a perfect job for you and your team."

I still had some doubts, but the concept definitely had merit. This wasn't *Mission: Impossible* stuff. This was real. Emergency operations happening not overseas but right here in the US.

Team Rhino would be up for the challenge. I would give everyone a thorough briefing when they arrived in Nantucket on Friday.

As I trudged along the wet road toward the next bus stop, the green Range Rover crawled past me, Si in the passenger seat. The brake lights glowed and the luxury SUV came to a stop.

The driver's door opened and out stepped Si's dad, a powerful-looking fellow. I couldn't tell if he was pissed or happy, so naturally I prepared for battle.

"I understand you want my son to work for you," the man said without fanfare. "Who are you?"

"Nat Phillips," I said. "I just got back from a deployment in Iraq, but I live over in Sconset," I said, using the local nickname for Siasconset. "Could use some help fixing some stuff up around the place."

"Fair enough." He held out his hand as I approached. "Alan Wilson. Good to meet you. When can he start?"

"Well, sir, if you can give me a lift home, he can start as soon as we get there—unless this storm flares up again."

"Jump in."

Wilson's Rover was much nicer than my old Defender. The leather still smelled fresh from the showroom.

We chatted a little about my work, then turned to the state of affairs in Iraq. Wilson grilled me on the war effort and the details of the ambush I had mentioned to Si. Like his son, Alan Wilson nearly went into a trance when listening to a real story about battling terrorists. I liked him. He was a no-shit kind of guy—self-assured, intelligent, and on the right side of freedom.

I had to give him credit, too: Wilson seemed completely unfazed by the ridiculous events both his son and I had just experienced. The subject of the sunken Porsche never came up during the ride home. I liked him for that too.

Twenty minutes later, we parked in front of my house, now covered in remnants of yellow-and-black crime-scene tape. *Bet the local cops appreciated the chance to break out the tape for the first time in a while.*

I saw the elder Wilson glance at Senator Harrison's rental next door.

"That guy's always been an asshole, I swear," he muttered disdainfully.

Si and I grinned at each other and then back at his dad.

Alan and I made plans to have a beer that evening when I dropped Si off. After making me promise to repeat my ambush story to his wife later on, he gave Si a slap on the back and drove off.

CHAPTER 5

Harrison Campaign War Room
Baxter Road, Nantucket

"What the fuck were you *think*ing?!" Coleman Harrison's campaign manager, Walter Fitzgerald, screamed. Harrison watched as Fitzgerald's face flushed and spittle flew from his mouth. "You selfish *fuck*ing bastard, you have *fuck*ing ruined the entire *fuck*ing campaign!"

After almost ten years, the senator had withstood many of his campaign director's legendary tirades, but he had never seen Fitzgerald so angry.

"She wants *what?*" Fitzgerald hissed. He was almost apoplectic after hearing Harrison relay his press secretary Aimee Sullivan's demand.

"I hope like hell you enjoyed yourself," the campaign manager spat as he frantically paced the room. "You tell that bitch that it takes more than her tits, ass, and a Princeton degree to get a seat on the National Security Council!"

Harrison was careful not to make eye contact with the possessed man in front of him as Fitzgerald poured himself three fingers of scotch without offering any to the senator. He took a sip.

"Tell Aimee I want to talk to her. Just the three of us. You sit there and keep your mouth shut unless I tell you to speak."

Harrison watched Fitzgerald undergo a familiar transformation as the velvety liquid slid down his throat. The campaign manager's features softened as he went into hunting mode. Harrison, Fitzgerald, and Sullivan all agreed on one goal: Getting Coleman Harrison through the gates at 1600 Pennsylvania Avenue in a position of power. Secrecy was at a minimum in the political world, especially when all eyes were on the campaign trail. But Harrison had deluded himself into thinking that Fitzgerald would succeed in keeping the senator's affair with Sullivan under wraps. Fitzgerald would fix the problem and, in a few days, probably even press Harrison for some of the sordid details.

"When do you want to see her?" Harrison asked with new enthusiasm.

"Give me about twenty minutes, then bring her in. I have a few phone calls to make first."

The senator was already walking out the door when he realized that Fitzgerald had basically just dismissed him from his own office.

★ ★ ★

Coleman Harrison held the door as Aimee Sullivan walked confidently into the meeting. She carried herself like a woman in a strong bargaining position.

Walt Fitzgerald was sitting behind the large mahogany desk, cleared of all but a single sheet of paper.

"Aimee, please have a seat." He gestured to an overstuffed chair. "We're here to talk about how we can keep you engaged with our team."

"Walt, where I want to be is the true power center of this country," Sullivan said. "I want to broker policy options for the president. That means a significant position on the National Security Council. I will accept nothing less."

Fitzgerald leaned forward at the desk.

"Aimee, I mean no disrespect, but your limited credentials would not withstand the vetting process." He spoke softly, almost like a father talking with his daughter, looking to find her way in the world.

"None taken, Walt. My résumé is as good as any other member on the staff. I studied at the Kennedy School and my internships more than support the *fresh blood* mantra that we've been pushing the past year. You'll think of something, Walt. I have confidence in you."

She never blinked an eye.

Fitzgerald shifted his body and paused, as if deep in thought. Then he rose from the desk and handed her the sheet of paper.

"This is a nondisclosure agreement between you and me, Aimee. Though Senator Coleman is present, he can never be mentioned as a witness to anything we discuss today."

Sullivan started to speak, but he held up a hand to silence her.

"We will guarantee you a position on the National Security Adviser's staff under the following conditions. First, you agree to accept the position of a deputy undersecretary and promise to execute your duties with total support for the Harrison administration. Second, your personal relationship with the senator is officially over, as of now. Third, you agree never to mention this agreement. Got it? That's it. You sign it and we're all friends. But, Aimee, I must warn you: If you renege in any way, shape, or form, I will personally see to it that not only will you never work in politics again, you will spend a very long time in prison."

Walt Fitzgerald let his last comment linger, then smiled before breaking the silence.

"You've done great work, Aimee, and we want you with us for the next eight years. None of us can afford a slipup now. Our team is strong, and we'll work hard to get you up to speed in the switch from press to national security. In fact, let's do that on Friday. We'll also make an announcement of your new role at that time. Are we all in agreement?"

Beaming, Aimee Sullivan scribbled her signature and handed the agreement to Walt.

"Thanks for taking care of this, Walt. I'm excited to work for the president. And since we're all being honest here, you should know that I do have a video — you'll get it when we win. And by the way, I went to Georgetown, not Princeton."

She smiled at both men and left the room.

★ ★ ★

Aimee Sullivan walked through the elegant living room of the Nantucket cottage on Baxter Road, pulled out her cell phone, and tapped a number. A female voice answered.

"We're all set. Friday night. I'll give you the details later." Sullivan ended the call and headed to the kitchen in search of some coffee. There was a lot to do before the debate.

★ ★ ★

The woman who took Sullivan's call immediately made another call relaying the identical information.

The man in Paris said nothing.

Elise Courville hung up.

★ ★ ★

Walt Fitzgerald walked over to the door and slammed it shut. He stood over the cowering senator and fumed.

"You are a fucking idiot."

"I didn't know she had a video, I swear on my life." Coleman Harrison was almost in tears.

"Never mind," Fitzgerald said in disgust. "Asking you to grow a backbone is like asking a fish to use its feet. Get your head out of your ass and try to go one goddamn day without fucking me over, okay? I've got this taken care of. Just do your thing at the debate so we can get on with everything."

Harrison had a moment of clarity. "I still don't understand. How on earth can we pull off getting Aimee the job? There's no way in hell she'll pass confirmation." His personal life might have been a disaster, but Coleman Harrison did know his politics. "How are we possibly going to get this to work?"

"I don't think you really want to know, Coleman."

"Of course I do."

Fitzgerald moved in front of the senator and looked him directly in the eye. "Easy: We kill her."

"*What?!*" Harrison felt his stomach drop. His chief of staff was ruthless, but this was insane. "Walt, this has gone too far—I won't allow it!"

Fitzgerald poured himself another couple of fingers of the

brown liquid. He looked at Harrison with icy contempt, took a long pull from the tumbler, and smiled.

"Listen, Coleman, here's the deal: Your girlfriend is a drug addict."

"What? That's *bullshit,* Walt. What the hell are you talking about?"

"There are two kilos of Colombia's finest inside her apartment in Boston at this very moment. Believe it or not, she has it hidden in her closet—right next to all those toys you've both enjoyed so much."

Fitzgerald smiled as he watched the senator's incredulous look.

"That's right. See, what's going to happen is that your luscious lassie seems to have double-crossed some drug-dealing bandits—who, incidentally, have been sending all their cash back home to support the cause. Maybe the IRA. My guess is that they'll want to settle up on Saturday."

The speed of events Fitzgerald had set in motion plunged Harrison into shock. He needed a drink. He reached for the decanter and poured himself a stiff one. He took a long draw, swallowing hard as the liquid scorched his throat.

"We desperately need to get Elise back on the campaign trail with us," Fitzgerald continued.

Harrison looked up from his chair. "Who?"

"Your wife, you moron—*that's* who."

Fitzgerald sighed.

"Look, Coleman, you have two choices: One, you decide to be a stand-up guy all of a sudden, putting the White House out of reach, plus Elise cuts you off from her money and kicks you to the curb, leaving you with two things—jack and shit. Or two, you follow my plan, play by my rules, get what you want, and no one gets hurt. Well, *almost* no one."

Walt Fitzgerald laughed and drained his drink.

It took Senator Coleman Harrison exactly three seconds to make his decision.

"Tell me what I need to do."

CHAPTER 6

Baxter Road, Nantucket

Through the morning fog I saw a team of Secret Service agents posted on guard along the perimeter of the property. Though he hadn't yet secured his party's official nomination, Senator Coleman Harrison qualified for protection as a major presidential candidate.

The agents were dressed casually—save for the MP5 submachine guns strapped across their chests. I gave them a playful wave and watched as they immediately started talking into the palms of their hands. *The bad guy was back.* I figured one of them would be over to test the waters once whoever was in charge got wind of my arrival.

I tasked Si with his first job—making coffee—while I went to my garage to check on the concealed gun safe I had hidden underneath a workbench. I opened the biometric lock and pulled out my HK USP .40 pistol.

Just as I pulled the slide to the rear, I heard a female voice say sternly, "Put the gun down and turn around slowly."

No way this happens a second time in less than twelve hours. I put the pistol down, raised my empty hands, and turned around to see... a smiling face.

A fit, tan woman about five foot eight with shoulder-length blond hair and green eyes was standing in my garage dressed in khakis, a polo shirt, and hiking boots. She was alone and didn't have her gun drawn.

"Too soon?" she teased. "Sorry, I couldn't help it." She held out her hand. "US Secret Service Special Agent in Charge Rowan Anderson."

How could I forget the woman who'd had me arrested? She looked to be in her mid-thirties and had a drop holster and a pistol strapped to her thigh.

"Funny," I snorted. "The senator still alive?"

"For at least one more day," she said. "Look, I'm sorry about last night. But you *were* skulking around in the dark with a bevy of weapons."

"I'd hardly call it a *bevy*. It was more like a tiny collection of guns. And I wasn't *skulking*—I was moving quietly and deliberately."

She flashed me a grin. Anderson had a lovely smile and wore no ring that I could see.

"We had to take the potential threat even more seriously than we do the usual whack jobs running around these days, especially given the ruckus you caused with that state trooper. The rear security detail enjoyed that bit of excitement."

"Can't believe I missed the rear security clowns. That

was sloppy. I guess I deserved the beatdown," I muttered sheepishly.

"Well, we had you dead to rights for sure, but you were formidable. I will give you that." She chuckled. "I'll have your *tiny collection of guns* back here this evening. I assured my boss that we would take good care of you. My ass still has bite marks from the chewing, by the way. You've got some mighty powerful friends. Peace?"

She moved closer and once again extended her arm. She had a good handshake.

"Peace."

Anderson checked a lot of boxes for me: intelligent; funny; gun-toting; tough. Plus she was really pretty, and when she turned around I checked her ass for the bite marks she'd mentioned; it looked perfect, from what I could tell. My teammate Wolf would approve.

I was suddenly tongue-tied. At work, on the job, even during a gunfight, I could talk to women as equals and friends. Out in the regular world, however, I always seemed to be too much or too little—a clueless train wreck, always somehow getting seventeen steps ahead of myself and messing things up before they even started. It was worse than an Achilles heel—I probably needed some kind of romance therapy to cure my Achilles *leg*.

Just then, Si rounded the corner into the garage holding two cups of joe.

Oh, thank God. Perfect timing.

I introduced the two. "Josiah, this is Special Agent in Charge Rowan Anderson of the United States Secret Service," I said in my best radio-announcer voice. "She's the one who arrested me, beat my ass, and stole my guns. She isn't a very nice person, but she is the reason you now have a summer job."

Si laughed. "Thank you for beating his ass so that I can have a summer job, ma'am."

"Hello, Josiah. As you can see, I do like to steal and pillage and get into fights. But as much as I'd like to hang out with you two desperadoes," she said with a smile and a wink, "I've got important work to do."

"Speaking of desperadoes," I warned her, "the rest of my crew will be heading up later in the week to create havoc. Be on the lookout for suspicious types."

She took it like a champ and headed off to do her Secret Service duties.

When Si and I caught each other staring as she left, we laughed self-consciously, clinked our coffee mugs, and headed out to fix my house. The big renovations would start later, but Si seemed as excited as I was to get cracking on them.

We spent most of the day replacing the front door and doing small cosmetic jobs. The kid had a keen work ethic and never once sandbagged it. He was pretty decent with a hammer and surprised me by even knowing the basics of wiring and electricity.

Seeing him in action, I asked how he had acquired such an impressive skill set. It seems the Wilson family was not afraid of hard work.

According to Si, while his parents employed a large staff, they preferred—when possible—to personally handle the maintenance on both their homes.

Young Wilson was also a competitive sailor, fluent in French, and apparently a top-rated squash player. Most of all, he had a desperate need to be part of something meaningful.

We had a good time together, and by the end of the day I had offered him another job: working for me at CSTC until he returned to college. A trip or two over to the sandbox would give him a lifetime of challenge and direction.

I just needed to convince Alan and Constance Wilson that it was a good idea for their baby boy to go to Iraq.

CHAPTER 7

Colorado Governor's Residence
Denver, Colorado

"You're twelve goddamn points down, do you hear me?" The veins in Mark Larson's neck were throbbing as he glared at his wife, Governor Theresa Larson, from across the room. "And if your run for president is finished, then I will be finished with you."

The Larson machine was not a force to be underestimated. Mark had made sure of that. Plenty of people out there would like nothing better than to take a swing at him. People who would be only too happy to tie him down and make him confess to all the conniving and scheming and shitty things he had done.

His wife included.

Governor Larson silently counted to ten, exhaled audibly, and reached for a cigarette. She continued to stare at him as he paced the room. With each step she pictured smashing his handsome face with the big crystal ashtray on the coffee table in front of her. But she knew it was too heavy, and that she wasn't fast enough.

"Twelve points is a steep deficit," Theresa admitted. "A lot of stars will have to align, but I know it can be done. Senator Harrison is a joke of a candidate, but somehow he's leading. What's the force behind him? I know his wife's family is connected, but that much? I don't think so."

Before her husband could interrupt, Theresa continued.

"We know him for what he is: a social-climbing parasite and a philanderer. But the public loves Harrison's charm and his lifestyle; they consider him the closest thing to American royalty since JFK. And his campaign expertly feeds that *Kennedy redux* story to a willing electorate desperate for another fairy-tale narrative."

"Well, Harrison's running a smart campaign," Mark argued. "It's you who cannot afford another mistake. We've worked for this very moment for years, yet you play it like it's no big deal—like it's a game," he seethed. "It's not a fucking game, Theresa."

"Mark," she answered earnestly, "everything has been fine with our strategy so far. I don't understand—why are you so upset over an off-the-cuff comment?"

The governor had been boxed into a tight corner in a recent *Morning Joe* interview about her policy toward Taiwan and microchips, and whether she would or would not defend the island from the Chinese. Of course she wouldn't let the Chinese have free rein over the island, but all she'd said was that the current administration hadn't figured it out yet, and that such a complicated foreign-policy decision would require the expertise of her future advisers. She never said anything about independence. Case closed.

ROCKET'S RED GLARE

It was a safe answer to a loaded question. Any other politician would have given the same vague answer. But apparently that wasn't good enough for her husband.

"We only have one chance at this!" Mark yelled, his face crimson with rage. "It is real, and it is war, and like I said, if you are out then I am out."

He stormed out of the room and slammed the door hard enough to make several paintings rattle against the wall.

The governor lit another Marlboro, took a drag, and indulged in her recurring fantasy: killing Mark herself. She pictured him on his knees, crying, begging her not to pull the trigger as she stood over him with a Walther pistol. She imagined the whispered sound of the .22LR bullet leaving a suppressed barrel, and the sight of the small hole in his forehead as he fell backward to the floor.

Then she'd shoot him in the balls.

The thought made her smile. She would make him pay one day.

Yet she had to admit that Mark was right about how far they'd come together. Her rise from local school board to the state legislature to the governorship—and now, the national stage—had been swift and magical.

With Mark or without him, Theresa Larson had to believe she could still grasp the prize. As her uncle liked to say, *Bad things happen to bad people.*

CHAPTER 8

Wilson Estate
Cliff Road, Nantucket

It was time to meet the Wilsons on their home turf.
Si gave me directions to his family's "cottage" on Cliff Road, which overlooked the most stunning expanse of waterfront I had ever seen on this island or any other.

I admired the circular cobblestone driveway, the manicured lawn as lush as the putting greens at Augusta National, and a flagpole flying Old Glory, POW/MIA, and the Wilson family crest.

Si introduced me to his mother and went to get cleaned up. Connie Wilson was clearly happy to have her wayward son home.

She was a natural beauty with a genuine smile. Like her husband, she was a fit, tan fifty-something with a few light streaks of gray in her hair, and looked like she'd stayed active with years of tennis and maybe some Tae Bo or spin classes, definitely a lap or two down at the club. She wore a high-end version of the Nantucket summer uniform: red shorts, a white tee, and flip-flops.

We chatted comfortably, comparing favorite spots on the island, as Connie gave me a quick tour of their eight-bedroom place, which was as tastefully appointed as it was architecturally impressive. It had to have cost north of $15 million.

When we moved to the large veranda overlooking the Atlantic, Alan brought us each a beer in a green bottle. I liked that despite their clear wealth, the Wilsons were down-to-earth, beer-in-a-bottle kind of people.

Straightforward, no bullshitting around, right up the gut without a chaser, I sprang my plan on them.

I suggested that effective immediately, Si come work directly for me and CSTC until he went back to college in January. I explained a little more about what I did on a normal day, then laid out a timeline: In a few months, we'd take stock to see if he wanted to make a deeper commitment.

"Would he be carrying a firearm?" Connie asked somewhat nervously.

"After sufficient training he would be licensed to carry a weapon, but only if he traveled overseas with me."

Alan was smiling. "I think it would be a great opportunity for him, Nat. Hell, I still remember going through airborne school at Benning."

I'll be damned. Alan Wilson, scion of the financial world, was a member of the Benning Boys Club.

To my relief, Connie was all smiles too.

When I mentioned that some of my team members were coming to the island this weekend, she went directly into party-planning mode. Before I knew it, a CSTC welcome-to-Nantucket party at the Wilson shack was on the calendar.

When I dipped inside, I encountered the youngest Wilson — a handsome devil now that he'd cleaned himself up. The peach fuzz was gone; his sandy hair was neatly combed; and he was dressed in a summer uniform much like his parents'.

I updated Si on his new job, which would officially begin after we fixed the drywall, rewired the garage, repaired some leaky faucets, and painted all the windows.

He smiled as brightly as his parents had out on the veranda.

Who knew what the future might hold? But maybe I had just hired the next Tristan Dent.

★ ★ ★

As Alan brought out a second round of beers, he pointed to another palatial estate farther down the beach and told me it belonged to Senator Coleman Harrison. "I can't believe we're neighbors with that asshole."

Connie shook her head, smiled, and gave her husband an embarrassed look. "Nathan, my husband seems to have forgotten his filter this evening."

"What, Connie? Coleman is without a doubt the most pretentious asshole I have ever met on this island — which is saying something. And he may be our next president."

"Commander in chief," I noted.

Alan gave me a look that reminded me I had promised to relate my ambush story to his wife. I hesitated. Telling a member of the Benning Boys Club a war story was one thing, but giving a blow-by-blow description of a firefight to Connie felt a little different.

I didn't want Mother Wilson getting cold feet this early in the game.

FOUR DAYS EARLIER
Operation CODEL

CHAPTER 9

Baghdad Forward Operating Base

Operation *CODEL* was a special one for Team Rhino. All participants, military and civilian alike, agreed on one point: This engagement carried the weight of history.

The occasion: a meeting among both Sunni and Shia sheiks and the US Army's top command to solidify the American commitment to peace and security throughout war-torn Baghdad Province.

The location: the Russian nuclear power plant on the banks of the Euphrates River, southwest of Baghdad. Long abandoned by the Soviets, the mammoth half-completed facility had been commandeered by Al-Qaeda when the war began as a place to commit torture and murder.

In late 2006, when US forces delivered a healthy load of lead to the enemy and mounted a final push toward the west, Al-Qaeda's safe haven had been taken over, and the badlands of Baghdad became a little safer.

This seemingly impossible feat was in large part due to an unlikely alliance of Sunni and Shia tribes throughout the region southwest of Baghdad. With a lot of north-south headshaking, countless cups of chai, and a homicidal quantity of cigarettes smoked with the local sheiks, the US forces had been able to convince the two tribes that the definition of success was playing nicely together.

Since then, the abandoned power plant had been the only setting where US, Sunni, and Shia forces worked under practically the same roof. There was the pesky issue of total trust—never completely solidified by all members of the tribes. But with a limitless supply of US dollars for all who renounced Al-Qaeda and demonstrated their support for the cause, the Sunni and Shia were at least civil to one another. In fact they made it a point of honor not to allow any terrorist attacks in the area.

Still, foreign fighters often crossed into Iraq from Syria, then traveled unmolested to the western banks of the Euphrates River. For years the local village near the power plant had been sympathetic to the terrorists, its surrounding sands stained with a good deal of American blood. It was another nasty place for the enemy to hide.

★ ★ ★

The civilian guest of honor at tonight's meeting was Congressman Martin Jennings, chairman of the House Armed Services Committee. As a statesman, Jennings was well regarded on both sides of the aisle: He was a social liberal but a military hawk.

Jennings's father had been an island-hopping Marine during some of the fiercest fighting in the Pacific theater of the Second

World War. A Silver Star recipient at Tarawa, Private Jennings had lost a leg protecting his fellow Marines.

The one lesson Jennings senior instilled in his young son: "You don't fuck with soldiers, sailors, and certainly not Marines." Martin Jennings remembered his father's message. Even with his otherwise left-of-center ideals, he was fiercely committed to those who had served—including Lieutenant General Chase Montgomery, commander of Multinational Forces/Iraq. General Montgomery had invited Congressman Jennings to the Russian power plant to acknowledge him as a military ally back on Capitol Hill.

A consummate warrior and a skilled politician, General Montgomery was in it to win it. His thirty-year career in the Army had been nothing short of historic. He'd served in the toughest units. He'd done hard tours in Korea and Germany. He'd taught at his alma mater, West Point, and had earned a master's degree in National Security and Strategy at the War College. The general had even made time to get an MBA from Georgetown while on assignment at the Pentagon.

Montgomery had collected his third star after successfully leading the infamous 82d Airborne Division to many victories in the war on terror. The president and the Secretary of Defense had handpicked him to assume the lead in Iraq.

Jennings would be flying to the meeting in a Black Hawk helicopter. Team Rhino would follow in our CSTC armored vehicles, traveling approximately one hundred meters behind an eight-vehicle convoy of US Army forces.

Among the mission VIPs riding in the Army convoy were some CNN reporters and a few straphangers looking for face time with the boss.

Two deputies working for Congressman Jennings—William McKay and Travis Hunter—were less than enthusiastic about being relegated to the trailing vehicles with the likes of mere security contractors. Back on 15th Street in Washington, bragging rights would be in play at the Old Ebbitt Grill when this congressional delegation—or CODEL—returned, so a photo op with the top brass was career gold. A photo op with CSTC did not offer quite the same cachet.

After the briefing from the Army commander on routes and protocol, the drive would take about an hour. Thankfully there had been no significant activity along the routes in the past twenty-four hours. In fact, Army supply trucks preparing for the big day had made the trip several times in the last week without incident. There was some good supporting firepower, should things go south.

Always a good day when you don't get blown up. The odds were in our favor.

CHAPTER 10

The road to the Russian nuclear power plant

We had driven over to the Army HQ at noon in order to make the final coordinations prior to our 1 p.m. departure. Now, as we eased our convoy of SUVs into the armada of other Humvees in the staging area, I was acutely aware of the tense stares soldiers were giving our custom-built Range Rovers.

We parked our CSTC SUVs a safe distance away from the Army's Humvees. *This won't be so bad,* I thought as we approached the command group, Meg Fuller walking beside me. *The soldiers understand.*

I quickly realized they weren't at all happy to see me—but they were very happy to see Meg. For a variety of reasons, we had done well in hiring her—not least of which was that as an attractive woman, her mere presence could sometimes help defuse testosterone-laden situations. Sexist? Maybe. But still true.

I found the captain in charge of the convoy and reintroduced myself. He was a good guy, and I could sense the stress he was carrying under his ninety pounds of gear. He gave me a quick update, careful not to roll his eyes with contempt. As usual, the powers that be had decided a mission of such high visibility would be better led by an officer more senior than this paltry captain. A major from HQ would assume the role of commander for this trip. The captain had been relegated to passenger status.

Shit happens, was all I could muster.

I found the major walking to his vehicle in his way-too-clean uniform, looking pleased with himself and his new status as convoy commander. He was less pleased with the responsibility of lugging my team along as I half-trotted to his side and put on my best façade of *You're in charge and I'm here to follow.*

We did a quick plan rundown from A to Z. I handed him one of our CSTC encrypted mobile radios so that he and I could stay in contact over our own frequency as a backup. Then he begrudgingly asked if I needed anything.

"We're all good here, sir," I replied. "See you at the power plant. Keep it under ninety—and don't walk off with my radio, okay?"

The look the major gave me as he headed to his Humvee telegraphed *You're an asshole.*

As I walked back toward my SUV, Rhino 2, I gave Team Rhino the hand signal to mount up and get ready to depart. I could see Meg, Oliver Smith, and John Paul Kennedy laughing at me for playing Mr. Nice Guy. They knew exactly what had transpired with the new commander. I shook my head and smiled as I made my way to where my VIPs were waiting for their ride.

I beckoned the two congressional staffers, William McKay and Travis Hunter, over to the hood of Rhino 2, where I unfolded my map and began my brief. Neither one had the slightest idea where we were heading, but both bravely attempted to look like they did.

"Bottom line," I said, "is that, unless I tell you otherwise, you touch nothing and you do nothing. Put on your helmets and enjoy the ride."

With that, I donned my Kevlar helmet and sat down in the front passenger seat. With a simple touch of a button, I could talk to all the members of our team internally or communicate with the major in his vehicle, as well as with our command center. I made checks with all of our vehicles. So far, so good. Even the major was kind enough to answer my radio call.

Wolfgang "Wolf" Kerr was my driver. Whether it was regional pride or a love of Mozart, his German mother had never explained naming her firstborn son *Wolfgang*. But for as long as he'd been alive, his American father had called him *Wolf.*

The nickname fit perfectly. Wolf served ten years as a Green Beret before leaving the US Army. He enjoyed some time in the reserves, but found it somewhat unfulfilling. After finishing his bachelor's degree in Colorado, he floated between federal jobs with the FBI and the Secret Service. He knew Oliver and JP via Special Forces, and when he heard that Tristan Dent had opened the door to CSTC, Wolf came running.

"Rhino Base, this is Rhino 2, preparing to depart for Russian power plant, two PC for delivery, eighteen total. Over."

"*Roger, Rhino 2, good copy. Break. We're tracking through GPS and monitoring command frequency from this location. Over.*"

I watched as the wheels of Rhino 1 started to roll forward. We were on our way. The excitement, fear, and challenge of the mission hit me all at once, as usual. I said a quick prayer for safe travels and gave the command to move out.

I would have felt better knowing that CSTC's Team Eagle was on standby. We had a fleet of armed helicopters for convoy protection, each one equipped with six-barreled mini-guns capable of neutralizing just about any armed threat we could face on the ground. But we wouldn't have access to the helicopters today.

Moving a convoy of twelve vehicles out of a base with fifteen mile-per-hour speed limits is a clumsy endeavor. The goal is to get everyone spaced evenly, moving at the same rate of speed, and functioning as one large element. Of course, it takes some time to get synchronized. Inevitably, a young driver throws off all the vehicles behind him by driving too fast or too slow.

Those at the tail end of the convoy—as Team Rhino was today—feel every mistake made by those in front. Profanity becomes an art form in the community of arms. My drivers immediately began cursing into my earpiece.

"Okay, children," I answered as nicely as possible. *"Everyone calm down, pay attention—and shut the fuck up."*

CHAPTER 11

Once Rhino 4 cleared the last gate of the base, we started to flow. My gunners in all four vehicles gave running observational commentary. Everything was a threat to us until proven otherwise: cars moving at the wrong speed, a man standing where he shouldn't be, kids playing too close to the highway.

North of Baghdad, US college names were used for highways; east of Baghdad it was baseball teams; and to the south, where we were headed, were NFL teams. The plan was to drive south from Baghdad along Route Cowboys and then head west along Route Ravens, split southwest along Route Packers to the Euphrates, then head north along the river on Route Steelers.

The trip down Cowboys was pretty easy. We hit Ravens and headed west. The convoy had to slow down considerably on this two-lane road. Most roads in Iraq ran parallel to a system of canals and small rivers. The mixture of soil and constant irrigation allowed invasive reeds to grow incredibly tall and so thick that it's impossible to see more than six inches beyond them.

They also grew right up to the road, providing ideal hiding spots for the enemy to place IEDs or rocket ambushes.

★ ★ ★

The chatter on the intercom picked up. My team was on their game. We made it onto Route Packers safe and sound.

We passed the market in the village of Yusufiyah, then the outlying shops and derelict structures that bordered the street. It was not out of the ordinary to see women dressed head-to-toe in their black burkas walking next to donkeys pulling carts, while a gaggle of men sat under the shade of the buildings watching them work.

The locals were mostly immune to the sight of American Humvees, but they took instant notice of CSTC's armored Range Rovers. Some of the men reacted as if they'd seen spaceships.

I called back to John Paul Kennedy in Rhino 4. As usual, everyone had already noted it.

"Roger, boss—I got it covered. Break. They're still sitting there. Rhino 1, anything ahead?"

"Negative, Rhino 4—we're about seventy-five meters behind the convoy," Oliver replied. "It opens up about fifty meters ahead. Nothing but an old garage on the north side. You should be passing it about now. Over."

Oliver Smith was as cool as they come. The six-footer looked like NFL Hall-of-Fame linebacker Lawrence Taylor. During a fight he had ice water in his veins.

The sun was high in the sky and the temperature must have been about 120 degrees as we headed north along Route Steelers.

I could see the huge cooling towers of the old power plant ahead. We made it there in just over an hour.

"Okay, kids, we're here," I said over the intercom. "Rhino 1, just follow these cats wherever they go. Break. I'll get out with the PC and link up with you all once I figure out what's going on for the trip home."

As the vehicles came to a stop in the parking area, I gave one last command. "Go make some friends—and don't let anyone steal our shit. Meg and I will be back in a few."

I turned to William McKay and Travis Hunter, the two junior VIPs wedged in the back seats, and waited as they unfolded themselves.

"Congratulations, gentlemen, this leg of the journey was a success," I announced.

They'd been upset at the prospect of traveling with us before, but now they were proud of their first trip off the Forward Operating Base as part of Team Rhino for the day. Though their L.L. Bean rugged outdoor clothing was drenched in sweat, Hunter and McKay posed happily in front of the Range Rover.

Meg and I left our gear in the vehicle and headed off to find the major.

CHAPTER 12

Russian nuclear power plant

I could hear the distinct sounds of Black Hawk helicopters in the distance. Two helicopters were designated for transporting the general and his crew, while four others served as armed escorts. I was certain the fast movers were also on standby.

The F-14s and British Tornadoes would be able to drop a ton of bombs and cannon fire on any unfortunate creature attempting to make a statement. I'd put money on other government agencies also being out in abundance, and countless hordes of infantrymen set up in concentric circles of security around the plant.

Nothing unexpected was going to get near, let alone inside, this place in the next four hours. I saw silhouettes of the guards in their tower perches and knew anyone trying to move toward them would suffer certain death from one of the .50-caliber sniper rifles.

Meg left my side to find the command center to check in with the intelligence officer. She knew the ropes; she almost always returned with some golden nuggets of information that higher echelons had purposely denied us. She was like that.

I was feeling a bit out of place with all the soldiers around. It had been different when I wore the uniform. Now I was an outsider.

In Baghdad I had spotted a few familiar faces around the FOB from time to time, but today I recognized only Chris Miller, the command sergeant major. As the senior enlisted guy, he was the big cheese. And he was a warrior for sure.

Miller stood about six foot eight and lived on coffee and tobacco, yet he could run a six-minute mile without breaking a sweat. I heard he got a Distinguished Service Cross for a fight in Afghanistan on one of his seven deployments. Across the globe, it was leaders like Chris who made sure American soldiers remained in good hands.

Given all the shit Chris had going on today with the dog-and-pony show, I stayed out of his way. I found a chair in the back of the meeting area and took a seat.

The press pool was in one area, the sheiks in another, the soldiers all around. And then there was me. I could feel more eyes on me with every passing moment. My baseball hat bearing the embroidered rhinoceros must have been the giveaway that I was "one of those." Half of those assembled saw me as a special operator; the other half thought I was really cool.

I almost fell out of my chair when someone barked at me loud enough to be heard in Baghdad: "What the fuck are you doing in my AO?"

I looked up to see Command Sergeant Major Chris Miller speaking directly to me. I could feel my face flush as I reached for a witty comeback.

"Sergeant Major," I said with a grin, "I have those little blue pills you ordered." A private standing beside him did a double take and tried to stifle a smirk.

"You," Chris said, pointing a large finger at me, "had better drink some water, since the heat has obviously fucked up your cranial algorithms." The Alabama native gave me his best Chattahoochee River smile. "And you," he said, switching his focus to the hapless private, "do some fucking push-ups till I get tired."

The private hit the floor.

After a quick reunion, Chris told me to head over to his command center for a cup of coffee while he gave the last few orders for the Iraqi gala. We'd heard the Black Hawks land during our tête-à-tête, so we knew Congressman Jennings and General Montgomery must have arrived at the helipad.

As Miller walked away, I noticed the private still knocking out push-ups. I leaned over and told the soldier to get up.

"Stay the fuck away from my men, asshole." Chris Miller had eyes in the back of his head. "Recover, stud," he ordered the private without missing a beat.

The young man jumped up, straightened his uniform, and went about his business.

Woe to the terrorist who meets this dude in a dark alley, I mused.

CHAPTER 13

It was quite the welcome party. The CNN crews were busy trying to get clear pictures of the group, including the diplomatic entourage. The soldiers were standing in formation, trying not to take a peek, and the Iraqis were hanging around trying to figure out what the hell was going on.

I headed off in the direction of the coffeepot in the ops center. Five minutes later, Command Sergeant Major Chris Miller showed up again, shaking his head. I could sense his frustration.

Some things never change. The soldiers in the operations room immediately tried to look busy, hoping to avoid any unpleasant encounters with their annoyed command sergeant major.

We sat down in the air-conditioning and had a cup of stiff, black, Army coffee. Chris was tired. This was his fourth combat tour in Iraq. We caught up on news of friends we knew in common—who was where and who had done what.

With her own impeccable timing, Meg Fuller walked up. She had finished her intelligence-scavenging hunt and saw me sitting with Chris. As I made the introduction, I saw the sergeant major's slightly raised eyebrow, the imperceptible reconnaissance.

"How do you do, Sergeant Major?" she said as she shook his hand. "I was just over with the S2 guys—super helpful."

Classic Meg.

Obviously, Chris had not given anyone in the intel shop the authority to speak to her, but there was nothing he could say now other than *You're welcome.*

They exchanged pleasantries and took jabs at me for a few minutes before Meg hit Chris with a question: "What's the latest on the Jaysh al-Mahdi cell in Yusufiyah? Any issues these days?"

Yusufiyah had been the site of some significant firefights. When the surge came to town, most of the foreign fighters had fled west of the Euphrates. Unfortunately, the current inhabitants still maintained a risky loyalty to the Shia leader, Muqtada al-Sadr, who also controlled the militant Jaysh al-Mahdi, aka JAM or the Mahdi Militia.

JAM were ruthless killers who followed al-Sadr's directives to a T. Outwardly, al-Sadr cautiously supported the new Iraqi government. But there was always that lingering tension between Shia and Sunnis. We all knew that if al-Sadr ever gave the word, sectarian violence would escalate uncontrollably.

Chris gave me a hard look out of the corner of his eye, then smiled.

"About two weeks ago, we started hearing interpreter chatter that JAM had returned to Yusufiyah and was setting up a cell for future operations."

Over the last six months, a ceasefire declared by al-Sadr had held, but it was a tenuous decree. If JAM had reentered Yusufiyah, a mixed village of Sunni and Shia farmers, the chance of violence increased exponentially.

Apparently, the US and Iraqi forces had hosted a sit-down with the local Sunni sheiks. The thought was that a focus on pacifying the Sunnis would help keep the tension low and the roads wide open for future Iraqi commerce and good old-fashioned nation building. Unfortunately, when news of the unilateral meeting made its way back to the Shia Muqtada al-Sadr, the lug nuts started to come off the wheels. Within twenty-four hours, JAM flags and black-pajama-wearing militiamen were spotted throughout the small city.

Nothing good was ever going to come from men in black pajamas, Chris said. The bottom line seemed to be that everything was fine for now, but the potential for carnage was back on the radar. The local sheiks were here today to do some damage control without alerting Congressman Jennings to the potential disaster. Ostensibly, they would talk general peace terms and the usual money issues, but in the off-the-record comments, the sheiks were going to be instructed by General Montgomery's emissary to get their collective shit straight and keep the peace.

"After three years in this soup, I don't trust a single one of them," Chris sighed. He leaned back as if in deep thought and rubbed his temples. Then my giant pal rocked forward on his chair and looked at me and Meg.

"You watch your ass, Nathan, Miss Fuller. This shit is on the edge, right here and right fucking now. It's been too quiet, and the locals are tired of watching the goons we're paying off get rich. I fucking feel it, my friend. Someone in one of these tribes—don't know which—is going to blow this whole deal right out of the water. Keep your eyes wide fucking open and don't take shit for granted."

With that, my old friend stood up and said goodbye.

Meg and I looked at each other. We both understood that of all the intelligence she had acquired from the officers, this last bit from Chris, a true warrior, was the most important.

CHAPTER 14

The road to Baghdad

I caught a glimpse of the obligatory photo ops with Congressman Martin Jennings, Lieutenant General Chase Montgomery, and the sheiks. The Iraqis seemed genuinely impressed to be hosting a man of Jennings's distinction.

Montgomery looked pleased, though I guessed that he was ready for the group to head back to Washington. As if watching over the lives of more than 100,000 soldiers wasn't enough, dealing with inquisitive politicians from Congress and the State Department—not to mention the continual diplomacy with the Iraqis—was a tall order for anyone.

As usual, my team had already repositioned our vehicles in the proper order and was waiting in trail behind the Army Humvees. As I ran through my pre-mission checklist, I listened on the internal frequency as Meg gave Wolf, JP, Oliver, and the rest of the team a summary of the sergeant major's earlier comments.

Team Rhino was an experienced group, well aware of the dangers lurking in the shadows here.

My two junior VIPs were already suited up in their protective gear, ready for the return trip. Just like earlier in the day, our convoy began to creep forward toward the gate. We inched along as the vehicles made their way through the security perimeter and onto Route Steelers.

Through my front passenger window, I could see the riverbank along the roadside. The slow flow of the river seemed so peaceful. It could easily have been a scene from rural America along the banks of the James or the Potomac.

But as soon as we passed the first cluster of shacks, I remembered where we were. This was no Shenandoah Valley in Virginia; this was a war zone in Iraq. *Get your game face on, asshole.*

We made it south down Steelers and turned left on Route Packers. As soon as we made the turn, Oliver in Rhino 1 radioed us all with a reminder about the men we had passed near Yusufiyah. "Keep your eyes peeled, guys," he said.

Roger that, buddy. Good call, Oliver.

The convoy was moving at a decent speed. Oliver was careful to allow the last Army vehicle ahead of him about thirty meters of space, and gave us all constant updates. We were about a quarter mile from Yusufiyah and approaching the dilapidated old garage where we'd received the stares earlier.

"They're slowing down ahead—watch your speed," Oliver commanded. "The trail vehicle has stopped. Break. Not sure why. Okay, the gunner in the turret is standing straight up. Looks like there might be some local traffic mixed in the formation."

It wasn't uncommon for local farmers to jump into our formation, anxious not to get stuck behind a long, slow-moving military convoy. Over time the Army had slightly loosened its traffic protocols, usually giving the wayward driver a siren blast or a menacing look to remind them who had the right-of-way.

"*Break break break!*" Oliver suddenly shouted. "*Got a Bongo truck on the north side of Packers. Five military-age males in the back. It's backed up near the road.*"

In theater-of-operations vernacular, any vehicle not clearly a passenger car was dubbed a *Bongo truck*. That label likewise described any vehicle doing something it shouldn't.

As soon as I heard Oliver's tone, I knew Chris Miller's premonition was about to come true. The knot in my stomach tightened. I could feel my heart beating through the body armor. The blood in my temples thumped against the frames of my Oakley sunglasses. It was like watching a car wreck in slow motion.

Then I heard the explosion.

I actually saw it a split second before I heard it. A bright flash from an RPG sent a rocket directly into the side of the last SUV in the convoy, just above the roof and next to the machine-gun turret.

It must have hit at an oblique angle, because I saw the ricochet sail off from the roof toward the north side of the road. The sound was deafening. The side of the turret was mangled. A moment later came the muffled sound of small-arms fire from both sides of the road.

Whoever the bad guys were today, they had trapped an American vehicle in a deadly cross fire.

CHAPTER 15

Yusufiyah, south of Baghdad

Instinctively, we drove our vehicles into a protective formation. Oliver went to the left side of the road; Wolf pulled our SUV in closer on his right while Meg and JP mirrored us from behind. We now had eyes on the entire mini-perimeter of Team Rhino.

I could see exactly what was happening. The Humvee was dead in the water. Five bandits on the north side were peppering the vehicle with AK-47s, while two on the south side about twenty meters away were likewise shooting their weapons at the vehicle.

The soldier in the Humvee's roof-mounted machine-gun turret had either been shot or had dipped down to protect himself. Either way, the crew was sitting ducks.

I heard another explosion farther ahead of us. Strangely, though we were only about fifty meters away, none of the gunmen were paying any attention to us.

ROCKET'S RED GLARE

I called the Major on my radio to give him an update. No answer.

Was he hit? Did they get the whole convoy?

I couldn't see beyond the trapped Humvee. My best guess was that the bad guys had ambushed the last vehicle of the Army convoy, then created some sort of diversion for the vehicles that had already passed through the kill zone.

Time was not on my side. Through the dust and disorder, I could feel the fear, tension, and anxiety emanating from every member of my team.

Though we were technically a part of this military convoy, I was not in command, and I was not receiving any guidance from the commander. Nor were we being engaged by the bad guys, who had still not even looked in our direction. There is a strict protocol for contractors in a combat zone: Fire only when fired upon, or run the risk of creating a serious international incident.

I could hear shots from the AK-47s plinking off the armored vehicle. *Fuck.*

I tried again to reach the major on the radio. Nothing.

Come on, pal, just give me the word, I thought to myself.

Again, dead silence on the radio. No sounds of American gunfire came from up ahead. Maybe the entire convoy *had* been hit.

"Rhino Base, this is Rhino 2, *troops in contact. Over.*" I called our headquarters to give them an update. At least they would have the ability to make headway over the military command frequencies.

"Roger, Rhino 2," they replied. "*We've alerted Eagle 6, break. Stand by.*"

Stand by? Shit. "Stand by" did nothing for any of us, though I knew the guys back at HQ would be doing everything they possibly could to help support the whole convoy.

The last thing anyone needed was a free-for-all on this battlefield. The Army command would get the situation fixed—they were damn good at that—but the chaos of the moment made seconds seem like hours.

One of the bandits on the south side of the road lifted an RPG launcher toward his shoulder. *Fuck!*

"*Break, break, break, all units, THUNDER,*" I said over the radio as calmly as I could. "*I say again: THUNDER.*"

"*Roger, THUNDER,*" I heard in unison.

THUNDER was the CSTC code word for *immediate attack.* No matter what the situation, when an operator heard that word, he or she immediately went into assault mode.

THUNDER was the equivalent of *Mayday* on the high seas.

CHAPTER 16

I felt the safety switch on my Colt M4 Commando move from the safe position to semiautomatic as my right foot hit the ground.

It was instinctive. In one fluid motion, my left arm brought the gunsight to my field of view. I slightly adjusted the ACOG's tritium-illuminated reticle pattern to directly in line with the head of the guy with the RPG. It was only a forty-meter shot. I pulled the trigger without hesitation. I actually launched a controlled pair, which hit the target in a nanosecond.

Without taking a second breath, I moved my sights to the target beside him and squeezed another two. I felt the rounds from John Paul Kennedy's gun whistle by my right shoulder at the same time. There was no doubt that his bullets hit the mark as well.

As we ran toward the passenger side of the disabled vehicle, we could hear Meg and Oliver shooting on the opposite side. No talking, no radio communications, just the sounds of deadly American gunfire. JP and I made a quick search for other hostiles in the area. Nothing to the south.

As JP scanned the area for signs of the enemy, I approached the vehicle. I could see some movement.

I ripped off the American flag Velcroed to my body armor and pushed it to the view of the passenger. I didn't want him getting more spooked and inadvertently shooting me.

I over-enunciated through the window: "We're the good guys. You're gonna be okay."

Oliver reported from the north side of the vehicle. *"I've got three enemy dead, one enemy wounded we're taking prisoner, and one fucking got away."*

"Roger, copy, we have two enemy dead on the south side. Anything ahead?" I asked.

"Negative. I see some movement, and—stand by, I see some troops coming."

About the time I heard the call I saw some soldiers moving in a tactical formation toward us, weapons raised. I waved my arms and shouted, "Americans!" I held up my flag again so they wouldn't send any rounds in my direction.

Fortunately, I saw them lower their weapons. Rudy, our medic, was already inside the vehicle, checking on the wounded soldiers. I heard him say no friendlies were dead, but the machine gunner was pretty banged up.

The approaching soldiers moved toward us in a fan so as to cover the entire area and provide security. I recognized the leader of the group, a staff sergeant who immediately gave the scene a once-over. He trotted up to me. "You okay, sir?"

"Roger. What's the status ahead?"

"Fucking ambushed the convoy. Put a decoy between the last vehicle and the rest of the convoy, then hit us. They hit a secondary on the major's truck. He's a little hurt but gonna be okay.

I told the major I'd check back here. Our comms suck and we have the damn CNN reporters up there too."

"Yeah, no shit—I couldn't reach anyone on our net. No other casualties?"

"Nah, they hit and ran," said the sergeant, glancing around. "At least some of them did. Good shooting, sir. We need to get this unfucked and head out. I got another vehicle backing up to tow this thing home. Fucking lucky none of us are dead, that's for sure. All the air is tied up with the fucking general's bullshit. Fuck me, this sucks. Savages. Where's the prisoner?"

I pointed to where Meg was kneeling over the captured terrorist. She and Oliver had secured his hands behind his back with plastic zip ties. Her knee was resting squarely on the guy's back as she scanned the area for more targets.

The whole place was deserted—not an Iraqi man, woman, or child in sight. They had scattered either right before the ambush or as soon as the fireworks began. No matter what any of the locals knew or had seen, none of them were going to give us any information about the attack.

"No doubt they were gonna snag one of us." The staff sergeant spoke into his radio and gave a quick brief to someone on the other end. I could see his face wince when he was finished.

"Sir, we're going to tow this thing back to the base and bring you all to the brigade headquarters."

"Got it," I said. "We'll figure something out. Thanks for the support."

"For what it's worth," the soldier said, "thanks for helping Sergeant Carnes and his guys. No shit they'd be dead and gone if it wasn't for you all."

CHAPTER 17

One of the other Humvees backed up and the crew quickly attached a long iron tow bar between the two SUVs. We'd be out of there in no time.

As I climbed back into my Range Rover, I clocked the faces of my two VIPs. William McKay and Travis Hunter, the young congressional staffers, were not quite white with fear, but they were definitely struggling to process the events of the last few minutes. I gave them both a thumbs-up and closed the door. "Let's get ready to roll," I told Wolf.

Regardless of the political fallout and the shitstorm that was sure to follow, I knew I had made the right call. There was no way I could've just sat back and watched the enemy kill or maim an American soldier. Any levelheaded soldier would've done the same in my place.

I also knew that my CSTC partner Tristan Dent would back me 100 percent. But it's all relative when trying to explain chaos to people who've never witnessed the brutal reality of war.

The drive back to the base was silent except for Oliver

making the checkpoint calls. Otherwise we all just sat and contemplated our future.

We followed the convoy directly to the unit headquarters. There were plenty of soldiers running around, ready to assist the men who had just evaded death. I saw a group of medics with their stretcher teams and medical gear moving the wounded to the triage site. Rudy was still helping with the casualties.

As we parked the fleet and I exited the SUV, I spotted a phalanx of Army officers and one civilian walking over, moving with a sense of purpose. I suspected they were coming to apprehend me. Where the fuck did they think I was going to run off to, anyway? Syria?

Before they reached me, Oliver, Wolf, Meg, and JP moved into a semicircle behind me, more as a show of solidarity than anything else. The two VIPs were still getting out of the Rover when the leading officer spoke up.

"Sir, I need everyone who participated in the event to come with me." His tone was even, rehearsed. He had probably spent the past hour practicing this line-in-the sand moment.

"Hold on a second," I ordered.

The command seemed to catch everyone off guard. I was starting to feel somewhat put-upon. In no way, shape, or form was I going to have my team muscled by these guys—even if they were in charge.

"Let me check all my shit first, okay? Once I have my gear accounted for, then I will come with you for the inquisition." I didn't attempt to hide my slightly pissed-off tone.

"Sir—um, Mr. Phillips—yes, of course. We just need to get everyone into the briefing room ASAP. Colonel Knapp wants to speak with you immediately." Knapp must have been the brigade commander.

"Sorry, Major—it's been one of those days," I said, searching for some empathy.

Travis Hunter, one of the congressional aides who'd been in our Range Rover, tapped me on the shoulder. He was probably twenty-six or twenty-seven, but he projected a confidence beyond his years, completely composed and totally sure of himself. He put his right hand out for a shake.

"Thank you for what you did back there, Mr. Phillips. I promise you that Congressman Jennings will get a full briefing on today's, uh, *events*. Do not despair."

His counterpart, Will McKay, stood behind him nodding.

"Do not despair?" I thought to myself. *Who says that kind of shit?* Still, the guy was friendly, and the gesture was sincere.

"Thanks, Mr. Hunter. I appreciate your help." I shook the aide's hand. He had a good grip. "Sorry for the excitement, but now we have to face the music."

As the staffers walked off toward the civilian who'd been waiting behind the officers, I saw Hunter whip out a cell phone and punch in some numbers.

Hopefully some good will come from that call, I thought.

CHAPTER 18

Baghdad HQ

Colonel Dave Knapp stood waiting for me outside his office. "Mr. Phillips, this way," the colonel said, gesturing with one hand. No smile. No handshake. He was all business.

I faced a gigantic desk while Knapp moved around it to take a battle position in his comfortable desk chair. He looked at me coolly for a few seconds, then motioned for me to sit. On a bookshelf behind him stood a huge bust of a bald eagle that peered menacingly at the unfortunate souls forced to sit before the colonel. It was two against one.

Knapp let out an audible breath and began. "You and your crew saved some of my men." He was still almost expressionless, but the temperature had warmed up a little. "Some of your fellow contractors are pretty fucking"—he enunciated the *ing* for effect—"cavalier around these parts. They run around with complete disregard for the rules and fuck things up more than they help."

Another pause.

I figured my best course of action was a direct assault. "Sir, I know I have just made your life much more difficult. But no way could I stand by and allow those terrorists to execute American soldiers."

The colonel's secure phone rang. He picked it up with a gruff "Knapp." Still no sign of emotion. He continued to give me the hard stare while delivering monosyllabic answers to his caller. "Roger that, sir. Will do," he concluded and put the phone down.

"Here's the deal. You have indeed caused a massive storm of bullshit for me, Mr. Phillips. It will probably mean weeks of paperwork and investigations and all kinds of shit that I will have to deal with personally."

He let the words sink in, then continued.

"But trust me when I say this: I would rather deal with a shit ton of paperwork than write another letter to another spouse or parent about their dead son or daughter. I can't lie to you, son: There is going to be a massive investigation. But if this was a righteous kill and you all were by the book, I can't see it turning into anything more than a pain in the ass for my staff and yours."

Colonel Knapp leaned back in his chair. "That was General Montgomery on the phone," he explained. "He and Congressman Jennings want us to escort you to his office in a few minutes. Apparently a legal team from your outfit will be there, along with Army criminal investigators and Army lawyers." He shook his head as he stood from his chair, blocking me from the eagle's gaze.

Nothing more needed to be said. I stood and started to move

toward the door. But first I felt obligated to express my gratitude. "Sir, thank you for shooting straight with me. I really appreciate your help."

"No, Mr. Phillips, thank *you* for everything," Knapp said with a knowing nod. "You be safe out there."

CHAPTER 19

Outside the colonel's office, I looked around for the escort detail and was surprised to recognize the sergeant who'd been riding shotgun in the wounded Humvee, as well as the staff sergeant who had taken control of security at the ambush and directed the vehicle's recovery.

"Sergeant Jeff Carnes," the man from the vehicle said as I approached. Before I could give him my hand, he leaned in for a bear hug. "Thank you, sir. You guys were awesome. Sorry I couldn't do a damn thing."

Though he had recovered from the daze of the blast and his adrenaline surge had ebbed, the reality of what had just transpired was sinking in. Sergeant Carnes knew that disaster had been narrowly averted. He was scared and thankful at the same time.

I patted Carnes on the shoulder and shook his hand. I knew at that moment that whatever the higher-ups did to me no longer mattered. I could rest easy knowing that we had saved not only the sergeant's life, but the lives of the men in his charge.

"Hey, man, a direct hit from an RPG at ten meters is gonna rock your world," I reassured him. "You don't ever need to apologize for anything to me or my team. I'm just glad we were there."

We all knew that the endgame would've been nasty had the ambush been successful. Despite the liberal rhetoric spouted by anti-war types, this enemy had never agreed to follow the rules of the Geneva Convention.

The staff sergeant held out his hand. "I'm Sergeant Ben Hilton, sir."

I gave him a good shake. Hilton was probably in his early twenties but looked a decade older. He'd already done a year or two of fighting in Iraq while most of his peers back home were finishing college or working entry-level jobs.

"Good to meet you, Ben. Nat Phillips. Guess you guys are the ones taking me to see the old man," I said.

Hilton looked at me sheepishly. I could sense his discomfort. An hour ago, we were fighting for our lives and now we had to go plead our case to a man who'd been miles away from the battlefield.

"I just want you to know that I really appreciate all you did for us," Hilton said. "That place always sucks, man. Every time I drive by there, it gives me the creeps."

"I hear you, Ben. The whole damn place gives me the creeps." I smiled, gave him a brotherly pat on the shoulder and nodded toward the door. "It's cool, Ben, don't give it a second thought."

"Well, um, thanks, Sir."

We walked outside, where a huge Chevy Suburban was waiting. Sergeant Carnes opened the door in the back for me to enter.

"You're not gonna cuff me, are you?" I asked with a smile.

He gave me an awkward smile and shook his head. I could tell he felt uncomfortable being a party to my sentencing.

"Every little t'ing's gonna be alright, mon," I said in my best Rasta voice, trying to lighten the mood.

I started to realize that I was hungry. No—make that *starving*. Shit, I hadn't eaten since early that morning, and though I'd had that one cup of coffee with Miller and had drunk a ton of water, I couldn't lose the battlefield cottonmouth. Oddly, instead of my impending career doom, all I could think about was the growling of my stomach.

Before long, we pulled up to division headquarters, home to Lieutenant General Chase Montgomery. The division HQ was housed in one of Saddam Hussein's former palaces, a structure that loomed at least four stories high and must have been as wide as a football field. The military had commandeered it right after the US invasion of Iraq; when Saddam went underground, the good guys moved in.

As we drove by at a glacial three miles per hour, I craned my neck to look out the window at the palace. Huge pillars supported a peaked dormer over the entrance, while atop the roof rose a magnificent dome reminiscent of the US Capitol. All statues of the former owner had been removed, though plenty of Babylonian figures remained perched on stone foundations, standing watch over the grounds.

A crowd had gathered—thankfully, not a reporter among them. I noticed that it was almost 8 p.m. and the blazing sun had nearly set. I immediately started to feel sleepy.

Hungry and *tired—fuck my timing.*

The Suburban rolled to a gentle stop. Sergeant Carnes popped out and rushed around to open my door.

"Good luck, sir. We'll be here till you're done."

I handed business cards to both Sergeants Hilton and Carnes and told them to give me a call when they got back home. Poaching Chris Miller's guys was sort of breaking the rules, but it was the least I could do for them.

"Don't tell Miller I gave you two my card. He'll kick all our asses. Thanks for the ride."

And off I went to meet my fate.

★ ★ ★

The first person I spotted was Jed O'Reilly. He was CSTC's chief legal adviser in-country and always had his act straight. It was good to spy a friendly face among the crowd of unknowns. Tristan Dent had lured him away from a pretty fat private practice in DC to work as our consigliere — *The Godfather*'s Tom Hagen in the flesh.

Jed shook my hand and pulled me aside. "Glad to see you in one piece, partner. Good job out there. I know it was legit. You did the right thing."

Jed's reassuring posture made me feel better.

"Thanks, Jed. Don't think we had a choice. Oliver, Meg, and JP were on their game today, that's for sure. No shit, they did great. Anything from the prisoner?"

"Nothing that anyone is telling me here. Everyone is holding their cards close on this one. Fuck 'em, though. I'll be in there with you the whole time."

A one-star general walked over and gestured for us to follow him toward the massive palace doors.

As much as the daily scenes of poverty had numbed my senses, the excess I saw here threw my barometer way off the charts. No kidding, a chandelier hanging from the distant, fifty-foot-high ceiling sparkled with what must have been ten thousand crystals. I couldn't help staring at the spectacle of lights like it was Disney World.

As the general turned to speak to me, I spotted my two junior VIPs, William McKay and Travis Hunter, standing against the wall with a group of their colleagues. They were both sipping coffee and looking surprisingly refreshed. Hell, I think they may even have showered.

We locked eyes and Hunter, without smiling or otherwise changing his poker face, gave me a faint wink. I couldn't tell from his expression if it was a sign of caution or comfort, but I smiled and followed the general.

The one-star read us a page from the legal playbook. I was to go in one room as investigators interviewed the rest of my team individually in other rooms.

I was about to say something about my team's right to legal counsel, but a slight bump in the small of my back from Jed's hand persuaded me to let it go. I guess he had a plan in mind.

I walked off with Jed and the general. We headed down one of the mammoth corridors toward Montgomery's office. I could feel my mouth getting drier by the second, and of course my stomach was still growling. I wondered if the others could hear it.

CHAPTER 20

Office of Lieutenant General Chase Montgomery

"Ridiculous, isn't it?" came a deep voice.

I hadn't immediately noticed the silhouette of the three-star general when I crossed the threshold into his inner sanctum. Lieutenant General Chase Montgomery waved a hand around at the palace room's ostentatious touches. "Actually, it's pretty much an embarrassment. Every day I'm here, it reminds me why we needed to come to Iraq. This had to be stopped," he said with a somewhat cordial voice.

"Yes, sir—I couldn't agree with you more."

"Chase Montgomery, please, Mr. Phillips," the commander of all forces in Iraq said, throwing me off with his rank-less introduction. He gestured the three of us toward the center of the cavern, to some overstuffed chairs arranged on top of a Persian rug that must have cost a mint. In addition to Jed and myself, a handful of other civilians had gathered in the general's office, including Congressman Martin Jennings.

Jennings strode across the room, hand outstretched. This was the second time in the past thirty seconds that I'd been thrown off guard. The congressman grabbed my hand and shook it before I could say anything.

"Please, please sit down," he said, then quickly turned back to Montgomery as if to apologize for usurping the general's authority.

"Yes, Mr. Phillips, please, let's sit. May I call you Nathan?" Montgomery motioned to have coffee and water brought for us all. I immediately dusted the seat of my pants and sat down on the front edge of a chair. After introductions, Jed O'Reilly sat next to me. He pulled out a small notebook and readied himself for a fight.

Jennings and the ranking general looked at Jed inquisitively.

"General Montgomery, if I may...?" the congressman began. Montgomery gave a nod as he reached for a cup of coffee from the platter his secretary had returned holding.

Jennings smiled at me and Jed. "Do you know where I live? When I'm not in Washington dealing with that mess," he said with a grimace, "I live outside Pittsburgh. Do you know where Sergeant Carnes happens to live?"

I didn't, but suddenly found myself hoping it was Pennsylvania.

"He was born and raised in Oakdale, about ten miles from my home." Jennings stopped for a moment to let that information sink in.

I didn't want to jinx anything, so I played it cool. I purposefully kept any expression off my face.

"You can put your notebook away, Mr. O'Reilly," the congressman said. "There will be no grand inquisition here today—or any other day, for that matter. Mr. Phillips and his team saved not only the life of one of my constituents, but undoubtedly the lives of every soldier in that vehicle—maybe even the lives of everyone in the convoy. Who knows what we'd be doing right now had those terrorists succeeded? I can assure you we wouldn't be sitting here drinking coffee."

The air must have involuntarily left my lungs with a whoosh because both Jennings and Montgomery smiled. They looked almost proud, like parents watching their kid do something remarkable for the first time.

"See, we're not all so bad in DC," Jennings said, chuckling. "Now, here's the plan. I am pleased to find your legal counsel present for this part. I have already alerted the president, State, and SECDEF, as well as the appropriate members of the Armed Services Committee. The attorney general is in communication with Mr. Dent in Maryland—good duck hunting, by the way—and we will begin the process of removing your team from this theater most expeditiously."

My relief immediately fell to the bottom of the well. Even though I had done the right thing, CSTC was having its contract terminated and being sent home. Hit with a wave of nausea, I set my coffee cup down to steady myself.

"Congressman—with all due respect—" I began to stammer. "I made the decision, and I made the call to fight back." My voice started to rise with each word. "Please don't pull the plug on the contract just because of me."

"Hold on a second, Nathan," General Montgomery reassured me. "We're not pulling any contracts. But we do have to switch teams. Believe it or not, the Iraqi government realizes they still have a huge problem with JAM and the other militias, not to mention Al-Qaeda. But, as you know, we have to show them something. And there's been bounty chatter, too. I believe the congressman has already alerted the folks at State to work with your guys to get another team back out here ASAP."

"The general is correct," said Jennings. "One of my aides, whom you delivered to and from the gala today, gave me an immediate recap of the ambush. I may be a lot of things, Mr. Phillips, but I am not one to forsake any single man or woman in uniform, period. And that includes you and your team."

I heaved another audible sigh of relief, then picked up my coffee and took a long pull. It was the best coffee I had ever tasted. I eased myself back into the seat a little deeper and said thank you.

"Now, Mr. O'Reilly, I would like to excuse you to begin coordinating the departure of Mr. Phillips and his principals," Jennings said to Jed. "One of my staff, Will McKay or Travis Hunter, will assist you with the process. I can assure you that there will be no hiccups whatsoever. So if you will excuse us, the general and I would like to speak with Mr. Phillips in private."

Jed stood uncertainly, but I motioned to the door with my head. He thanked the two men and followed the secretary to the large door.

"Okay, Nathan," the general said after everyone but Jennings and I had departed, "it's just us girls here—plain and simple, no bullshit. What happened, why did it happen, and what do you think is going to happen next?" He crossed one leg over the other and leaned back in his chair.

I noticed the congressman seemed to relax as well. *If this is some kind of trick, at least Jed heard the bulk of the good stuff.* I didn't think they could take it back, but you never know with some people.

I unspooled the saga from beginning to end.

By the time I got to the part about seeing the RPG hit the Humvee, both men were leaning forward in their seats. As I described stitching the first Iraqi, Congressman Jennings seemed so fired up that he was ready to clap his hands.

I also made sure to put in a plug for the calm professionalism of both Sergeant Carnes and Sergeant Hilton.

The bottom line, I said, was that something screwy was definitely going down. It was clearly not news to either gentleman, but it made me feel important to give the distinguished pair my two cents.

"So, sir, Congressman, that's about it. Umm, what should I do next?"

The general stood and thanked me again. He mentioned the need for operational security, as well as the most obvious *Don't go talking to the press or writing a book anytime soon* guidance. Congressman Jennings looked at his watch, then at me.

"We will have another plane here tomorrow morning to transport your team back to Maryland. You'll get the itinerary shortly. We will see you when you're back on the shores of the greatest country in the world."

This time it was Jennings who passed out business cards. I thanked both men effusively and headed toward the door.

"By the way," Montgomery said, "Command Sergeant Major Miller and I have served together off and on for almost twenty years."

I smiled, recognizing that Chris must've gone to bat for me with the old man.

"He wanted me to ask you, and I quote him verbatim, *Why the fuck did you let one escape?*" General Montgomery laughed a little. "Don't worry about it, Mr. Phillips—I'm sure we'll get him another day."

I grinned and gave a half-wave.

"Thank you, sir," I said. Then I walked out of the cave and into the tunnel to begin the trip home.

CHAPTER 21

CSTC Headquarters, Baghdad

I headed off to my office at CSTC headquarters. Tristan Dent was expecting my candid report. While I knew part of him wished he was out here with us in the wilds of the foreign battlefields, his responsibility was back in the States, drumming up business and keeping the entire global operation running fluidly. Ultimately, even though we were close friends, CSTC was Tristan Dent's show and I worked for him just like everyone else.

I closed my door and picked up the satellite phone. The automated voice on the other end asked for the security code. I punched it in and waited for the connection to "go secure" and encrypt our call.

A few moments later, a real voice on the other end picked up. "Dent."

"Tristan, it's Nat. Can you hear me okay?"

"Natty, how the hell are you, my man? Great to hear your

voice, amigo. I've been on the phone all day with Jed and the State Department."

"I'm okay, brother. Man, I'm sorry for the heartburn I'm causing you today. Just got back from meeting General Montgomery and Congressman Jennings."

"You guys did the deed, and I'm behind you a thousand percent. I think this thing is a wash. Let everyone know they did a great job and we are all proud of them. We'll talk when you get back here. Been having some really interesting talks with folks in DC the past few months or so. I'll fill you in face-to-face, but bottom line, I think you'll really like what I'm gonna tell you."

★ ★ ★

It took a few hours to finish the Team Rhino debrief, but we all agreed the operation had been a good one overall. I passed along Tristan's thanks and told everyone to pack.

"One more thing," I said, "my house in Nantucket has plenty of room if anyone is interested in a few days up north. Last I checked, the beer was cold and I've got a pretty decent stash of bourbon."

I always tossed out an open invitation like this after a deployment, which always ended with ninety days of vacation, free to do whatever before the next rotation overseas. So far, no one had ever taken me up on the offer. Not that we didn't enjoy each other's company, but folks usually opted for some downtime away from one another in between return trips to Baghdad or Kabul.

The abrupt end to our time together must have changed the vibe.

Oliver, Meg, Wolf, and JP lingered after their teams left. It was just the five of us now.

Oliver spoke first. "Nat, you did the right thing. I just wanted to tell you I'm glad I work for you. No shit, dude—I would have lost it in that mess if I'd had to make the call. Hell, we'd probably all be in the big house if you'd been following me."

"Thanks, jefe, I appreciate it. I was lucky, no question. You guys did a fucking awesome job as usual. I didn't even know you were taking fire. Damn good shooting, that's for sure."

"Yeah, Nat," JP chimed in. "Thanks for grabbing the ring on this one. That was some hairy shit."

"Well, I don't have a clue what the hell you apes would have done without me on the ground."

We all laughed, Meg most of all.

It was impossible not to have a soft spot for Megan Fuller. Deep down, none of us ever really understood why she chose to work with us. She was brilliant, no doubt about that, spoke four languages fluently, and was good with a gun. She'd proved again today that she could handle herself in just about any situation. No matter which way you looked at it, Meg was a rock star.

"By the way, I'm in for that vacation on your island, Nat. I get my own room, though." She grabbed her rifle and headed to pack.

CHAPTER 22

CSTC Headquarters, Maryland

Back stateside in Maryland after a long-ass flight, Tristan and a fleet of CSTC Range Rovers were waiting for us at the airport in Easton.

I rode with the boss in his Maserati, while the rest of the team piled into the spotless Rovers. We all headed off to the compound. No reason to wait around for our baggage; I saw our things getting loaded directly into a large cargo truck parked outside the fence.

Tristan and I drove straight to his private office. The rest of the teams would begin end-of-tour administrative work, getting paid and processed out.

We sat on one of the office's leather couches and reviewed every detail of the ambush. Tristan asked a lot of questions—more than usual. He wanted to make sure we had followed the rules of engagement to the letter of the law.

I was about to ask some questions of my own about why my

team had been brought back early when Tristan threw a fastball directly over the plate.

What he told me about our next mission kept the two of us talking for longer than I had expected.

★ ★ ★

Still processing my conversation with Tristan, I walked out to give some last-minute instructions and say goodbye to the team, who'd been waiting for me to finish with our boss.

Oliver, Meg, Wolf, and JP all assured me they'd be descending upon my place in Nantucket by the weekend, so I thanked them all again and headed to our parking garage to pick up my Defender. My bags and guns had been stacked neatly in front of my parking space. I loaded my gear, cranked up the old engine, and began the almost nine-hour drive up the Eastern Seaboard. With any luck, I'd catch the last ferry to Nantucket and be sleeping in my own bed before midnight.

I arrived at the Steamship Authority loading dock in Hyannis with an hour to spare before the last ferry. Though it was beach season, not too many cars were going across. The motor vessel to Nantucket was an old ferry capable of transporting fifty passenger vehicles and two hundred passengers each way. While one ferry was leaving Hyannis, its sister ship was leaving from Nantucket.

I always wondered why there never seemed to be any searches of passengers or vehicles by TSA or the local cops. I guess islanders were beyond suspicion when it came to matters of national security. At least it meant I wasn't going to be bothered about why I was transporting an assault rifle, a submachine gun, two pistols, a few knives, and way too much ammo.

A little over two hours later, I rolled off the ferry at the boat basin. Even on a weeknight, the sidewalks were packed with vacationers in search of late-night food and drink. The contrast between this wealthy island and Baghdad was dramatic. Instead of burkas, the women sported Prada. Instead of ox-drawn carts, they drove Porsches.

I wove through the cobblestone streets and made my way past the cranberry bogs to Sconset. The eastern side of the island was famously quiet compared to the hubbub of town, which was why we year-round residents liked it so much.

I fell into a category somewhere between the wealthy summer vacationers and the locals. I had fallen in love with the place the first time I ever came out here, then used my first bonus from CSTC to buy a humble house on Baxter Road. This island was my sanctuary between deployments.

There was a stretch of about six miles where the land on both sides of the main road had been saved from development by a land trust. There were no other cars on the road this time of night. With no streetlights and no moon—only my headlights to show the way—the sense of isolation was relaxing. It was nice to finally be alone.

I rolled past the rotary and the market and made the turn onto Broadway. I was almost home.

The reflective paint on the Nantucket Police car up ahead on Broadway took me by surprise. I couldn't remember the last time I had seen a police vehicle out here. Was there a fire? I slowed to look around. I couldn't see any flames or smell any smoke. Another police car sat farther north at the next intersection, but no fire trucks or ambulances.

The state trooper shined his flashlight and headed toward me, signaling me to stop. I hadn't been speeding, and my headlights worked fine. This was odd.

"I'm sorry, sir, but this road is closed for a few more hours. There is an event," he said with as little enthusiasm as he could muster. It was late, and he was stuck on a shit detail. I knew the feeling.

"Hey, sir, that sucks. But that house right over there, like fifty yards from here? That's mine, and I'd really like to go home."

The officer shook his head from side to side and gave me the mean-mug stare.

"Listen, bud, the road's closed until they tell me it's open—probably a couple more hours. Come back then."

The guy was really starting to piss me off.

"Officer—"

"Buddy," he interrupted. "The place is locked down for people more important than you. You're not getting by, so turn your ass around and go away. They went house-to-house and told everybody all last week. Guess you missed the memo."

"I just came home from fucking Iraq." I knew I was about to get sideways with this guy. "Listen, you can walk me to the door. It's right there. Just give me a break here, man."

"I'm not gonna tell you again: Get your ass out of here, and don't come back bothering me." Another dose of mean-mugging.

I tried to throw daggers with my eyes, but he wasn't budging. Defeated, I started to back up, muttering profanities at the dashboard.

That's when I noticed the cop pointing at me and laughing into his radio.

CHAPTER 23

Baxter Road
Nantucket, Massachusetts

*P*lan B.

I was going to sleep in my own bed tonight. Fuck that guy.

I drove back to the market and parked the Defender well out of the cop's line of sight, then reached into the back seat and grabbed my two gun cases. I slid my .45 into an outer pocket of the SMG bag and tucked the Sig into my belt behind my back.

Everything else could stay until morning.

Keeping to the shadows, I made my way up Front Street. At its north end, I ducked between two of the cottages, walked east for about ten yards, found the footpath along the bluff, did a left face, and began the walk to my house.

Thankfully it was pitch-black along the path, and the odds of anyone being out for a late-night stroll were nil. The silhouette of my house emerged as I took a knee at the edge of my property.

ROCKET'S RED GLARE

I scanned my backyard as if on patrol in the bush. Only about twenty yards of open lawn to reach the back porch.

From my concealed position, I could see light glowing inside the house north of mine. That must be where people more important than me were hanging out tonight. I had never met the owners, but had heard they were doctors from Boston who rented out the place year-round.

I made my way across the lawn to the veranda, then quietly climbed the four steps to the deck. I tiptoed to the door and gently placed my gun bags at my feet. Like every longtime Nantucket dweller, I had wedged a key to the dead bolt beneath a loose cedar shingle. *So far, so good.* The back door swung open without a sound.

It was pretty dark, but I easily felt my way through the living room and into the kitchen, where I placed my bags on the table. My eyes adjusted to the ambient light, and I walked over to the bar, grabbed a lowball glass, and poured a couple of fingers of Kentucky's finest.

I win.

Taking my first sip, I thought I saw movement outside my window. I squinted and noticed that my front door was ajar.

That's strange. Why is my front door open? Was it left open the whole time I was deployed? No way.

In slow motion, reality started to sink in. *Intruders.*

Good thing I had a career's worth of experience at close-quarters battle.

I put down my glass, pulled my Sig, and assessed the situation. There were three avenues of approach to my house: the front door, the back door, and the kitchen window. In two steps I could move into position to cover two of the three entrances, but I could not defend them simultaneously against multiple teams coming through multiple breaches. Just knowing this gave me a momentary advantage.

Still, my sixth sense told me something didn't fit. As I scanned the room, I heard an unmistakable sound—one I'd heard a million times—as an object bounced off an interior wall and rolled across the floor. I knew what it was: a small metal canister containing a flash-bang grenade. The disorientation device was harmless—except for its ability to produce an explosion so loud and a flash of light so bright that I would be unable to react.

Whoever was on the throwing end of that meant business. I had about three seconds.

I spotted the grenade near the front door and instinctively turned my body toward the back door. There was a momentary flash of light, followed by an explosion. They had me.

The attackers knew what they were doing. They were good but not great, lacking the polish I'd come to prize in the people I had worked with over the years. Whatever the reason for what was about to happen, discretion was the better part of valor: Dying was not in the cards for me tonight.

To protect myself, I dropped face down on the floor. That's when I heard voices.

"Don't move, motherfucker."

I heard my screen door being ripped from its hinges and heavy boots pounding across my pine floors. For about five seconds, there was complete pandemonium. Lots of yelling and shouting among the intruders. Flashlight beams stabbing the dark all over the place.

These people were not great at executing the entry. But they definitely weren't robbers. I heard my furniture being overturned and someone running upstairs as softly as a buffalo.

"He's got a gun!" someone screamed at the top of his lungs as the lights came on.

Oh, shit. I was lying face down on the floor, my hands spread wide in front of me, but my Sig was lying next to my right hand—and the barrel of a submachine gun was now pointing in my face.

"Move and you're dead, asshole." The assailant was dressed in black from head to toe. He wore a Nomex hood that concealed his face and night-vision devices on his helmet.

Someone put their knee on my back, while a second person roughly frisked me from the waist down. I then felt strong hands forcing my arms behind me and applying plastic cuffs to my wrists. I was being manhandled exactly the same way Meg had treated the second Iraqi assassin.

I was someone's prisoner.

"Easy on the Rolex, asshole," I spewed.

"Shut your fucking piehole, dickhead." My captor bounced my head off the floor for good measure. *Fucker.*

I was pulled to my feet. There were almost twenty people with guns in my kitchen. Judging by their black uniforms, half were some sort of tactical team; the others were dressed like they were on vacation. The plainclothes guys had badges hanging from their necks. Multiple guns were pointed at me.

There were no police uniforms, so they must have been Feds. FBI? Why the hell would any of those people be here? It made no sense. I saw a group rummaging through my wallet and bags, then heard the wail of a siren. Presumably the Nantucket Police responding.

"Who the fuck are you guys?" I barked. "Would someone please tell me what the fuck is going on?" No one answered me, instead firing questions of their own left and right.

"Why do you have all these weapons? Are there others here with you? You were told to stay away from the senator. This is a secure area."

Senator? What senator?

"I don't know what the hell you people are talking about. This is my house, for Pete's sake. What the fucking fuck? I want to speak with my lawyer."

A five-foot-eight blond woman wearing civilian clothes approached me. She flashed her badge for me to see.

"I'm Special Agent in Charge Rowan Anderson, and you are under arrest."

TWENTY-FOUR HOURS LATER

Operation Nantucket

CHAPTER 24

Wilson Estate
Cliff Road, Nantucket

For forty-five minutes as I recounted what had gone down in Iraq, Constance Wilson said not a word nor displayed any sign that I had crossed a boundary by sharing too much. When I finished speaking, she leaned forward from her chair and gently took my paw in her tan hands.

"We're so lucky to have men like you protecting us, Nathan. Thank you for all you and your brave men and women do for us." She was so sincere I thought she was going to cry.

I thanked her for her thoughtful words. At a loss for what else to say after that, like an idiot, I complimented the Wilsons on their beautiful rosebushes.

I should have taken them up on their offer of dinner—it would surely beat whatever I was going to cook—but I was on overdrive. I desperately wanted to get home and finally get a solid night's sleep.

I called Tristan as I headed back across the island. CSTC had issued us all encrypted phones with satellite capabilities so that we could talk securely from almost anywhere in the world. CSTC had a high-powered server and wireless network that could operate not only encrypted but also when other civilian networks were down. Don't ask me how that stuff works. All I knew was that it was a rare occasion when we couldn't communicate with each other.

Tristan approved of my plan for Si Wilson, and said he'd send a plane next week to fly us both down to Maryland for a look around. He even invited Si's parents, with the extra incentive of knowing there might be some synergy between CSTC and Alan Wilson, who managed billions in assets.

We made plans for next week and said sayonara.

I realized that I'd stayed at the Wilsons' longer than I'd planned. It was coming up on 10 p.m. by the time I made it home.

I went inside, closing all the window shades and locking all the doors before opening the gun vault in my living room. I wanted to make sure the Secret Service had not monkeyed around with the rest of my guns.

Inside one of the closets, I had built a false wall and hidden one of the safes. A push of the recessed button sprang the door open. Either I had done a really good job of building the trapdoor or maybe they were just sloppy, but all my weapons—an assortment of assault rifles, shotguns, and pistols—were secure inside the miniature arms room. I checked another Colt M4, an MP5 submachine gun, and a Remington 870 shotgun, as well as a Benelli that I used for duck hunting, along with a few cases of ammunition. Everything looked good. I locked up and headed for bed.

No sooner had my foot hit the top step than there was a knock on the front door. Who the hell would be coming by at this hour?

I opened the door to find Special Agent Rowan Anderson standing on my doorstep with two rifles slung over her shoulder and a six-pack of beer in one hand. Sleep would have to wait a little longer.

CHAPTER 25

Baxter Road, Nantucket

Rowan Anderson handed me the six-pack and came inside, placing the weapons on the kitchen counter. We each cracked open a beer and sat down on the couch.

Was this a social visit? Reconnaissance? Either way, the last thing CSTC needed was some federal agency sniffing around, so I kept it light. We talked about the job and she told me some behind-the-scenes stories—unreported items that the tabloids would kill to hear. I was determined to keep one card close to my chest: how it was that I'd been released from jail by the attorney general on behalf of the president.

I didn't press Anderson on her current assignment with Senator Harrison, but I did ask if he was aware of the ruckus I had caused. *He's been briefed,* she assured me, *and seems relieved there was no threat to his life.* The senator's handlers, however, did want to track my whereabouts.

The exchange was no big deal—until she asked for my weekend

plans starting on Friday. I eyed her suspiciously. *Where was she going with this?* Playing it safe, I replied that I had dinner plans with some friends on the other side of the island and left it at that.

Though I had mentioned my fellow desperadoes earlier, there was no sense in making her life that easy. She could deal with my four gun-carrying guests once they arrived. I thought about calling lawyer Sam Starnes—*that* would be an interesting showdown—and smiled.

"You look like the cat that swallowed the canary. What the hell's so funny?"

"Nada—just thought of a friend of mine. So what's new on the campaign trail?" Focused on staying alive in Iraq, I hadn't been paying much attention to events outside that country.

She seemed to believe her guy was a lock for the primary. Politely dancing around any sensitive topics, Anderson gave a sharp overview of the campaign from her vantage point. She did dangle one interesting tidbit: Another big party was scheduled at the senator's place for Friday night.

So that's why she'd asked about Friday. Security reasons.

Again I kept it light, giving my answer a real estate spin. "I was just over on that side of the island, visiting Harrison's neighbors. Pretty nice digs."

Rowan Anderson looked confused for a moment but quickly recovered. "You must mean the Wilsons."

I hadn't mentioned them by name. Another sharp move on her part. She turned the conversation back to politics.

"It's the last big deal before we pack up this circus and head to Chicago on Monday. Anyway, the place on the other side of the island belongs to Harrison's wife, Elise Courville. But the party is going to be here." She pointed to the property next door.

So the senator was on one side of the island, while his wife was on the other. The official explanation for the separate sites was that the senator and his staff wanted a little breathing room as the campaign surged toward the convention finish line.

I didn't buy the *breathing room* spin. *There must be trouble in paradise.* I wondered how that would play out if Senator Harrison did win the primary.

Something was fishy.

I could sense that Rowan Anderson was uncomfortable making even the smallest reference to Mrs. Senator, so I didn't push further.

We polished off the beers and, like an idiot, I looked at my watch as I tried to stifle a yawn.

A vaguely disappointed look fell across her face and then a smile crossed her lips.

I started to apologize like a madman, but she cut me off.

"You've had a long day, Nat. I really didn't mean to stay this late. Maybe a cup of coffee tomorrow? I'm off for once, so I have the whole day free to keep you out of mischief." She gave me a playful punch on the arm.

I walked her to the door and thanked her for the beer. I was debating—*handshake or a kiss?*—when she suddenly planted a quick one on my cheek.

Before I could react, she was out the door.

Tomorrow was looking like a much better day than yesterday.

I closed the house down for the night and went upstairs to bed. Three seconds later I was out for the count.

CHAPTER 26

Paris, France

At the sight of the number on his cell phone, the man looked out through the dingy window at the Arc de Triomphe and held his breath. The brief message from Elise Courville contained joyous words.

It was almost time for the call to prayer, but the man decided to praise Allah immediately. He quickly typed a message into his phone and pressed Send. The recipients of the text would read six numbers: *052200*. Friday, 10 p.m.

The man looked at himself in the mirror as he loosened his custom-tailored Italian tie. He resembled any other European banker.

Unlike most of his followers, the Algerian's face was clean-shaven and his hands were manicured. He exercised his thirty-year-old body past maintenance and musculature to the point of near-exhaustion daily. Punishing himself in everything he did was simply his way.

The Algerian removed his suit and gently folded it over an old plastic chair in the dilapidated room. He slipped a threadbare garment over his head and pulled out his prayer mat. As soon as he began the first rak'ah of his five-times-daily Salah, he could almost feel the gracious and sweet air of Allah's breath entering his body.

He begged forgiveness for his many transgressions on his way to the first chapter of a new life — a life controlled by Him, and Him alone. By Saturday morning, the confluence of anger and hatred would be put to rest, bringing an end to his current torment.

But there was much to be done before he could step onto his future path. The pig, the whore, and the infidel must begin their painful journeys to hell. One by one, they would all pay for their shameful sins.

CHAPTER 27

Baxter Road, Nantucket

I woke on Thursday to the sound of a ringing cell phone. After a few fumbles trying to find the damn thing, I answered and heard the familiar automated instruction: "Go secure."

I punched in the code and waited.

Soon the automated voice was replaced with a human one. One of the CSTC computer guys was on the line, reminding me of the systems upgrade scheduled for this morning. I must have missed the memo, but I needed the boost in order to receive additional updates from the smorgasbord of national intelligence agencies. I took the phone downstairs to the kitchen to make some coffee, and fired up my laptop as the tech on the other end fiddled with the behind-the-screen gibberish.

The vast sums Tristan had invested in our IT infrastructure bought quick results: The guy back in Maryland was able to make the necessary adjustments by simultaneously interconnecting the computer of every CSTC principal across the globe.

As the software was downloading, Rowan Anderson waltzed back into my house without knocking. *Since when were Secret Service agents authorized to walk into my living room at will?* Another memo I must have missed. But she was very good-looking, so I didn't complain too much.

I waved her over, and motioned that she should help herself to some coffee.

As Rowan made her way to the kitchen, I noticed she was wearing her pistol. Her radio gear was strapped to her belt too.

"Sorry, Nat—just came by to let you know that it turns out I *do* have to work today. Dinner tonight instead?"

"No sweat. Come on over when you're done—I'll be here."

She was clearly trying to get a look at my laptop screen, but CSTC operations were none of her damn business. I especially didn't need the Secret Service prying into our operations, so I obscured her view of the screen by tilting it down a little.

"Sorry, Curious Georgette," I said with a smile, "the Man in the Yellow Hat says you lack the clearance to see the stuff I'm working on."

Rowan gave me a grin, flipped me the bird, and blew me a kiss. Then she marched out the door, waving goodbye over her shoulder.

Guess I'd have to prove myself over dinner.

I finished the computer download and decided to check in with Tristan about his latest endeavor. He could hardly contain himself as he asked what additional equipment we would need. Tristan was practically bubbling over with the new operational possibilities we would have to be prepared to execute.

We talked for almost an hour, giving me plenty of time to make some lists. I told Tristan that we would review the concepts in detail when the team arrived on Friday.

That's when my boss mentioned the information in my third missed memo of the day: He was flying the team up on one of the CSTC jets to maximize our time. He had already drawn up the itinerary; all I had to do was collect them at the airport.

At least we wouldn't be working *all* weekend. We had the party at the Wilsons to relax a little.

Si Wilson pulled up in an old Jeep CJ-5, then jumped out and jogged to the door. He told me how much his parents had enjoyed meeting me and thanked me again for the job offer. Si said he was anxious to get to Maryland to see the compound—and, hopefully, get in some trigger time on the shooting range.

His excitement reminded me of when I began my career with the Rangers. That kind of enthusiasm was contagious and I knew he would do well.

★ ★ ★

The Special Agent in Charge looked incredible. She was wearing a sleeveless summer dress that showcased her bronzed shoulders and muscular arms, not a tan line in sight. The simple design—plain enough not to reveal too much, but figure-hugging enough to draw attention—complimented her athletic body perfectly.

We headed to the Rope Walk, my favorite restaurant in town. A dinner that fit my budget at a table overlooking the million-dollar boats lined up along the docks and mooring buoys of the Nantucket Boat Basin was my idea of pure capitalist fantasyland.

We enjoyed a sunset cocktail and talked like old friends.

Like most people in her profession, Rowan Anderson was never really off duty. She constantly checked her phone for messages from her fellow agents. After watching the way she related to her team, I couldn't imagine anyone other than her running the detail.

In a lot of ways, Rowan reminded me of Meg Fuller. Their personalities were so similar that they could have been sisters. Or colleagues, given the effortless way each slid into teammate roles in male-dominated professions.

We finished dinner and took a walk along the dock to admire the yachts. The sun was setting, and the view of the floating estates—and the generations of wealth they represented—was striking.

As we stood there admiring one of the mega-boats, Rowan leaned into me, inspiring me to go for broke: I put my arm around her and pulled her closer. Her firm body nestled against my chest and I felt her arm wrapping around my waist. We were a good fit.

I wanted to get to know her better. Of course, she was leaving for Chicago on Monday. And after that, who knew?

We drove back toward my place, still with the same easy conversation. We talked about relationships and recounted some of the more notorious dating disasters we'd each had over the years. Though mine eclipsed hers in drama, I was thoroughly content to imagine a positive outcome for the evening.

Until I almost killed us both.

About two miles from home, doing about sixty beneath a moonless sky, I suddenly spotted a lawn-service truck pulled only halfway off the dark stretch of road. I was almost a second too late.

I had to jerk the wheel hard to miss clipping the big Ford, the ass end of my Defender sliding left then right like it was on ice. I swear we came up on two wheels as I turned into the swerve, the vehicle barely under control and my headlights wildly raking the countryside. I cursed the lawn guys as I recovered from the fishtail.

"Guess they had a flat," Rowan deadpanned. She was calm enough given the situation.

"Probably." Though my adrenaline was amped up several notches, I was dead serious when I asked, "Still up for a nightcap?"

"Twist my arm," she said coyly. Nothing like a brush with destiny to get the heart racing a little.

We walked inside holding hands. Before the door even closed, I pulled her to me and kissed her. We stood in the open doorway for a good minute or two before she stepped away.

"Pour me a drink," she commanded matter-of-factly. Then she headed upstairs.

Tonight was shaping up to be a special occasion, so I went looking for the bottle of Pappy that Tristan had given me a few years ago. Once I found it, I poured us each a couple of fingers.

I turned at the sound of Rowan coming back downstairs. She was leaning against the newly repaired front door, beckoning me with a crooked index finger. She was wearing an old button-down of mine and clutching the fabric so close to her body that I was pretty sure nothing else was touching her skin.

I left the two glasses sitting on the kitchen counter and walked toward her, while she let the shirt fall open just enough for me to catch a glimpse of what was underneath.

Please don't screw this up, I told myself.

She placed a finger on my lips as she grabbed my hand and started to lead me upstairs.

We hadn't gone two steps when someone rapped insistently on my door.

"What the fuck?!" I yelled.

Rowan's come-hither smile disappeared. She dashed upstairs as I squinted through the peephole, then unlocked the door.

Standing on my front porch was a young man dressed in what I guessed was the summer Secret Service uniform: tan pants, blue polo, and pistol belt.

"Um, sir, is Special Agent in Charge Anderson here, by any chance?"

The little pervert knew damn well she was here.

"Bad timing, dude—but I'll go take a look." I gave him a hard stare, telegraphing my eternal grudge against the Secret Service for not only fucking up my door the other night but now fucking up my date night too. I shut the door and left him standing out there.

Rowan was already heading back down the steps, gazing at her phone. She shook her head sadly.

"I'm sorry, Nat. Apparently Walt Fitzgerald has called an all-hands-on-deck meeting at midnight to talk about security for the next few days. The fucking asshole wants me there too."

It was the first comment she'd made about Senator Harrison's staff. Despite my hope that missing an evening with me was the root of her frustration, I could sense that she and this Fitzgerald guy saw eye to eye on very little.

"I'll try to make it back," she said doubtfully. "But no promises."

Now *I* hated this Fitzgerald guy too.

"I understand: Duty calls." I knew we'd probably both be tied up for the rest of the weekend, but I made an offer anyway:

"Maybe we can grab a quick bite over the next couple of days, if you're free."

"Here's my card and my cell number. Call me when you can, okay? Please."

She had such a downcast look on her face that I couldn't resist giving her a hug and a quick peck, almost on the lips.

"No worries—of course I'll call you. I won't let you go that easily." She seemed to enjoy the encouragement.

Then Special Agent in Charge Rowan Anderson put on her boss persona: She flung open the front door and barked out an order to the junior agent, and the two of them headed across the yard to the big meeting.

If Harrison won the primary, she would be detailed to his campaign that much longer. If he lost, she would undoubtedly be switched to provide security for someone else, which would last all the way through the general election. Either way, I hoped we could see each other just often enough to provide a future where we always had something to look forward to. It wasn't perfect, but it was a start.

I gulped down the two glasses of bourbon and pouted my way up to bed.

CHAPTER 28

Nantucket Memorial Airport

The Hawker jet made a smooth landing on Runway 45 of Nantucket Memorial Airport on Friday afternoon. Standing outside the gate, I watched the sleek aircraft bearing the *CSTC* logo taxi around the airfield, finally finding its destination next to the other private planes. Tristan Dent had done well. This was no doubt one of his better toys.

No sooner had the cabin door popped open than I saw Oliver's eager face peeking out. Meg, JP, and Wolf followed, all of them smiling and waving as they trailed down the stairs.

I'd bet they might have had a beer or two during the short flight from Maryland on Dent Air. My team deserved a good trip, and I was happy to see them. We had so much to catch up on.

Without missing a beat, they pulled all their gear, including five heavy-duty gun cases, from the baggage compartment and made their way to the gate.

Seeing Oliver in his flip-flops and vacation clothes made me laugh out loud. His biceps were stretching the sleeves of his pink-and-white-striped polo shirt, while his tree-trunk legs strained the seams of his light-blue Bermuda shorts.

A huge preppy Black dude with a gun on Nantucket—I loved it. He dropped his gear and gave me a bear hug.

Meg was dressed in a pair of old green jeans and a lightweight yellow cotton T-shirt, accessorized by her signature jewelry: a gold cross around her neck and a men's Rolex Daytona on her wrist. Her sandy hair was tied back with a funky scarf and her classic Ray-Bans made her look like a hip movie star trying to avoid the paparazzi by dressing down. Intimidating and classy.

JP and Wolf were dressed like goofy twins. Neither could seem to shake the CSTC ensemble; both sported matching tactical khaki pants, hiking boots, and light denim shirts, with Oakley sunglasses wrapped around their temples.

Granted, unlike most summer visitors to Nantucket, they didn't give a shit what anyone else thought. But I resolved to persuade at least one of them to change before we went to the Wilsons' party.

After the abrupt end to the last Iraq trip, I was sorry the whole band wasn't together, especially Rudy. But life gets in the way of fun sometimes. Soon after learning Team Rhino had to leave Iraq, Rudy had found out about a trauma-medicine symposium he could attend in Dallas. It never occurred to him to take a vacation when he could be sharpening his medical skills.

As the five of us made our way to the parking lot, an unmarked Cessna Citation landed on the same runway as the Hawker. I saw a large black Cadillac Escalade with smoked windows waiting near the terminal. No alarm bells for now, but I'd keep an eye out.

We loaded the Defender and headed back across the island to

my place. I had them all in stitches over the jail story. I told them about meeting Si Wilson, and the little soiree planned for his parents' house this evening.

As we pulled into my driveway, I caught Wolf's gaze in the rearview mirror.

"No funny business with Constance Wilson," I told him.

"I promise to behave myself," he swore. *We'll see.*

I saw the guard detail at the senator's house looking over at us. It didn't strike me as a huge defensive showing—more of an overt display of power should one of the neighbors get drunk and decide to pay the senator a visit.

"Leave the guns in the car for a second," I cautioned. "I better go let them know you're here."

Nobody gave my words a second thought. They just pulled a cooler out of the back and headed inside as I walked over to give Rowan's crew a heads-up on my guests.

There were three agents on the perimeter out front. The peaked roof afforded no perch for a sniper. I figured there were probably one or two inside the house, as well as a few in back and maybe a couple on the beach. No doubt the rest of the team was either roaming the area or hanging out back in town, waiting for the next shift.

I immediately recognized the agent who had cockblocked me last night, so I gave him a wave. He said a few words into his communication mouthpiece and walked toward me. I told him I was hosting a few guests for the weekend; in the interest of being a good neighbor, I wanted to keep Uncle Sam informed.

The front door opened and Rowan headed in our direction. I noticed her looking at my house, where I caught all four of my misfits laughing. She gave me a glare.

"You didn't tell me you'd invited weekend guests. Do they have guns too?"

It wasn't a friendly question. She was pissed off. If there was a hint of intimacy left over from last night, it wasn't registering on my radar.

"Actually, I did tell you about my guests the other day. And yes, they all are carrying guns—legitimately licensed, I might add."

This set her off completely.

"Why the fuck would you have four people with guns here tonight? Of all nights, Nat—why this night? For Chrissake, do you have any idea what a pain in my ass this is going to be? Thanks a whole fucking lot, Nat."

She was practically spitting at me.

"Hey—what the hell, Rowan? Calm the fuck down. The guns are locked up, and I will put them in my safe with all the rest."

Her look of surprise registered immediately. She didn't know I had a gun safe inside. *Score one for the good guys,* I thought.

"You won't even know they're here, because they won't be. We're going to a party over at the Wilsons' tonight. What kind of shit day are you having, anyway?"

She exhaled and looked back at the house.

"Everyone around here, especially that dickhead Fitzgerald, has lost their collective shit over Harrison's stupid party tonight. You wouldn't believe the way he's ordering us around." She quickly regrouped. "I apologize, Nat. I'm really not a lunatic psycho. I swear."

The intimacy made its way back onto the radar.

"Listen, why don't you come over tonight when everything is done and have a beer with us? They're great people and you'll like them. Trust me." We were standing in the open, so I couldn't give her a hug. "I'll let you wear my shirt again."

Rowan smiled at that, which gave me a window to step back and offer my hand. As she shook it I said, "Have fun today—and I'll see you whenever." Then I turned as quickly as I could and walked back toward my house.

CHAPTER 29

It was time to spill the beans to the team about Tristan Dent's new project.

"A lawful, in-extremis operations network," Tristan had told me back at CSTC headquarters. "I've been working on this for a while, and it's a perfect job for you and your team. You're made for this kind of shit. You ran that *THUNDER* op like nobody's business."

He'd been approached a few months back by some hotshot DC players with an idea to establish a team of operators who could, if needed, augment the existing paramilitary and law-enforcement organizations within the United States during times of national crisis.

Much like the military's need for additional bodies to support its operations overseas, the law-enforcement community was in the same predicament back home. Rank-and-file officers were just not trained to deal with national security–level crimes. Translated loosely, the local cops couldn't stand toe-to-toe against terrorists on the home field. The president was restricted in the use of military forces domestically, and the federal agencies were simply overwhelmed.

"We're calling it *Rocket's Red Glare*," Tristan had told me during that private sit-down at our Maryland compound.

"What the fuck are you even talking about, bro? And who's this *We*?"

The recently formed Office of Domestic Strategy would be responsible for the program, he had replied. I'd never heard of it. Oversight would come from a board of select congressmen with national-security interests.

"'*Rocket's Red Glare*,' like the line from 'The Star-Spangled Banner'? Based on the Congreve rockets in the War of 1812—the ones that burned bright in flight and could be fired faster than a cannon?"

"Exactly," Tristan had said. "Just know that this thing has great possibilities. It's a game changer, and we are on point. It has your name written all over it in bold letters."

I'd thought about it for a few long seconds. "Interesting concept. Where's the rub?" For starters, I was concerned about the legality of the proposition. Though I knew CSTC would never willingly engage in anything even close to illegal, I could spot some obvious friction points. But I wanted to hear them from Tristan.

"*Rubs,* plural," he had said. "There are a few of them."

Rocket's Red Glare teams would ultimately answer to the president, but obviously in a completely unattributable way. The first point of contention would be dealing with operational security around state and local law-enforcement agencies. It had to be extremely compartmentalized.

In this new role, Team Rhino would be navigating a modern Wild West, our own take on Marshal Matt Dillon in *Gunsmoke*. The possibilities of fighting terrorists, human traffickers, drug smugglers, and dirty oligarchs were endless. We would be able to green-light almost any mission. We just couldn't ask for help or tell any of the good guys about it.

We'd have no overt support from anyone outside CSTC, federal guys included. Though the CSTC computer networks would be masked to allow for high-level secure intelligence feeds, that was about the extent of the support from Uncle Sam. If we got ourselves in a jam, it would be a toss-up as to whether we could expect help from the cavalry. We would be on our own, with thanks from a grateful government. Quite simply, we could not be compromised.

"Just taking a stab at this, buddy, but is Martin Jennings on the oversight committee?" I'd asked Tristan.

"Shit, the whole thing was Jennings's idea. His and the president's. Total happenstance that he was over there when you guys were getting after it, though."

Tristan had closed out our meeting by saying he and his wife would come up soon, and that I should take my time wrapping my mind around the enterprise.

That's what I'd been doing more or less continuously over the last few days.

When I was in the Army, there were always whispers of units outside the commands—back-channel spook shit that sounded too good to be true. Certain guys and gals would disappear from the ranks, only to have someone bump into them years later at LAX or Dulles or Kabul and receive a knowing nod that said,

Keep walking, buddy. You never saw me—got it? It was a fun fantasy, but I'd never believed such units existed.

Now I was being asked to run a completely off-the-books strike force for the President of the United States. *You can't make this shit up.*

CHAPTER 30

My team took the news about Rocket's Red Glare like the pros they were. If any of them had even an iota of apprehension about the program, I sure missed it. There were nothing but smiles and nodding heads all around as I walked them through all the friction points that had been stewing inside my head.

"This opens up a whole new world for us, guys," I said as I raised a beer. "It's staggering to think about what we can do with carte blanche to fight a domestic war on terror."

"Right on, Nat. It's a pretty wild idea. My only concern is getting real-time intelligence without the ability to vet any of it ourselves or ask direct questions." Meg, our intelligence chief, was a master at puzzle-solving. She had done enough real operations to know what separated good intelligence from great, actionable intelligence.

John Paul Kennedy smiled and shook his head. He wasn't one for deep discussions, but he might be the best listener I've ever known. He removed his John Deere cap, rubbed his eyes, and said, "Shit, with the fucking money Dent has, why don't we just make our own intelligence agency? Think about it: We're three-quarters of the way down this secret-army rabbit hole already, so let's take the fuckin' plunge and go all in. If we're gonna win this thing, let's stack the deck and kill these fuckers wholesale." He returned his hat to its rightful place, sank back, and smiled.

JP loved being a part of the team. He never doubted the nobility or validity of anybody or any unit in any country who stood against evil. He could quote great patriots from memory and tended to drop the words *kill* and *terrorists* in just about every conversation.

But his personal mission statement had come with a steep price tag. In fact, it had nearly cost him his life.

JP's younger brother, Mike, had been a fireman at Ladder 23 on September 11, 2001. He'd been lost in 2 World Trade Center, with only traces of his body ever recovered. JP had been a Green Beret at the time, on an operation in Belize. He'd been unable to get back to the States to join the search. Logically, he knew there was nothing he could have done, but emotionally he could not forgive himself. He had struggled mightily in the wake of the attack, experiencing severe depression. By the New Year, JP had left his beloved Green Berets and the Army entirely.

For two years, JP distanced himself from family and friends, did odd jobs around Las Vegas, and burned through most of his savings. One day he found himself on a park bench outside the Venetian, considering suicide. He knew he needed help. Fast.

That's when he'd called Oliver Smith, his old team sergeant. Oliver was already with CSTC by then, so he jumped in Tristan's G5 and flew to Sin City to gather up his friend.

Back at the CSTC farm, JP was given a room and access to

therapy. Tristan even flew in his old priest to spend time with the prodigal son. Thankfully, JP responded to treatment. On his own initiative, he started daily gym visits and began devouring books with a vengeance.

Eight weeks after arriving at the farm, JP knocked on Tristan's door and asked to use the rifle range.

Two weeks later, he asked for a job.

With Oliver's recommendation and my approval, John Paul Kennedy was assigned to Team Rhino as an operator and sniper on a six-month probationary period.

On his first security assignment in Colombia, JP killed a FARC rebel who'd been attempting to kidnap the foreign minister's six-year-old daughter. "I shot that fucking asshole twice in the head," he said afterward. "Didn't bring Mike back from heaven, but it sure made me feel like I was helping to make it right."

The foreign minister called the White House personally to thank the president for sending such a talented and brave American.

From then on, JP was a new man. He found peace and dedicated his life to hunting down evil.

★ ★ ★

"The problem with that," Meg said now about JP's suggestion, "is that it's such a huge, time-consuming process to develop our own system—one that will get us the shit we really need." She didn't want to hurt his feelings.

"But we could do it, couldn't we?"

"Yes, no doubt we could do it—with a hell of a lot of money."

"Leave that part to Tristan," I said.

Bottom line: As long as we were all 100 percent certain that this clandestine program was thoroughly legitimate—and that we couldn't be left holding the bag after a domestic operation—we were willing to jump in headfirst and immediately begin planning contingencies.

That settled, there was just enough time for everyone to get cleaned up before the party. Like most houses on the island, mine had both an indoor and an outdoor shower. When the weather was nice, I bathed outside and enjoyed the view of the Atlantic. The cedar wall afforded some privacy, and I'd even built an extra shelf perfect for holding a cold beer.

The boys immediately began a wrestling match to see who would get the first crack at the outdoor shower. Meg and I stood in the kitchen and laughed.

"So, Mr. Phillips, is there a new love in your life?" Meg asked, eyeing me appraisingly.

Her directness caught me slightly off guard. In every situation—a gunfight or briefing the SECDEF in a combat zone—Meg was poised and in control. I don't know if she was a card-carrying Mensa member, but she was certainly one of the most intuitive people I'd ever met.

"Uh, no, not really. I mean, no—I don't have any love life to speak of."

"Well, my friend, trust me when I say that *she* is definitely into you. Even from across the yard, I could see the way that agent was looking at you. You must have used the Jedi mind trick on her without her even knowing."

"There is definitely no Jedi stuff going on around this place," I assured her.

"Whatever you say, Obi-Wan. But you'd better recalibrate

your radar, because I'm pretty sure you're missing the signals. Then again, this is you we're talking about—you miss *all* the signals."

I looked across the yard and watched the protective detail outside the senator's house. The same three guys were still standing in front.

I finished my beer and got ready for the Wilsons' party.

CHAPTER 31

Courville Estate
Cliff Road, Nantucket

Charles Courville, the Ambassador of France to the United States, was the lone passenger inside the unmarked Cessna Citation that had landed behind the Hawker jet on Runway 45 at Nantucket Memorial Airport.

After last night's distressing phone call from his daughter, Elise, Ambassador Courville had canceled his appointments in Washington. For the past two months, she had rarely left the confines of her island estate.

Elise's marriage was over long ago. If only she could see that instead of indulging herself by playing the recluse.

Not long after joining his daughter at her Nantucket home, the respected diplomat had felt his resolve turn to shock. He had sat in her living room for the better part of the afternoon, witnessing her sorrowful tears and listening as she shattered his paternal dreams with stories of his son-in-law's shamelessly adulterous lifestyle.

"Coleman Harrison is finished," Courville shouted, his face flushed with anger. "How could he do this to you? On your mother's grave, Elise, I will ruin him. He will pay! I promise you, he will pay."

Elise Courville had more than enough money to last two lifetimes. Her father had seen to that. After her French mother died when Elise was a little girl, Charles had raised her as best he could, with the help of boarding schools and private tutors. He had also opened a trust in Switzerland for her.

The day after her thirtieth birthday, Elise had begun drawing her monthly dividend of almost $50,000. Given the structure of the investments and the financial acumen of her father's trusted advisers, it would be nearly impossible for her to deplete the fund before her 127th birthday.

Despite her privilege, she had always dreamed of an uncomplicated life. She was accustomed to living by herself. But upon meeting then–Congressman Harrison at a London polo match sponsored by the Duke of Windsor, she had fallen in love with the politician immediately.

Coleman Harrison, a rising star in the party, was said to have a real shot at the White House someday—but was virtually unknown outside the United States until Elise Courville granted him connections around the globe, courtesy of her ambassador father. Between Coleman's charisma and Elise's natural beauty, political insiders christened them America's answer to Charles and Diana.

Shortly after their marriage, Harrison ran for office and was easily elected to the US Senate. In no time, he became not only more famous than any of his ninety-nine colleagues, but was being courted by heads of state on several continents. He had even remained faithful to his bride — for almost a full year.

"I just want it to be over, Papa. I just want to leave and go back to Paris." She moved to her father and hugged him.

The ambassador shed tears as he held her, then cupped her face in his hands.

"When I finish serving the president, we will return to Paris for good. As I stand here today, I promise you that."

"Oh, Papa, I love you. I knew you would take care of me."

"I have many friends who will do whatever I ask. I swear to you that I will call in every favor to make sure he never hurts you again. Now I must ask you, Elise, how you found out about this latest affair."

"One of his staffers told me in confidence."

"Let me make a few calls. And then we can talk about Paris."

His phone in one hand and his briefcase in the other, the ambassador bid his daughter a tender goodbye. As he turned away, his expression hardened. He knew what he must do to help her.

CHAPTER 32

As soon as her father left, Elise Courville's expression hardened as well. She walked across the room and picked up a cell phone from the mantel.

She pushed the Disconnect button. For the last two hours, it had been transmitting their conversation to another phone halfway around the world.

It was through her father that Courville had first met the man in Paris. On an earlier trip to forget her problems, Charles Courville had hosted a dinner party for some up-and-coming Parisian elite.

Among the guests was a handsome and well-dressed man—an Algerian who'd found early success directing one of the city's large financial firms. Haracat al Marrak was thirty to her thirty-five, and was polite, respectful, and confident in everything he said and did.

From that first meeting, Courville had felt like she had known him all her life. During their brief encounters, which almost never happened in public, he was such a good listener—so quick with reassuring words for her troubles—that she wondered why he had no other woman in his life. He kept a low profile and encouraged her to do the same.

Only when she told stories of her life as the wife of a US senator did the Algerian show the slightest impatience, and his temper would almost imperceptibly flare.

If she mentioned her hurt and anger at her husband, he'd remind her that personal and spiritual growth outweighed any discomfort from her challenges. *Be a dutiful wife,* he urged her.

As their relationship grew stronger, Elise Courville would lie awake at night contemplating the Algerian's latest advice. She didn't agree with everything he said, but she couldn't dispute its logic.

When Coleman Harrison decided to run for president, the man in Paris told her what she must do.

At first she wasn't sure she could go through with it. But night after night, as she listened to his persuasive voice on the phone, Courville slowly came to terms with the reality he presented.

Every week she received a new cell phone. It was used to communicate only with him. He assured her that it could never be traced, that she would be safe from any repercussions. As each new package arrived, she destroyed the old phone and separately trashed its broken parts.

Courville trusted the man more than she had trusted anyone in her life. *So long as you follow my instructions and we finish the plan,* he promised her, *our lives will be complete.* He considered her one of his most faithful, he told her, and promised that he would lead her to glory in Paris, where they could continue their journey together. Allah would welcome her.

She looked forward to the day when she could be with him in Paris.

Now Elise Courville stood on her balcony and watched the late-afternoon sun descending. Almost every day at this time, she would sit on this very balcony and warm her body in the rays of light.

She looked at the people on the lawn of the house not far away. The owners seemed nice enough. They lived mainly in Florida, where he was a banker of some kind and had a son in college. In their years as neighbors, they had exchanged pleasantries every so often.

She could see a group gathered, obviously enjoying the company of weekend guests. They all looked so happy—so oblivious to the troubles of the world.

She dreamed of the future in Paris, when she could invite the new friends she would make to a party just like theirs.

CHAPTER 33

Steamship Authority Ferry Docks
Hyannis, Massachusetts

He answered to the name of David, but that was not his real name.

The man in Paris had sent him here to do a mission. David knew there were others, but he had never met any of them. Tonight that would change.

He had been living in Boston for the past twelve months, secretly rehearsing for this very night. He had repeatedly made the trip across the water, traveling on every boat that the company used to transport passengers to and from Nantucket. He knew every dimension, every function, of every vessel.

This evening, he would ride across on the *Eagle*. The oldest of the ferry fleet was also the easiest target.

David had proven himself useful many times before, yet in the thirty years he had lived, he had never felt as needed as he did tonight. The man in Paris demanded perfection, and David assured him that by Allah's grace, it would be.

Chechen by birth, David had a talent for destruction. He was a bomb maker who could fashion the most unremarkable everyday items into projectiles that could kill or maim, depending on how he adjusted the formula.

Tonight he had only one job to do: sink the Hyannis ferry before it made its way into Nantucket Harbor.

David guided the U-Haul truck gingerly across the ferry ramp and found a parking spot beneath the passenger berths. The guards at the security checkpoint never looked inside the cargo compartment. If they did, however, they would have discovered nothing more than antique furniture, expertly packed to avoid damage in transit across Nantucket Sound.

Twenty minutes later, the last of fifty vehicles was loaded onto the ferry. The *Eagle*'s captain eased the throttles open and began the twenty-six-mile journey from Hyannis to Nantucket. The ride would last a little under two and a half hours.

David checked his watch. He had ninety minutes to wait.

He allowed himself to dream of his next assignment. When this job was complete and he had proven his worth, his reward would be great. He would join the others back across the ocean for the next wave of the battle against the Great Satan. Perhaps he would be chosen to plan a new attack against the infidels.

CHAPTER 34

At 9:45 p.m., David casually walked belowdecks to his U-Haul. No other passengers were around. The sun had long set, and the dim lighting in the vehicle berths bolstered David's confidence as he made his way to the rear of the truck. He slid open the roll-up door and climbed into the cargo area to survey his masterpiece.

In a most diabolical fashion, he had designed this particular bomb by applying the simple laws of physics to create an indefensible projectile.

He had custom-made a series of copper plates—each one about an inch thick and a foot in diameter—and installed them in the truck. Ignition of the almost 1,000 pounds of Semtex packed inside the furniture would propel the plates with such force, energy, and heat that the metal would, in a nanosecond, transform from solid to liquid and melt its way through whatever was in its path.

The ferry's hull might withstand a single plate, but not the ten that David had positioned in the U-Haul's undercarriage, which would cut a ten-foot hole in the ship's steel body. Another ten plates that David had built into the truck faced upward, toward the passenger deck. He had angled the ceiling plates to maximize the fan of death that would further escalate when the U-Haul disintegrated into the ferry, becoming its own lethal weapon.

David would soon have the honor and pleasure of firing the first shot in the battle waged from across the ocean by the man in Paris, sending the children of the Great Satan to hell.

He took one last look at the ignition device he had concealed in the closest disk, then worked his way down his checklist:

Turn on small cellular phone attached to fuse igniter and check that it has network capability.
  Make sure second cell phone is turned off; place that phone inside waterproof bag, then put bag inside small backpack.
  Slide shut truck's roll-up door.
  Walk to aft end of vehicle berth.
  Signal boat waiting to make pickup.

Making sure he wasn't seen, David slipped over the railing and onto the fantail, then ducked behind the vehicle ramp. Pulling out a flashlight with a red lens covering the bulb, he started pushing the On/Off button in a series of flashes toward the darkness.

When red flashes began to reply in kind, David breathed a sigh of relief. His pick-up boat was on time. Soon he would meet a man like him—one who believed it was Allah's will to blessedly destroy the godless heathens.

David took one last look at the armed U-Haul and jumped into the water.

CHAPTER 35

Wilson Estate
Cliff Road, Nantucket

The Team Rhino welcome-to-Nantucket party at Alan and Constance Wilson's house was in full swing—and a roaring success.

The hedge-fund giant had found his second lease on life and was eager to meet Tristan to discuss some "possibilities." Si seemed impressed by the team, and relieved of whatever stressors he'd been facing at home before the sunken-Porsche episode.

Connie charmed my team as much as she had me. Wolf, as I'd predicted, was especially intrigued. Oliver made sure he stayed on his best behavior, while I hung out with Meg and JP, sipping cold beers and bullshitting about life and Rocket's Red Glare.

JP wouldn't let up. "Let's talk to Tristan when we get back down there, Nat. Meg knows the deal."

Meg smiled and agreed that if it ever reached Tristan's desk, she would back JP's play. Then she gave me a punch on the arm and said, "Enough about rockets and secret agencies—let's talk about Nathan's new girlfriend."

I halfway stood from my seat next to her and in a split second pushed her back onto the grass, then pinned her down with my foot. She was caught off guard and laughing so hard that she dropped her beer bottle, making her laugh even louder and call for help from JP and Oliver.

"Let's *not* talk about Nathan's new girlfriend," I said, enunciating each syllable as I stood over Meg. "Because there *isn't* one."

"You're gonna pay for this, Mr. Phillips," she said.

I was formulating a smart-ass reply when Oliver broadsided me, knocking me off everybody's favorite little sister. The wrestling game was on, right there in the Wilsons' yard.

I tried to roll with him, but his momentum carried us another full revolution and he assumed a Brazilian jujitsu position known as the *mounted guard*. Oliver immediately began slapping me—and not softly, either. I tried to escape, but he had me at a perfect disadvantage.

Not to be outdone, JP launched himself across the grass from about six feet away and landed on top of both Oliver and me. I was now at the bottom of almost 400 pounds of idiot and knew it was only a matter of time before the others joined in.

Our hosts looked on, incredulous, as Wolf Kerr went down in Nantucket history as the first man to perform a perfect somersault onto a pile of humans. With a thundering cry of *Dogpile!* Meg leaped on top, and we all burst into hysterics and rolled away on the grass.

I assumed such a spectacle had never occurred in the backyard of the Wilson palace. Whatever concern Alan and Connie might have been feeling about their unusual guests and their behavior, their curiosity won out.

Si clapped and cheered, and his parents joined in.

That seemed the signal to leave. We helped the Wilsons clean up, then said our goodbyes and climbed into my ancient Defender for the twenty-minute ride back to my place.

CHAPTER 36

Senator Harrison HQ
Baxter Road, Nantucket

An important announcement concerning the next phase of the campaign read the invitation from Walter Fitzgerald to the ten most senior members of the Harrison staff.

Fitzgerald took the tack of a coach reviewing the starting team for a Friday-night game. They would play according to the rules—*his* rules.

"At this point in the campaign," he reminded staffers over cocktails, "we have three weeks to play ball. Both sides are scrambling for the win. What we need is one key play that will send our candidate to Pennsylvania Avenue."

In the large living room of the borrowed house, the staffers waited expectantly to learn what that play might be.

Fitzgerald stunned them with the reveal.

"There are favors that need to be repaid," he said. "Donors and high-ranking members of the party demand that a young female fill a key role, so the Harrison campaign is launching a preemptive strike before the primary."

He marched directly to a beaming Aimee Sullivan and shook her hand. "Everyone, please welcome the youngest National Security Adviser in the history of the United States."

His tone left no room for debate or further discussion. The silence was deafening. But the more the staff reeled, the better Fitzgerald felt. Their turmoil perfectly set up the next and most critical piece of the exit strategy he had planned for Aimee.

"We'll officially release word on Monday," Fitzgerald explained. "Friends of the campaign have arranged for Aimee to take an immersion course in foreign policy at the Kennedy School in Cambridge. They will stack the deck with Harvard's heaviest-hitting intellectuals—the greatest strategists in the world.

"You know the saying, people: It's Christmas in July for the Harrison campaign," Fitzgerald said. *No reason why the coach shouldn't finish with some cheerleading.*

The aides lined up with their hands extended, and Aimee Sullivan graciously shook them. Coleman Harrison glided into the room. Sullivan took both the candidate's hands in hers and squeezed.

The show of loyalty complete, the party started to fade.

What only Walt Fitzgerald knew was that the redheaded bitch would never make it to Monday. By the time she reached her apartment in Boston tomorrow night, the appointment charade would be over. The only thing left to do would be the spin required to distance the Harrison campaign from the woman soon to be revealed as a coke-addicted former staffer.

By 9:30 p.m., the house was quiet. Apart from Harrison, Fitzgerald, and Sullivan, only the Secret Service agents and a senior aide remained. The campaign manager and his aide left for the study to work on the press release, leaving Sullivan and Harrison alone for the first time in days.

Without a word, Harrison walked across the room toward the staircase. Sullivan followed him upstairs to thank him in her own unique way.

CHAPTER 37

Nantucket Memorial Airport

The men could have been any of the many itinerant workers who flocked to the island every summer. The ones who toiled the fishing boats or tended the lawns or performed any of the backbreaking manual labor needed to keep this island of the super-rich functioning.

These three men happened to be Mexican. They had arrived a year ago on visas purchased with the help of a man in Paris. Since then they had been sharing a one-bedroom apartment on the island and working as truck drivers, hauling away the trash of the wealthy.

Tonight they drove toward the airport in their big green garbage truck, then pulled off the road on a dark stretch away from any streetlights. The first man looked at his friends, checked his cell phone, then jumped out of the cab. He walked to the back of the truck and reached underneath the bags of trash to retrieve his gear. He grabbed the military-issue green duffel bag and slung it over his shoulder.

ROCKET'S RED GLARE

He headed down the street in the direction of a motel. The motel maids were his neighbors, and he had easily gleaned from them the intelligence that this was where Senator Harrison's Secret Service agents stayed when he was on the island. The agents slept in shifts, four to each of two adjacent rooms.

He looked at his watch. It was 9:55 p.m. In five minutes, he would kill all the infidels.

The second man jumped out of the truck and walked across the road toward the airport, stopping by a cluster of small trees. The full summer foliage would shield him from the streetlight but still afford an unobstructed view of the control tower. A clear line of sight meant he had a clear shot at the structure, which housed the communications equipment necessary to direct incoming and outgoing aircraft. He checked his watch. It was 9:58 p.m.

The last man drove the garbage truck at a crawl, turning off the headlights as he approached the airfield's last utility gate. The chain-link fence was secured with a heavy gauge lock that held the gate shut and denied intruders access to the runway. He reached behind his seat and pulled out a pair of bolt cutters.

His was the easiest job of all. When given the signal at the appointed time, all he had to do was drive the garbage truck onto the tarmac and park it at the intersection of both runways. So positioned, the huge garbage truck would effectively block any fixed-wing aircraft from landing on the island.

The last man was also armed with thermite grenades and a dozen lightweight antitank weapons—all of it stolen equipment that had been earmarked for destruction two years prior, before disappearing from a National Guard armory in Brownsville, Texas. Records of the subsequent investigation had been lost.

CHAPTER 38

Nantucket Harbor

The fishing boat drifted lazily in the dark night about half a mile north of Nantucket. The lone boatman had been watching the long, slow approach of the Nantucket *Eagle* ferry and patiently awaiting his signal.

Just over one hundred yards from the *Eagle*'s route, the boatman noticed a blinking red light on the port side. His contact was ready for pickup. The boatman tossed his cigarette into the dark water, pulled a flashlight from his duffel bag, and blinked back a series of lights.

The boatman started the engines. Compared to the *Eagle*'s massive engines, the twin Mercury 250-horsepower engines barely made a sound. Pointing the sloop's bow in the direction of the ferry's wake, he guesstimated the position of his contact. In about four minutes, he spotted a red light just above the water. The boatman slowed the sloop and allowed it to drift downwind until he was positioned to make the rescue.

ROCKET'S RED GLARE

The boatman hung a dive ladder over the side, then shifted the motor into Neutral. The man in the water waited for the boat to stop rolling in the *Eagle*'s wake before attempting to haul himself aboard. The boatman held out his hand to his brother-in-arms and helped him into the craft.

The men did not recognize each other, nor did they expect to. Even in the beam of the flashlight, both could see that the boatman was darker-skinned than the man who had jumped off the *Eagle*.

Without saying a word, the swimmer pulled off his backpack, settled himself on the deck, and reached inside for a waterproof bag.

Engrossed in the setup of his mission's next step, he failed to notice the boatman's movements near the cockpit. The machete blade hit the back of the swimmer's neck with such force that it sliced easily through his vertebrae and stuck in the deck of the boat. The swimmer's head tumbled into his own lap.

The boatman had followed his orders exactly. Now to make the call. He picked the waterproof bag out of the pool of the swimmer's blood and extracted the preprogrammed cell phone.

The boatman used one of his own phones to quickly send a one-word text: GLORY. Then he pulled out the SIM card and threw the phone, the machete, and the tiny chip into the black seawater, along with the swimmer's head and body.

As the ferry glided toward Nantucket Harbor, the boatman tacked in the direction of Martha's Vineyard and gave the engine all the gas he could. He needed to put at least half a mile between his sloop and the *Eagle* if he was to escape the brunt of the coming explosion.

At 10 p.m., he found the number in the speed dial of the swimmer's phone and called it.

The war was about to begin.

CHAPTER 39

Nantucket Eagle *ferry*

The cell phone rang inside the U-Haul. The voltage in the ringer function was more than enough to send a charge of electricity into the fuse igniter and through the blasting caps buried in the Semtex charges.

The blasting caps instantly ignited the explosive, which in turn generated enough force to lift the U-Haul off the deck even as the copper disks embedded in the vehicle cut through its cargo hold, through the deck, and into the hull of the ferry directly beneath it.

Sound travels roughly 350 meters per second.

By the time they heard the explosion, every person on the Nantucket *Eagle* was either dead or about to be.

The boatman looked at his watch. Everything was right on schedule. He kept the sloop on a westward bearing toward Martha's Vineyard. In a few minutes he would change course, turning east toward the west coast of Nantucket, the location of his next assignment.

CHAPTER 40

Nantucket Memorial Airport

One minute earlier, the man stationed at the motel—the first man to exit the green garbage truck—had pulled two grenade launchers from his duffel bag, extending both LAWs to ready them for action.

Standing less than fifty feet from his target, he raised the first launcher to his shoulder, armed the firing device, and took aim.

The instant the grenadier heard the sound of the ferry exploding, he squeezed the trigger. The door to the room where the day-shift Secret Service agents lay sleeping was an easy shot. The 40mm grenade exploded on contact.

The grenadier never looked up. He quickly armed and aimed the second LAW and fired directly into the room next to the first. If all the agents weren't killed by the explosion of the round impacting the room, the overpressure would be enough to render them incapable of responding to the impending attack.

The grenadier targeting the airport control tower—the

second man from the garbage truck—had simultaneously prepared his weapon. His first shot found its target, punching a hole about a foot wide in the side of the tower, the shrapnel scattering into a fan-shaped pattern as the grenade exploded. The air-traffic controller standing at his post observing the peaceful Nantucket sky never knew what hit him.

The second round hit the tower halfway between the ground and the roof. It penetrated the framework and started a fire between the interior and exterior walls. Fueled by the persistent Nantucket breezes, the blaze soon spread throughout the structure, causing it to spontaneously combust.

No response from anyone at the airport. Another strategic prediction proving dead right.

The grenadier saw a bright flash of light on the runway, signaling that the third partner had used a thermite grenade to melt the engine block of the garbage truck he had parked there. It would have to be towed off the runway in order for any plane to land. He waved to his first accomplice down the street at the motel and started to jog away from the airfield toward their next location.

The helicopters would be landing soon. They needed to be ready to attack them.

CHAPTER 41

Baxter Road

"Did you hear that?" Meg Fuller asked. I was driving all of us back to my place in Sconset, with Oliver sitting shotgun and Meg wedged between JP and Wolf in back. "It sounded like an explosion."

"I'm pretty sure you're right," I replied. "But what could have blown up on or around this island? Gas tank, maybe?"

The oncoming headlights of a truck swerved briefly into our lane, then raced past us. My mind switched into reasoning mode as I continued to drive. I thought about that big Ford lawn-service truck I had almost hit—in almost the same location—on my way home with Rowan Anderson from our dinner date at the Rope Walk.

Either intuition or cynicism tripped an internal alarm. "Hold on—something's fucked up." I hit the brakes hard and stopped.

The five of us slipped right into tactical mode. Spontaneously, the doors flew open and we all climbed out of the vehicle, scanning the perimeter for security. Our guns were drawn. We all felt it: the innate warnings of danger that soldiers like us had experienced time and again in battle.

"Anybody see anything?" I asked.

"Negative," said Wolf.

"All clear at six o'clock," said Meg.

"Twelve o'clock, forty meters, Christmas-tree lights," JP said clearly. He was pointing like a Labrador to a string of wires sitting on the road.

On examination, it appeared that these particular lights were in fact a type of IED: It used a simple open-circuit electrical system with a power source, in this case the modified string of Christmas-tree lights. If a vehicle ran over the seemingly harmless cluster of wires on the road, its weight would force the wires to touch, completing the electrical circuit and igniting the firing device inside the projectile.

End result: a flaming mass of molten lead hurtling through the air, instantaneously decimating whatever unarmored automobile stood in its path.

"Very nice, Nathan," said Oliver. "I make it home from our little shit show in Iraq only to get blown up by an IED in Nan-fucking-tucket." Serious as the situation was, he was grinning.

"You're killing me, Smalls," I replied without hesitation. "What do you think?"

"Don't think we have much choice." He nodded to the self-designated clearing team. "Go get 'em, boys."

Wolf took one side of the road and JP the other, each scanning the area and watching for any sign of enemy triggermen while moving slowly and deliberately toward the string of lights. It was important that they identify the location of the projectile so it could be separated from the firing device.

I held my breath, a thin defense against the prospect of witnessing two of my best friends vaporized before my eyes.

CHAPTER 42

Senator Harrison HQ
Baxter Road, Nantucket

United States Secret Service Special Agent in Charge Rowan Anderson had just finished walking the perimeter of the senator's de facto campaign headquarters. Now that she'd checked each of the sentinel's security positions, she paused in the side yard to look at her watch. The illuminated dial showed 10 p.m.

She looked at the two agents posted in the front yard, standing about three feet apart in the darkness beyond the glow of the porch light. The men were obviously deep in conversation, likely catching up on the latest behind-the-scenes gossip. Doubtless they were talking about the news that had swept the Harrison detail: The senator's young aide, Aimee Sullivan, would be joining the National Security Council.

"It's all part of the job," Agent Anderson muttered to herself, checking her watch again.

ROCKET'S RED GLARE

The periodic gusts of wind blowing from the North Atlantic masked the whisper of the sniper's 7.62mm bullet. It hit the first special agent squarely between his right ear and eye, killing him instantly. He did not blink, he did not cry for help, he just crumpled to the ground. As the agent next to him spun on instinct to search the blackness for the threat, the sniper's second shot tore through the second agent's larynx and nearly severed his head.

Anderson saw it all unfold right before her eyes. She could sense the unknown, silent killer—or killers—racing toward her from the darkness. Whoever they were, she knew they were coming. She drew her weapon and began to run, adrenaline pumping through her body, her senses on overdrive. Had she not been running so fast she would have seen a third agent fall as swiftly as the others.

The surge of adrenaline impaired her motor skills. The doorknob wouldn't turn in her sweaty hands. She had to get to Harrison. It was her job.

Anderson finally gained access and raced inside. She thought she heard footsteps on the porch but kept running up the stairs, her legs pumping as fast as she could force them to. She knew where he was. She had to get there first. It's what she was paid to do.

The door to the bedroom was closed. Without missing a beat, she forcefully kicked it open. Her tactical training took over immediately, her actions all muscle memory. In one sweep of the room she saw two naked people on the bed. A woman on top, straddling the senator.

The agent, two steps inside the room, paused for a second in her attack posture, her pistol leveled at them, just as she had been taught at the training center in Greenbelt, Maryland. The senator—quite possibly the next President of the United States of America—was lying spread-eagle on the bed of a wealthy donor, one hand cuffed to the headboard while his dominatrix and future National Security Adviser administered as much sexual pain as he could withstand.

It was insane—the whole episode was insane. It was almost more than Anderson could process. Seconds counted.

"Get the fuck out!" Aimee Sullivan demanded.

The two women's eyes met. Instantly Anderson realized that Sullivan was less angry at the interruption than mortified by her vulnerable position, naked save for a tight leather corset.

The shame of it was beginning to register when the first round from Anderson's 9mm hit Aimee Sullivan in the left shoulder and spun her counterclockwise. As she fell off the senator, the second round hit Sullivan just above her exposed right breast. Anderson never took her eyes off the target as she walked carefully toward the body crumpled on the floor.

Harrison started to hyperventilate with shock at the act he had just witnessed.

Anderson shushed him, putting her non-firing finger to her lips. Aimee Sullivan's mangled left arm was hanging by only her bloody bicep. She was trying to breathe, but so much fluid had filled her lungs that she was drowning in her own blood.

"Is...she...dead?" the senator stammered.

The sound of the bullet discharging at such close range inside the bedroom was deafening.

"Now she is."

Anderson looked sympathetically at the senator, whose eyes

showed fear beyond belief. He had never heard or seen anything like this—including the indeterminate noises from downstairs.

Movement at the bedroom door caused both Anderson and the senator to turn. Silhouetted in the doorway stood a person in green overalls and a black ski mask, holding a strange black gun with a long pipe on the barrel.

Anderson holstered her weapon and stepped away from the bed. "He's all yours."

The masked figure nodded. Without a word, he pulled another pistol from his hip and pointed it at Coleman Harrison, sending a thin dart into the senator's pectoral muscle.

Harrison started to wheeze as the powerful tranquilizer coursed through his bloodstream, causing him to lose control of his muscles and his consciousness, even as his hand remained cuffed to the bed.

The masked man pulled a large hunting knife from his belt.

"What the fuck are you doing? You can't just cut off his hand!"

The man paused and glared at Anderson. "Quit fucking around—we're short on time!"

A second masked man appeared in the doorway, his gun raised toward Anderson. The dart hit her in the meaty part of her thigh. She tried to lunge at the former ally, but she was overcome by nausea and felt the muscles in her body spasm.

Anderson's mind raced. *This wasn't the way they'd planned the job.* The man in Paris...or was it China, she couldn't remember...wherever he was, she needed to talk to him...

The second man grabbed Anderson's arm as she collapsed. She tried to punch and claw him, but her arms would not move.

Her body went limp, and he swept her onto his shoulders in a fireman's carry.

The last sound Rowan Anderson heard was Coleman Harrison's delirious cry as the first intruder began the gruesome task of freeing the senator's hand from the cuff.

CHAPTER 43

With practiced motions, the attackers unfolded two collapsible stretchers. In less than thirty seconds, the senator was strapped onto one and moved down the stairs. Rowan Anderson was placed in the other.

Her stretcher was loaded into the back of an oversize Ford pickup and neatly covered with bags of grass and lawn trimmings. If they were stopped—and they wouldn't be—no one would see the body that was bound and gagged in the back of the lawn-service truck. They had specific orders for this cargo. The man in Paris had given them very detailed instructions.

They knew that the Coast Guard ship positioned off the senator's backyard had been diverted to assist with the sinking ferry. They also knew a boat was idling just beyond the international water line. But that was all they knew.

The truck had driven exactly one mile when the driver stopped. The two men jumped out, holding a large spool of wire between them. In fifteen seconds they unrolled the wire across the road, then attached an explosive charge to one end and a battery to the other. *The man in Paris would be happy.*

Inside the black ski mask, it felt stifling hot. *What would it hurt to remove it for a few minutes?* The effort of pulling at the tight Nomex hood with one hand distracted his driving. The big truck drifted across the road into the oncoming lane.

"Watch out!" yelled the passenger in the front seat. The driver panicked when he saw headlights in front of him and turned hard to the right, tromping on the gas. As they sped past, the driver noticed that the headlights belonged to an SUV packed with five or six people.

Too bad for them, he thought. *They'll be dead in a few seconds anyway.* He maintained speed without waiting to witness the IED's work.

The remaining team moved toward the ocean. When they reached the edge of the bluff, the team leader looked for the worn path that led to the dark Atlantic. The men stealthily made their way down the same path that wealthy tourists took to the beach.

As they neared the water, the team leader turned on a flashlight with a red lens covering the bulb. He saw the reply — a green glow from a flashlight about fifty meters away in the dark water.

A few seconds later, they watched a Zodiac rubber raft crest the last breaker and reach the sandy beach. As the group quickly turned the inflatable assault boat around in the shallow surf and climbed aboard with the stretcher, the team leader lifted the severed hand of Senator Coleman Harrison and tossed it onto the beach. Maybe the crabs would eat it, or maybe some seagulls. Perhaps some infidel would stumble upon it. It didn't really matter — that's what the man in Paris had told him to do.

The 150-horsepower Yamaha motor was running and the Zodiac headed back out to sea. From his pocket, the team leader opened a small mobile phone and texted two people the same single word: PROPHET. Then he threw the device as far into the ocean as he could.

One more rendezvous and the mission would be complete. The money the man in Paris had promised would be deposited by the next morning. He watched as the lights of the kill zone faded from sight and they sped toward the vessel.

CHAPTER 44

Baxter Road, near Harrison HQ

"Fortunately, that was the shittiest IED I've ever had the pleasure of disarming," Wolf said.

"Fucking Christmas-tree lights. They barely even connected them to the battery. What the fuck is going on, Nat?"

"My spidey sense tells me this isn't your typical Nantucket episode," Meg observed, looking over her shoulder.

She and Oliver formed a security perimeter around us as the rest of Team Rhino huddled over the failed explosives laid out on the hood of my truck. JP, Wolf, and I surveyed the pieces of the killing device.

My mind raced over the intelligence we'd gathered. A loud fucking explosion behind us. A near miss from a runaway truck. An IED on the road to my house and Senator Harrison's HQ.

We solved the absurd calculus simultaneously. *It's gotta be about Harrison.*

I jumped back in the driver's seat as everyone climbed inside.

ROCKET'S RED GLARE

Wolf scooped up the pieces of the IED and slammed the back door. Everyone assumed combat posture, scanning in all directions for another threat as I drove while coming up with a plan on the fly. In case of another IED, I kept my high beams on. It seemed a safe bet that whoever had left the first one wasn't sticking around for a fight.

"Get Tristan on the phone and give him an update. The unbelievable is happening. Though we have no idea what it is, we know it means bad news."

I didn't address anyone in particular, but knew that Meg or Oliver would be on the phone immediately. I could hear them punching in the codes as we headed toward the senator's house.

The immediate threat was about half a mile ahead. We would have to be prepared to drive straight up the gut with zero backup.

"Watch your asses and let's see what's up there."

I cut the lights as we made the turn onto Baxter Road. I could see my house near the corner. It looked intact, though I had no idea what lay ahead.

"Okay, guys, eyes open. Clear the perimeter. Oliver, you and JP go left. Wolf, Meg, and I are going right."

I stopped the Defender just past my driveway. We slipped out of the SUV and began our movement toward the senator's house. There was no movement anywhere. Guns at the ready, we searched for threats particular to close-quarters battle.

"Two KIA, they look friendly," Oliver called out. Meg and Wolf were a few steps ahead of me.

"One KIA on the south side," Meg whispered. "Definitely Secret Service."

Despite the subpar IED, taking out a Secret Service protective detail was clearly the work of professional killers. *Holy fuck—what about Rowan?* I blinked my eyes to clear my mind. *Where was she?*

I paused for a second at the porch steps, keeping my weapon trained on the front door while the team cleared the perimeter. In less than a minute, they joined me back at the steps.

"Oliver, Wolf, and JP, take the first floor. Meg and I are going up."

JP slid past me to assume the lead position in entering the house. Wolf was right on his back while Oliver, Meg, and I followed. I felt a familiar tightness in my stomach as my team flowed toward the open door. *Here we go again, guys,* I thought.

JP went left and deep, Wolf went right, and Oliver took two steps inside the doorway, leaving room for Meg and me to slip past him toward the stairs. I heard JP's voice calling out casualties as they took down the first floor. Meg was on my hip with her weapon over my left shoulder, prepared to eliminate any threat around me as I focused on our movement toward the second floor.

Stairways suck no matter how good you are at close-quarters combat. The enemy has the higher ground, and fighting against gravity is difficult.

We reached what appeared to be the main bedroom and immediately saw signs of forced entry.

I did a half-assed scan, taking in handcuffs on a headboard and dark bloodstains on expensive white sheets. As I moved farther into the room, I saw a body on the floor. Meg followed behind, finishing the cursory search as I moved to get a better visual.

I regretted it immediately. It was as gruesome a sight as I had ever seen.

A woman's lifeless body, executed at close range. Her left arm was nearly severed, but her torso seemed intact. Aside from her ginger hair, however, her head was barely identifiable as human. It looked as though her attacker had set out to rob the woman of any semblance of individuality.

"Nat—look here!" Meg called out as she moved closer to examine the massive bloodstains. She studied the scene for a second or two, then turned to me: "They cut a body part off whoever was in here."

The senator was clearly long gone. Presumably abducted.

I nodded to Meg and we left the room to continue the search in tandem. The rest of the second floor was clear. The question was what the boys downstairs would tell me about the bodies they had found. This enemy was determined. Whatever they had done, they had done it with great violence.

"Friendlies coming down," Meg called out, alerting Team Rhino that we were moving to join them.

"KIA in the house," whispered Oliver. "No senator."

He looked at me for a long second. "She isn't here either, Nat."

CHAPTER 45

Okay, I thought, *time to call in the police.* This clearly was more than we could deal with in any legitimate fashion. It was certainly a crime scene, and most probably some sort of national-security issue.

I pulled out my cell phone and dialed 911. I tried to speak as calmly and clearly as possible, but the voice on the other end belonged to a person in distress.

I could tell the communication process was not working when the emergency operator asked me if I was still on the ferry.

The ferry?

"No, ma'am—I'm over in Sconset. I'm standing on the beach outside Senator Harrison's rented house on Baxter Road, where there has been a mass shooting."

This sent the dispatcher into orbit. "Senator who? You're not on the ferry?"

Why was the dispatcher asking about the ferry? Was the explosion we'd heard somehow connected to the ferry? It was becoming clear that more than one bad thing had gone down on this tiny island.

The dispatcher was struggling and the connection was getting garbled, so I hung up. Hopefully someone would review the call and send officers out eventually.

Like the ambush in Iraq, it was up to me to step up and make some crucial decisions. My guys were pros, and I knew we could develop a battle plan much quicker than the local cops could.

First, though, I dialed Tristan Dent's secure number. While I waited for him to answer, I had the team do another quick search around the house, looking for anything that might help us figure out who was behind the carnage.

"This is not a robbery gone bad," I told Tristan after giving him an overview of the crime scene. "Hell, there hasn't been anything even approaching this level of violence on Nantucket in probably a century. There are a lot of rich people here in the summer, but hardly anyone significant enough to attract a Mafia-type revenge hit. There's no drug trade beyond recreational use, and no real reason for premeditated crime."

"Somebody on that small island in the shitty, cold, North Atlantic has to know something," Tristan said. "See what you can find in the house."

"Will do. And let me know if you learn anything about that explosion we heard."

Next I dialed Si Wilson. "Hey buddy, it's Nat."

"We heard a real loud bang or something from down near the harbor," Si said. "Is something up?"

"No shit something's up. Listen, for the next hour or so, I need you to keep your eyes open, keep watch on the nearby houses and roads. Especially your neighbor Harrison's place. Don't go anywhere or engage with anyone—just be my eyes and ears over there. I need to know what you see. Write shit down and be as detailed as you can. We'll be over later."

In a crisis, people not used to living in chaos tend to panic immediately. They move disjointedly away from threats. It's the ones who seem unfazed that you need to keep an eye on. It was a long shot, but I hoped that Si might be able to catch a glimpse of some type of orderly movement somewhere.

"Tell your mom I said hi too," Wolf called.

"Asshole." I shook my head and chuckled.

Getting his first real assignment had Si as excited as a rookie stepping onto the football field for the season opener. He quickly ended our call so that he could start keeping an eye out for any movement around that side of the island.

My first instinct was for all of us to get back to my house on the double, but then I took a moment to reconsider. We weren't in a gunfight, and a few minutes to gather the facts would pay bigger dividends in the long run. I instructed Meg and Oliver to peel off and do a final security sweep of the house, collecting anything that looked useful.

"I got a blood trail, boss!" Wolf cried triumphantly. Without hesitation, he shined the beam of his gun light down the steps of the porch and into the side yard. JP and I immediately spread out with our gun lights and followed Wolf's slow and methodical inspection of the dark stains on the grass. They were heading away from the road and toward the ocean.

Wolf was a stud in every sense of the word, but particularly with regard to his tactical prowess. Whether it was spotting IEDs or booby traps or just finding shit hidden in plain sight, Wolf had a sixth sense that I had never seen in anyone else.

He zigzagged across the yard and in no time was leading us

down a well-worn path toward the beach. The white lights from Team Rhino showed recent footprints in the sand heading toward the water. I couldn't tell how many sets of tracks, but it was clear that at least three or four people had moved in the same direction from the path to the ocean.

Wolf spotted something in the sand and JP moved to investigate. "Check this shit out," he called over. "It's a fucking hand—like in *Jaws*. These SOBs cut off some poor bastard's hand and just left it on the beach."

By the time I reached him JP was down on his knees, examining the bloody appendage in the soft wet sand.

It was a surreal tableau.

My mind raced in a feeble attempt to classify what kind of enemy would commit a series of acts that could only be described as pure evil.

We moved in tactical formation back up the hill. Oliver and Meg returned from their thorough search of the downstairs, and we took one last look at the bodies. All told, the final count was three dead agents, two dead staff members, and one dead (and nearly naked) female in the bedroom upstairs. We had no way to identify these people by name, but it was obvious who was Secret Service and who was on Harrison's staff.

Back at my place, Meg fired up her laptop and connected to the CSTC secure site to see what she could find. Oliver dumped a bag full of cell phones and notebooks onto my kitchen counter, all of which the team had collected from the senator's place, and began to inventory them. JP and Wolf took notes, gathering the facts we knew.

My phone rang. Tristan calling back. "Hey, buddy, have you heard anything?" I asked.

He had — and it was bad. A ferry from Hyannis to Nantucket with at least 100 people on board had exploded just inside the channel to the Nantucket Boat Basin. Every Coast Guard ship was out searching for survivors. What's more, Nantucket Memorial Airport was on fire from multiple explosions on its east-west runway.

A small motel near the airport that the Secret Service was using as an alternate command post and temporary barracks had exploded as well. With the fire and rescue vehicles all at the harbor, the airfield was completely shut down; no fixed-wing aircraft could come in or take off.

Had I not just walked off a kill zone myself, I wouldn't have believed a word he said.

"Listen closely," my boss instructed. "I've got two birds in preflight right now. They have your number and will be in touch on the secure frequency."

"Tristan, I think whoever did this has kidnapped and tortured Senator Harrison. I don't have all the proof, but we can confirm multiple KIA and a human hand down by the ocean. They must have headed out to sea." I gave him more details as quickly as I could to fill in the blanks. "I also have reason to believe they may have abducted a Secret Service agent, probably the special agent in charge."

We were in unprecedented territory. However we decided to respond to these attacks, it was clear the decisions were going to go straight up the chain of command.

"Nat, I've already spoken with the people in DC," Tristan confirmed. "Rocket's Red Glare is a go, immediately. The secretary of defense is working with the attorney general and the

White House to green-light other special-operations forces to interdict any future attacks by what they are calling a terrorist threat. But for now, buddy, Team Rhino is all we have to save this man's life. You have command of this rescue mission. Bottom line, brother: You need to figure out pretty fucking fast how to find this ship and take it down. Do you copy?"

"What about the missing Secret Service agent?"

I knew the answer already, but it was one of those preprogrammed questions we always ask.

"Senator Harrison is the priority."

CHAPTER 46

International Waters
Twelve miles east of Nantucket

The Zodiac sped over the surface of the Atlantic. The ocean was unusually calm and the team of assassins had little difficulty navigating the dark waters. Even with the light chop of the waves, the visibility was good.

The team leader scanned farther to the east, looking for the signal in the dark night. He checked his watch. They had been on the water for forty-five minutes. The linkup should be close.

He pulled out a cell phone and hit speed dial. After two rings, the call was answered and two red lights appeared over the bow. The Zodiac was a quarter mile from the ship.

The next phase of their operation was more critical than the last.

CHAPTER 47

Baxter Road

"We need eyes in the sky, Meg. How soon can you connect?"

My team had transformed my living room and kitchen into a working operations center, almost as functional as the one we'd left in Baghdad.

Meg was furiously pounding the laptop keys. I was counting on intel from CSTC's secure satellites, knowing that every second mattered. Oliver was standing at the living room wall, using a Sharpie to draw a map of Nantucket and the surrounding areas. Wolf and JP were taking inventory of our weapons and gear, checking radios, batteries, and of course ammo.

That left me desperately trying to gin up some semblance of a plan. I had to admit I wasn't doing too well at the task.

Time was on the side of the unknown enemy. Every minute that elapsed put them half a mile farther away. And no one was chasing them at all. How did that happen?

"Oliver, why isn't anything flying? Shouldn't the Coast Guard or the state police or someone be all over this by now?"

Tristan certainly was. My boss had already dispatched two modified OH-6 helicopters.

This attack team was legit, obviously well-funded, and wasn't playing the fuck around. But who were they? Who the fuck blows up a passenger ferry, takes down an entire Secret Service detail, shoots multiple campaign staffers in the face at point-blank range, kidnaps a senator and possibly a Secret Service agent, chops off a man's hand, leaves a shitty IED on the road, and does it all without meeting any resistance?

It was a plan of violent simplicity—and I had to admit it had been well executed. They had hit fast and hard, ensuring that the good-guy resources would be limited. It made sense: Snatch the poor guy, jump on a boat, and head out to sea while the Coast Guard is forced in the opposite direction for a search-and-rescue mission and the airfield has been blown up.

They had a big lead on us, but the only play was to follow the trail to the ocean. Every minute we weren't on the offensive lowered our chances of recovering the senator.

"Okay, Nat, I've got Bigfoot and will have visual in a second." Two years earlier, CSTC had successfully launched a Jericho V satellite known as *Bigfoot*. It was virtually unheard-of for a commercial company to put its own satellite in geosynchronous orbit, but Tristan had made it happen. The asset was closely guarded; even at CSTC, only a few operators had clearance. Meg, of course, was one of them.

"Good going. Let's see what's happening due east of here."

We all huddled around her screen, trying to will a glimpse of the boat on the big expanse of black.

My phone buzzed with the message that the two helicopters were wheels up, ETA sixty minutes. Some simple Phillips math told me these guys must've been pretty close by when they got the call, confirming rumors of the existence of another secure CSTC facility in the tristate area near the border of New York and New Jersey.

"Meg, the birds just took off. Give me something."

"Nat, *Bigfoot* is fucking five hundred miles above sea level, and it's a big fucking ocean. I'm working on it."

"Is that a boat?" Wolf asked. He was pointing to a darker spot on the screen. "If I'm right, that's a pretty big vessel."

Meg slowly zoomed the lens from 536 miles above the ocean to focus on the dark spot. The satellite images pulled from her screen weren't particularly clear, but they defined the craft's general size and length. A moment later, the screen changed to bright green as Meg switched the camera to infrared.

"Hold on—it's working." The images became much clearer. There wasn't one big boat. There were two.

In this part of the world, big boats were not uncommon. Wealthy seafarers with small dicks parked their 100-, 150-, or 180-foot-long monster yachts at the Nantucket Boat Basin every day during the season.

But there was no chance that two of these mega-yachts, in this position, at this particular time, had not been involved in the attack.

"Looks like we have our first target, boys and girls," said Meg. "Natty, what do you want me to do? Haven't seen any movement, and neither seems to be generating much heat."

Attempting a no-notice hostage rescue meant countless risks, but I felt strangely calm. If anyone had a shot at success, it was this team.

"Everybody, listen up. The birds are sixty minutes out. We need to be prepared to execute as soon as the helos land. Keep eyes on, get me a grid, and pray these bastards don't decide to jump too soon."

All eyes were on me and everyone nodded silently.

"We have two birds, two targets, and no time to rehearse the mission beyond a talk-through. Oliver, I want your first briefing in twenty."

We would be facing an unknown number of enemy, with no idea how well armed they were. Nor did we have one piece of intelligence that placed Senator Harrison on either of the boats. Still, it was the only plausible scenario.

"Assuming that the senator is on one of those yachts, his safety is priority. This is my call. I want two in overwatch and three on the assault. You are all cleared hot to reduce any threat. Shoot anyone with a weapon directly in the face. Roger?"

Before anyone could answer, Meg called out a warning. "Nat! Both of the boats have started their engines."

CHAPTER 48

Courville Estate
Cliff Road, Nantucket

Special Agent in Charge Rowan Anderson normally maintained a state of complete control, but she was rapidly losing it.

She tried to focus on her current situation while piecing together the incomprehensible events of the attack at Harrison's house an hour or so earlier, but the hangover effect from the tranquilizer was debilitating. As she struggled to keep the overlapping waves of nausea and panic in check, she realized that her mouth was gagged.

Anderson desperately wanted to rub the throbbing pain from her temples, but the plastic shackles around her wrists and ankles denied her that relief. She was still in her field uniform, her limbs flex-cuffed to the arms and legs of a chair inside someone's home—clearly one of the island's elegant mansions.

She was supposed to be on a yacht with the Russians. But

somehow all that had changed. *What happened? Why did they turn on her? Why was she even still alive?*

Breathe slowly, she reminded herself. As she started to take exaggerated inhales and exhales despite the gag, she felt a gun barrel press sharply against the back of her neck.

"Surprised?" Elise Courville sang out as she stepped in front of her captive.

Rowan Anderson's eyes widened with a mixture of distress and disbelief at the sight of Coleman Harrison's smiling wife standing two feet in front of her, pointing a Glock at her face.

"Shhh," Courville whispered gently, like a mother to her child, then pressed the gun barrel against the agent's forehead. "That's a good girl. Nod your head if you promise not to make a sound."

Anderson moved her chin up and down without breaking eye contact.

Elise Courville gently lowered the gag as Anderson gasped for breath.

"I am so, so sorry," Courville told her. "What was your name? Agent Anderson?" She enunciated each syllable in a sing-song, childlike voice. "I hope that wasn't too uncomfortable."

Without waiting for an answer, Courville then raised her left hand and struck Anderson hard across the face.

"Make a sound and I will kill you right now. After what you've done, you should beg me to kill you."

Anderson opened her mouth to speak but Courville raised her hand again in warning.

"Agent Anderson, your secret is safe with me—for now. I can see that your mind is racing to understand how you got here. No matter what you think, you will be wrong," Courville said with a Cheshire-cat grin. "You see, everything you did this evening was captured on video. We have footage of you watching your teammates die. We have video of you executing my husband's mistress. Thank you for that, by the way. We even have video of you ordering them to cut off the senator's hand."

Bullshit. It must be doctored, thought Anderson. *I didn't order that.*

"I'm sure you can appreciate just how serious this is, can't you, darling? Oh, and we also have recorded phone calls of you explaining how the murder and kidnapping were going to happen. Isn't life, well, how do you say, *a bitch*?"

Anderson started to reply but then stopped. She waited until Courville nodded her permission, all the while leveling the gun at Anderson's chest.

"I did everything the man in Paris asked me to," Anderson whispered. "That you all asked me to do."

Selling out for a large amount of cash was one thing. Getting set up to take the fall for it all was completely different.

"Well, things have changed. When the Department of Justice, the FBI, the Secret Service, and everyone else gets their hands on the turncoat, terrorist-sympathizing whore who planned the kidnapping and torture of my husband, a sitting United States senator, you'll wish you were dead. What do you imagine they'll do to you, Agent Anderson?"

Rowan Anderson, like most thieves, lived by two truths:

Living is better than dying.

Take whatever actions are necessary to avoid death.

Anderson bitterly acknowledged to herself that while she might still be alive, she was totally and utterly screwed. The first deposit had already hit her bank account in Switzerland, but the second payment was now clearly in question. She needed the rest of it to make her escape.

"Please—please tell me what you want me to do."

"It's very simple. First, we paid you an awful lot of money for your loyalty, but we need to know that we can still trust you. So tell me, why it is that you decided to sleep with the American operative?"

Anderson blinked her eyes repeatedly and tried to slow it all down. *What did Elise Courville mean by "operative"?*

"What operative? Who? I didn't sleep with anyone. I swear."

All good lies are 80 percent truth. She would have slept with Nat Phillips, had they not been interrupted.

"Agent, how could you have been so stupid? That man works for a private security company. He has a squad of mercenaries on the island as we speak. Hell, I watched them at my neighbor's house not two hours ago. Who knows what they're doing right now? You'd better pray they don't screw tonight up."

"You have to believe me," Anderson whined, even as she spun a white lie. "He never told me what he did." Nat and his friends were expendable, especially since they were probably dead now, strewn across the road from the IED blast.

The special agent looked at Harrison's wife with all the confidence she could muster. "You've got me dead to rights. But I swear to you, I am all in on this thing and I will do whatever you ask. I just want to get out of here. That's the truth."

The Glock remained pointed at Anderson's chest as the women locked eyes for a good thirty seconds.

"I want to believe you. But you'll have to prove it. Tonight." Elise Courville expertly cut the flex-cuffs off Agent Anderson's wrists and ankles.

As feeling returned to her extremities, Anderson listened in horror as Elise Courville laid out the new plan: *US Secret Service*

ROCKET'S RED GLARE

Agent Rowan Anderson was going to kill the President of the United States.

This lady is insane, Anderson thought. But Courville had her dead to rights.

Anderson needed a new plan, tout suite. She sensed Courville's confidence starting to falter and easily grabbed the Glock.

Now Rowan Anderson was the one pointing a pistol and presenting a new twist to the plan. On the wrong end of the turnabout, Courville saw no option but to agree. She nodded her head slightly.

Anderson slowly backed away, aiming Courville's Glock at the center of the door. She nodded to her new partner.

"Hey!" Courville shouted. "I need you. Quickly!"

On demand, two thugs opened the kitchen door. As they stepped through in tandem, they were hit in quick succession with 9mm rounds through their chests.

Before they hit the floor, Anderson put one more in each, then stuck the Glock in the small of her back and turned to Courville.

"Ready?" Showing no emotion, Rowan landed a huge right hook.

The perfect punch, it knocked Courville backward and sent her flailing onto her beautifully upholstered couch. Anderson had to give the woman credit: She lay there holding her face and quietly whimpering, but not once did she cry or scream.

Anderson surveyed the damage to Elise Courville's face: no breaks, no blood, but a decent bruise was already forming. Given the circumstances, it was believable.

She made a decision. It was time to call in the big guns.

CHAPTER 49

Wilson Estate
Cliff Road, Nantucket

Si Wilson laughed nervously to himself. *Some secret agent I am!* After a brief consultation with his father, young Si had walked into the Nantucket darkness, hidden himself by lying flat on the ground behind the boxwoods that surrounded his family's property, and started following Nat Phillips's orders to be his "eyes and ears."

It was exciting to have been given a mission, but knowing that Nat and his team were on high alert fourteen miles away planted a fear of the unknown that made Si start to doubt his courage.

The one rule his father had given him, though, was *Quitting is never an option.* Following that mantra, he might get insulted—he might even get his ass kicked—but he would not give up. And that reputation, he learned over time, became an asset and slowly boosted his self-confidence. People assumed that Si had grown up pampered, in the lap of luxury—*the silver-spoon shit,* as he liked to say. Obviously it was true to some extent, but not entirely. Si might never be the toughest guy on the street or the smartest guy in the room, but he would never quit. Ever.

He drew on that strength now.

As his eyes adjusted to the dark Nantucket night, he scanned up and down the road. All was quiet for thirty minutes.

Then came the sharp sound of gunfire and a lone figure burst out of the Courville Estate and ran into the front yard, gesturing with both hands and moving in small, panicked circles.

Si raised himself from the ground and into a low crouch. He started to move toward the house for a closer look.

CHAPTER 50

Atlantic Ocean, Nantucket coast

"Falcon 3, this is Falcon 4, target identified: eight hundred meters, zero-eight-five degrees. Over."

"Good copy, 4. We are seventy-five meters off your port side, confirm eyes on the objective."

We had been flying blacked out at 150 knots since Tristan's two modified OH-6 helicopters had picked us up on the beach at Sconset. We'd radioed ahead to let them know the latest plan.

"Falcon 3, this is Falcon 4, one minute. Over."

"Roger, Falcon 4, I copy one minute. See anything?"

I'll admit it was a dumb question. I'd known our pilot in Falcon 4, Tommy Lopez, for ten years and knew he would never shortcut any detail of a mission. He was as good as they come.

"Besides the really bright white lights inside the cabin of the really big fucking boat we are about to take down? Is that the sort of *anything* you mean, clown face?"

I laughed out loud. Even in the midst of a dangerous operation, Lopez was cool as ice.

One boat heading south and the other heading north. Both appeared to be about 150 to 175 feet in length, with access to the interior of each craft possible from the bow and most likely from the upper deck astern.

Tommy and his crew had planned our approach to the southbound yacht down to the second. In sixty of them, we would be sliding down fast ropes both forward and aft of the yacht in hopes of finding Senator Harrison—and, with any luck, Special Agent Rowan Anderson. Chances were fifty-fifty that we'd picked the right boat.

I had only four from Team Rhino to play with, so I'd put Oliver, Meg, and JP on Falcon 3 to clear from stern to bow. Wolf and I would rope onto the bow from Falcon 4 and rush the cockpit, stopping the boat and controlling the operation from there. Oliver, Meg, and JP would search and attack until they found Harrison—or anyone with guns.

Simultaneous insertion would be the key to success. It would enable us to maximize our firepower by putting five rifles on the ship at practically the same moment. The one thing I was confident about was our fire discipline: With all the unknowns in this harebrained scheme, I knew we could converge from opposite ends of the target at pretty much a full sprint and not shoot each other.

The modified OH-6s would hover overhead, shining their searchlights directly into the cockpit and covering us with the helos' MP5s. Not the most lethal protection, perhaps, but with surprise and speed on our side I figured we could get a jump on any bad guys who opted to fight.

We'd devised the master plan by hand-drawing the outline of the yacht on my living room wall and studying the crude schematic. Oliver gave a little color commentary based on some previous operations he had pulled. We could plan on there being at least two decks to clear from the stern down into the main cabin, while the cockpit would have a couple of breaching points from either side of the ship. Basically, we would make it up as we went.

"Falcon 3, ten seconds, I'm gonna hit the lights. Stand by."

Showtime. With one hand, Tommy and his copilot lifted their night-vision goggles and hit the cockpit of the yacht with the 1,600-watt xenon short-arc lamp at almost forty million candlepower.

Night instantly became day. I could neither see nor hear Falcon 3 as we maneuvered into our assault position, but I could feel the sense of panic radiating from our target.

Falcon 3 hit the insertion about two seconds before us. With zero hesitation, Oliver tossed the fast rope and led the assault. Within another five seconds, Meg and JP were on a knee with weapons up, scanning the deck for signs of movement.

No need to toss the fast ropes from Falcon 4. Tommy was able to bring us to a hover about three feet above the deck of the bow. I gave him a thumbs-up, double-checked where I'd land, unhooked my tether, and jumped.

"Rhino 3, this is Rhino 1. We are on the deck and moving toward your position. Over." Oliver nodded to JP and the hunt began.

"Rhino 3, this is Rhino 1—how copy? Over," Oliver said again.

I fumbled for the radio call button. "Roger, good copy."

Although the 160-foot Benetti yacht was rolling slightly with the ocean swells, I made a solid insertion. I was counting on my trusty pair of Adidas GSG-9 assault boots for traction. But as soon as my boots hit the wet deck, the combination of gravity, choppy waves, and slippery conditions knocked me down.

"You okay, Tinkerbell?" Wolf asked. I was on my ass and Wolf thought it was funny.

"Fuck you, Wolf." I wasn't quite seeing stars, but I would surely have a monster headache tomorrow.

Tommy Lopez continued to train the helicopter's powerful searchlight on the cabin. The tactic was effective against whoever was driving because the yacht's forward motion stopped, almost on a dime.

The sleek Italian design allowed us to run directly up the slight incline of the bow toward the cockpit. Wolf broke left and I ran to the right. I saw two people inside the cockpit but no weapons.

"Bang it!" I called over the radio.

Out of the corner of my eye, I caught a glimpse of Wolf with a flash-bang grenade in his left hand and his Colt 1911 in his right. He had decided to use his secondary weapon during the breach of the cockpit.

By the time he said "Roger," I was already outside the cockpit with my own flash-bang in hand.

"Execute, execute, execute."

Fuse pulled, I chucked mine up and toward the opposite ceiling while Wolf threw his low and right. Two seconds later, the deafening explosion and blast of white light forced our targets to the floor.

The crew members—two men, maybe mid-forties, covering their heads with their hands, their bodies curled into fetal positions—were clearly unarmed. And caught completely by surprise.

Tommy pulled pitch and began to fly his helo in a close orbit, still illuminating the ship for Team Rhino to search.

Sixth sense told me there was no threat here. Even so, I kept my HK MP5 trained on their heads while Wolf checked the spectacular cockpit. State-of-the-art navigation instruments were inlaid in teak and mahogany panels. The captain's chair resembled a royal throne. The radio and computer systems were powerful enough to control the space shuttle.

"All stations, cockpit secure."

"Roger," Oliver called. "Stand by for SITREP."

"Standing by."

Wolf began his interrogation and started with the basics. Gilligan and the Skipper had a vaguely Slavic look to them and didn't understand English well.

"Listen, motherfucker, if you don't tell me where the fuck the senator is, I'm just going to beat your ass with a club," Wolf threatened.

Nothing.

"Congratulations, you cracked the case, Wolfgang," I joked, landing my payback for his laughing at my spill on deck. "That one on the right was probably Bin Laden's fucking driver too."

Instinctively I knew this wasn't the right ship, but I needed Oliver to confirm that.

"We got one."

I looked at Wolf. "OBL?"

Wolf flipped me off in reply as we waited for Oliver to send the report.

"Target secure—dry hole. I say again, *dry hole*. We have one passenger, but no trace of precious cargo. Lots of coke but no Harrison. Moving to your location now."

Oliver strolled into the cockpit a few seconds later. Meg and JP had remained below with the lone passenger. He gave a quick recap of clearing the yacht. Apparently just another luxury craft, out for a cruise in the Atlantic.

"And what about the passenger?"

"Yes, we have some Russian dude down below. He literally stepped out of the stateroom while Meg was clearing. As only Meg can do, she kicked him right in the jimmy when he made a move on her. The bastard's lucky she didn't stitch him. Dropped like a sack of shit."

"That must've hurt. Is he talking?"

"Nothing I could understand, but I do believe he was calling Meg some very bad names. Anyway, he's flex-cuffed and gagged, so not going anywhere for a while."

"Can't really blame him, but it's the price one pays for getting in the lady's way. Anyway, gotta be the other one. I'll get Tommy back here. Wolf, see if you can find the other ship on radar. Oliver, go tell Meg to ask the Russki what the fuck is going on over there. Don't take any shit from him, either."

"I scooped up all the phones and guns I could find," said Oliver. "But what do you want me to do with all this coke, boss? He's got a shit ton of it—must be worth a fortune."

I nodded toward the ocean, smiled, and walked away to call Lopez. I gave the pilot a quick update, then quickly made a mental review of the details of this raid. Failed or not, it would be important data as we searched for Harrison.

"Didn't they teach you *Just say no to drugs,* comrade?" That was JP in his best Russian accent as my team tossed a few dozen kilos of Colombia's bumper crop into the cold Atlantic.

In a perfect world, I would have brought all three of these mobsters in for some one-on-one time with Meg. We would have rolled them up and done the whole drill, but we didn't have the time.

Still, I was feeling confident that we would see them again later. We decided on catch and release.

CHAPTER 51

Cliff Road, north of the Wilson Estate

Si was ten yards away from the figure he'd spotted in the front yard. He strained to hear what the person was saying.

What would Nat or the team do in this situation? he asked himself, trying to decide if his pounding heartbeat could be heard from thirty feet away.

From the shadows along Cliff Road, Si saw the silhouette of a lawn truck parked in the Courville driveway. As if gunfire on the island wasn't odd enough, a lawn-service truck parked in a Cliff Road resident's driveway overnight was completely out of the ordinary.

He set a goal: make his way to the far side of the vehicle undetected.

He looked again at what the figure was holding. *Is that a weapon?*

It was now or never. Instinctively he moved toward his left in a low crouch, then sprang from behind the hood of the truck. In a return to his ice-hockey days, he lowered his head and shoulder, then rushed toward the figure standing just three paces away.

He felt his shoulder strike the unknown person's torso just above the beltline. The perfect check. His feet kept moving, momentum propelling Si and his target forward into a natural somersault, with Si tumbling almost perfectly into a mounted position. He raised his hand to punch the face of his prey when suddenly he stopped.

Rowan Anderson?! Was Senator Harrison back home? Why else would the head of his Secret Service detail be here? What was going on?

Even with her hands in close, Rowan Anderson managed to hook Si's leg and buck her hips, throwing him onto his side. She let his momentum carry the two of them to the same position, except now she was on top. Then the agent clutched Si's shirt collar tightly against his neck and started to twist the fabric.

As Si's air supply shut off, he began to panic. He swung both arms wildly at the agent's head and face, but each blow only glanced off her shoulders harmlessly. He could feel himself losing consciousness.

"Rowan, please," he wheezed. "It's me, Si Wilson."

At the sound of her name, the Secret Service agent paused momentarily in her automatic combat response. The skirmish stopped as quickly as it had started. Rowan Anderson released Si's collar and rolled off to her side, breathing deeply.

"Where is Nat?" she demanded, fumbling for her phone and her gun. "It's the senator, Si—I know where he is. We have to get to Nat or they'll kill Harrison."

CHAPTER 52

Atlantic Ocean

Meg, Oliver, and JP were forty-five seconds ahead as Wolf and I launched from the yacht we had just searched.

Falcon 3 was holding steady at 130 knots and an altitude of 25 feet above the ocean. Falcon 4 assumed its position roughly 150 meters off the starboard side. The heading of both helicopters was slightly right of north as we scanned the horizon for signs of the second yacht.

I briefly considered the possibility that this could be another dry hole. But with time ticking, I had to believe this was our only chance. It was all too random to be a hoax. The other ship was the one.

"One o'clock, five hundred meters," came the call from Falcon 3.

"Roger, I see it," Tommy Lopez said, as calm as if he was ordering a cup of coffee at Starbucks. "I'm staying right and will circle your starboard side toward the bow, just like before."

From my position on the right bench, I could see the lights of the target ship in the distance. Had we missed the mark entirely? Did another helicopter fly Harrison away? Was he aboard yet a third boat? Shit, if they took that option we were screwed.

I felt the centrifugal force pushing my ass tightly against the seat as Falcon 4 banked hard to the right. I didn't know how high we were above the ocean, but in a nanosecond saltwater mist was splashing against my face.

Tommy deftly juked his course back to level and started to climb abruptly. "Troops in contact," he said in that same voice fit for the Starbucks line.

As Falcon 3 started its assault roughly fifty meters from the stern of the yacht, someone with an AK-47 walked onto the deck and started to spray the little bird.

Felix Green — yes, we called him "the Cat" — was flight lead on Falcon 3. Just as ballsy and calm a pilot as Tommy Lopez, Felix was tracking movement on the main deck aft and on the second deck as well. He knew Tommy was banking in the opposite direction, which gave him plenty of airspace to work some of the pilot kung fu for which he was known.

I was on the wrong side of the aircraft to see any of the battle. As a leader, not knowing what was going on was worse than the havoc of the engagement itself. I wasn't quite in panic mode, but the pucker factor skyrocketed and I had to talk myself back to calmness.

As soon as Felix identified a weapon on the second deck, he banked left and started to climb, giving the Rhino passengers the heads-up that the shit show was about to begin.

While Felix was on evasive maneuvers, Wolf on the right pod squeezed a dozen rounds toward the terrorist. Before he could assess his accuracy, Felix made a hard right—almost an aerial U-turn—and started a daring dive toward the stern of the yacht.

By the time Oliver and Meg were able to scan the deck, all they saw was a body on the teak.

"Second deck, movement!" Meg shouted.

"Roger—I saw it," Oliver yelled. "Hold fast till he comes out again. The senator is in there somewhere."

"Change in plans, Tommy," the Cat radioed from Falcon 3. "You guys better hit from the bow ASAP, or this dude is toast."

"Roger, good copy, I'm ten seconds from target," Tommy said. "Nat—you good, brother?"

I gave him a thumbs-up and without Wolf having to say a word, I knew he was prepared to execute this contingency. I just hoped they hadn't killed Harrison already.

The target was at least 150 feet long. It had three decks and what looked like a speedboat stored on the second deck. The first target with the Russian had been nothing to laugh at, but this beast was huge. I just hoped I could get onto the deck without bouncing my noggin off the floor again.

The good news: The boat lights were on, illuminating our targets.

The bad news: The boat lights were on, making us sitting ducks.

I gave my gun a quick check to make sure I had a round chambered and looked up just in time to see the skid of Falcon 4 nearly touching the bow. Nothing but deck below me, so I jumped.

So far, so good. Wolf was on a knee, weapon armed and ready, scanning for threats. Lopez was off in orbit in no time, with not a shot fired his way.

"We gotta find Harrison. Any other action is a threat. You take point, Wolf. Get us inside pronto."

He nodded and moved to the port side. I could see movement in the pilothouse, but the lights from inside were too bright. Those assholes from the first yacht must have called to warn them. Shit.

"Come on, Wolf. We gotta go."

"No shit, Sherlock."

We were crouched just below the pilothouse when I looked up and saw someone scanning the side of the boat, obviously looking for us. One hand held a pistol and the other was shielding his eyes, trying to block the light.

"Got one right above us, pistol," I whispered to Wolf.

Without a sound, Wolf spun slightly from his crouch and shot the guy right in the face. We immediately raced toward the stern, seeking a breach point before things got messy.

Now under cover, we found a stairway leading to the second deck. As Wolf darted up the stairs, I scanned the rear for signs of Falcon 3. I couldn't see anything past the light on the deck.

"Meg, Oliver, JP, are you in? Over."

No response. Nothing. Fuck. For all I knew, they could be in the drink. We had to keep going. I rushed to catch up to Wolf and join him in looking for any signs of Harrison.

Wolf was in a careful hurry, heading back toward the bow of the ship. From behind, I saw him point toward the pilothouse door with his non-firing hand. As I moved toward him, I pulled a flash-bang from my kit and prepared to toss it. I held it off to Wolf's right so he could see, pulled the triggering cord, and tossed it hard into the room.

We turned and halfway covered our eyes and ears as the

eruption of brilliant white light and deafening explosion announced our arrival. Wolf rushed in with me right in his hip pocket. The guy with his face shot off was slumped on the floor. Two idiots were dazed where they stood, covering their ears. They both had holsters, but their weapons had dropped to the floor, either when their buddy got iced or when the bang hit them.

I drop-kicked the first mate. Wolf took the guy on the left, maybe the captain. I guess the Russians forgot to tell them about the flex-cuffing part, because nine seconds later they too were flex-cuffed and lying on the floor.

While Wolf searched for phones and documents, I tried the radio again. No luck. Then I heard a voice yelling, "Friendlies down below!"

As I made my way down the steps to what must have been the main deck, I saw Oliver, Meg, and JP stepping over a dead body, clearing the rooms left and right as they moved.

It was great to see them safe, of course, but my first words were, "What the fuck is up with your comms?"

"Hey man, the comms went to shit as soon as we got inside," Oliver replied. "I couldn't hear anything except for the flash-bang. Who knows?"

"Harrison?"

"Haven't found him, Nat. Meg stitched this dude as we breached, but so far nothing. The floor below this one is crew quarters. Or the engine room back there, maybe."

I told them to clear the crew berth; JP and I would take the engine room.

This whole exchange lasted about five seconds. Then we literally passed each other in the hallway as they moved forward and we moved aft. JP was already pulling security on the engine-room entry door when I heard shots fired down below. The boys and Meg were in contact.

I didn't call anything on the radio; instead I looked at JP and nodded for him to continue. If Oliver needed anything, he would call me. Or at least yell really loud.

With the sound of sporadic gunfire continuing below us, JP pushed through to the right and I buttonhooked to the left in the tight confines of the room. We scanned for about two seconds before realizing it was another dry hole. No way could the injured senator be in here.

As we moved out of the engine room and made our way toward Oliver and his team, I heard the words I loved to hear: *Jackpot! We're good—you can stay up there!*

In this case, *Jackpot* meant Senator Coleman R. Harrison. What a relief. The second part of the message was odd, but I gave JP the nod to move on.

As we descended to the crew deck, I could smell freshly burned gunpowder from the firefight. Brass casings littered the floor, while the yacht's interior walls were paneled in splintered wood. Four dead bodies lay scattered around the stateroom.

"Senator Harrison is alive," Meg reported. "But just barely. Blunt-force trauma to the head and chest. His left hand has been amputated, and he's lost a lot of blood. We've got to get him to a surgeon ASAP."

Then I saw Oliver, his left arm drenched in blood, propped against a wall and facing an open door. As JP and I moved toward him, he spoke very clearly, enunciating each word for impact.

"As I said, I'm okay, just don't move. I'm serious: *Don't. Fucking. Move.* Harrison's wired."

CHAPTER 53

Paris, France

The man in Paris, Haracat al Marrak, watched the video for the third time. The movie cameras, laptops, and lights hadn't delivered the high production values he'd envisioned, but the message was clear: Senator Harrison's battered body was easily identifiable against a backdrop covered in Arabic script.

His mind was methodically reviewing the events of the past twelve hours. The attack on the beach house had been executed flawlessly. The men in the American waters had done their jobs exactly as he had planned. The woman had perfectly made the double-blackmail deal with the Secret Service agent. The last-minute change was also perfectly handled.

His only concern was the Russian. The Russian was not a believer by faith—only in the money and the power—and he was late for his call. Almost an hour late, to be more precise. Still, the Russian had fulfilled his end of the transition a week ago with the last delivery of explosives. Perhaps he was dead. If not, it could certainly be arranged.

It was time for the American infidels to pay for their sins and face the fearsome events he was about to unleash. It was time for the world to see his masterpiece.

CHAPTER 54

Atlantic Ocean

Senator Harrison lay on a gurney, wearing a vest outfitted with wires and explosives. His prospects looked bleak.

"Hang in there—it'll be okay," Meg reassured him, though no response was audible.

Wolf knelt beside her, surveying the mess of explosives and wires. "I'm cutting this shit off," he said. "No visible triggering device. No igniter. No blasting cap to power the explosives. I think this vest is a dud."

"Buddy, it's all you," Meg replied as she scanned the room, looking for a possible alternate triggering device.

It took Wolf an hour-long minute to carefully cut wires from the faux detonator and explosives attached to the senator's body. He gingerly removed each and placed the pieces on the floor, careful to separate the things that go bang from the things that make things go bang. His last chore was to delicately feel all over the senator's body one last time before he called the all clear.

"All clear!" Meg repeated.

★ ★ ★

JP was already at Oliver's side when the all clear came, helping him to a couch in the galley aft to begin first aid.

"It's just a flesh wound!" Oliver said, in his best Monty Python accent.

JP gave a quick assessment of Oliver's condition: "He's got a through-and-through, left shoulder, lost some blood but he's going to be fine. Looks like it cauterized itself on exit and didn't hit any bone. I'll give him an IV and bandage him up. He can still shoot."

"Wolf, what do you got for me?" I said as I moved to enter the room where he and Meg were tending to Harrison.

"That vest they put on the senator is worse tech than the IED we found on the road in Nantucket."

"Got it." I entered the room and in two seconds registered the whole event. Torture, videotaped, agony, horror, message to be delivered loud and clear. Everyone in the world with an internet connection would either weep or cheer over images they would never be able to unsee. The video would be a horrible blow to any successes our country had achieved.

The enemy had accomplished their mission by launching the most personal attack against the United States since September 11, 2001. A graphic assault against not just any American, but a sitting US senator and prospective President of the United States.

I pulled out my cell phone and turned it on to alert Tristan. As my phone came to life, a light blinked with fifteen overlapping missed calls from Si Wilson and Tristan.

As I hit Reply on Tristan's call, Meg looked up at me with bleary eyes and said, "Nat, we lost him."

CHAPTER 55

Fort Meade, Maryland

The headquarters of the National Security Agency are hidden in plain sight, but the inner workings of that government institution are just plain hidden.

The Baltimore-Washington Parkway south of Baltimore has signs directing AUTHORIZED PERSONNEL ONLY to the NSA complex, but there are no visitor rooms or facility tours on-site like those offered at the Smithsonian or the Capitol or even the FBI.

Multiple defense screening systems protect the facility from external threats, while internal protocols make the interior virtually impenetrable by anyone without a need to know. Every room is equipped with alphanumeric placards that monitor the multiple cyber and biometric locks on every door.

The formidable fortifications of the manmade iceberg are mirrored in multiples beneath the surface of the Maryland countryside, where operations remain in full swing every hour of every day throughout every week, month, and year.

ROCKET'S RED GLARE

The long and short of it? We, the good guys, can monitor almost every piece of information that gets digitally passed around the world. Phone calls, emails, even encrypted communications can be tagged for further scrutiny if they pose a potential threat to our national security.

How it all happens or precisely what they can see and hear was beyond me, of course. All I knew was that somewhere about five stories below the parking lot existed a room where really smart people watched, read, and listened for blips in cyberspace.

And it was one of those subterranean eggheads who caught a glimpse of a blip that had originated a few miles off the coast of Nantucket. Whatever triggered the blip was enough to alert a team of analysts, hackers, and algorithm wizards to focus all their efforts on tracking the anomaly.

Whoever was going to receive the electrons racing through the atmosphere was no dummy. Apparently, the signal was bouncing around from London to Hong Kong and everywhere in between. Some complex system of loops and retransmission sites had been staged for this specific piece of digital information to pass from sender to receiver. It wasn't impossible to track its journey, but it was almost impossible to pinpoint its final destination: The relays happened in a tenth of a second before traversing the heart of Europe and Asia.

At least, that's what Tristan told me when I got him on the phone. All the good guys knew was where it had originated and where it was heading. They had no idea of its content.

That, unfortunately, was the intelligence they were looking to us to provide.

CHAPTER 56

Atlantic Ocean

"Harrison is dead. Nothing we could do, man. I'm sorry."

"Got it," Tristan said. "Give me the basics and I will let them know."

Them, I assumed, meant the faceless and nameless decision-makers who protect the president's liability.

"Tristan, here's the deal. Harrison was snatched from his bed, moved offshore, tortured, and killed. And it looks like all of it was caught on video. We're collecting as much intel as we can right now, and standing by for whatever you need. Tommy and Felix are still on station, but they've gotta be running low on fuel. Do you have anything on Rowan Anderson, the Secret Service agent?"

"Nothing, sorry. Send Falcon 3 and 4 back home to refuel. Navy ships are heading to the harbor to aid the Coast Guard in recovery; I'll get one diverted to your position for extraction.

Still a shit show on the island, but latest word as of about half an hour ago is that no one on the ferry survived. The airport is still shut down, so nothing's flying but us and USCG."

I took in that breaking news, then asked Tristan what the local cops knew.

"Short answer: They know there's a national-security operation happening, and that a government unit is conducting sensitive missions. You're the POC."

I could tell there was more, and Tristan didn't prove me wrong.

"The NSA caught a glimpse of some electronic data—obviously the video—and traced it back to your approximate position. They're still trying to get a lock on it. Take everything you can back to your place, and call me when you get home. Put your thinking cap on, buddy."

No sooner had Tristan hung up than my phone jumped to life again with a new call from Si Wilson.

"What do you have, Si?"

"Nat, it's me. Did you find Harrison? I know where he is."

I was so shocked to hear Rowan's voice that I dropped my phone.

She's alive—and on Si's phone. As if in slow motion I bent to pick up my phone, seeing everything and everyone frame by frame: Meg exhausted and bloody next to Harrison's body; Oliver collapsed on a couch, nursing his wounds; Wolf and JP taking turns pulling security and stuffing everything they could into whatever bags or boxes they could find. And I had just heard the voice of a dead woman turned sole survivor.

"Nat, are you still there?"
"I'm here. Where are y—"
She cut me off. "Where's Harrison? Do you have him?"
"We have him, Rowan. He's dead. They killed him."
Silence.

CHAPTER 57

Paris, France

Even with the sound muted, he could almost hear the screams. Haracat al Marrak watched the last few seconds of the broadcasted video, closed his laptop, and smiled. The methods he had instructed his faithful to use were meant not only to inflict unimaginable pain but also to repulse and terrorize anyone who watched.

How had the American pig-dog president reacted when he saw his fellow infidel filleted with a knife, beaten with a pipe, then castrated with bolt cutters? Soon the president too would die. *Inshallah* — God willing.

This of course was just the beginning. Several more would die by al Marrak's hand before he was finished. The biggest prize would take some time, but the plan was designed for the long term.

The American traitor had reacted exactly as he'd expected. She was pathetically weak, even for a woman. Greed and fear were all he'd needed to turn her. For money she would betray everything in her precious American world.

Despite the contempt he felt for her, al Marrak had to admit that the traitor was adept at tradecraft. *By now she has seen the video,* he had no doubt. He had even less of a doubt that she would perform her next task without a second thought.

At certain moments he had considered sparing Elise Courville. Her eagerness to join his faithful was exciting, even to him. Surprisingly, he enjoyed their long conversations. Her beauty was a pleasing distraction at times, her dreams of a life together not at all disagreeable. But she was the daughter of an infidel, and though al Marrak had turned her quite easily, she still had infidel blood in her veins.

He always knew that he would kill her in the end. She had moved his agenda forward, but her life had no further purpose for him. Allah had brought her to fulfill his will and now, with events in motion, nothing would stop him. The woman deserved to die.

Haracat al Marrak dialed the next number from memory. The international call took a few extra seconds, but after two rings the man picked up and listened.

"Matar a la mujer." *Kill the woman.*

"Entiendo." *I understand.*

The man in Paris regretted being unable to witness her death, but he was too busy.

He looked at his watch and began to undress in preparation for the first of his five daily rak'ahs. Allah had rewarded him justly, and it was fitting that he continue to show his devotion even in the middle of battle.

CHAPTER 58

Nantucket Sound

The boatman surveyed the bloodstained deck of the Boston Whaler and tossed a second phone and SIM card—these belonging to the decapitated swimmer—into the water.

The twin Mercury 250-horsepower engines sprang to life as he pointed the bow back toward the beach on the western side of Nantucket. He knew the police and authorities would still be consumed with the ferry attack, but nonetheless he constantly scanned the water ahead and behind for anyone out at this time.

He estimated about a ten-minute boat ride to shore, then a four-minute walk to the woman's house. That would leave him a little over twenty minutes to find and kill her. He calculated that he had a forty-five-minute window before he had to be back on the Whaler heading south. The two spare gas tanks would give him just enough fuel to reach Long Island.

His instructions were simple, and he was paid well to follow them: *Kill Elise Courville.*

CHAPTER 59

Atlantic Ocean

It took a couple of tries, but on the third redial my call went through.

"Nat? It's Si. I don't understand what's going on."

"Where are you?"

"On Cliff Road, a hundred yards or so north of my house. This night is unbelievable."

"Let me speak to Rowan, buddy."

She came on the line. "What?" she said, sounding distracted.

"Rowan, you've got to get it together. Listen, I know you don't work for me, but I'm asking you to get over to Courville's place and get eyes on the wife. I think she's in danger. After what they did to him, they might be gunning for her…"

The phone went dead. Again. Thank God for redial.

Si picked up, saying, "Nat, Rowan's a little shaken by all this. What do you need?"

"Get over to the senator's place and make sure his wife is safe.

They fucked up her husband big time, and I bet they're coming for her. Can you do that? Tell Rowan."

"Got it, Nat. We're already here. I'm standing in the front yard. Rowan went back inside. There was a shootout, and she killed some terrorists."

CHAPTER 60

Atlantic Ocean

The Mark V SOC patrol boat pulled to our port side. The Navy master chief had called my cell shortly after I finished with Tristan, and like clockwork they were here, tying their boat to the yacht and climbing aboard much more gracefully than my earlier insertion.

The master chief seemed to have a vague understanding of the team's involvement in national-security operations, so he didn't ask too many questions. We exchanged debriefs while Meg and JP showed them to Harrison's body.

The Navy was better equipped than Team Rhino to deal with a high-profile casualty—beginning with preparing Harrison's body for extraction. Their plan was to carry him a few miles due east and rendezvous with a Navy helicopter, which would transport the remains to Walter Reed Medical Center in Bethesda, Maryland.

Rescue operations had ended; we were now in recovery mode. All local emergency services had been deployed to the Nantucket ferry docks, and the Navy had dispatched a mobile surgical ship that would arrive soon. Several more Mark Vs were en route from the Cape to patrol the waters immediately around the island.

Security on the island was in seriously short supply. The sleepy downtown and the Nantucket Boat Basin were locked up pretty tight and the airport was still shut down, but patrolling all of that was more than the local police could handle. Once Team Rhino got resupplied with food, water, and ammo, we could help. I planned not to involve the local authorities any more than necessary, and their operation in the harbor was not my concern.

As the chief and I finished our chat, my team emerged from below. Not all smiles, given the activity of the past few hours, but as if he had read my mind, Oliver piped up that he was mission-ready.

"Hey, Chief, hate to be a bother, but is there any way you can drop us on the beach by Sconset?"

"Aye, Mr. Phillips, hop in and we'll take you right over."

The Mark V was eighty feet long and had a max speed of sixty-five knots (about seventy-five mph). I'd never been in a boat like this, and I was impressed. The ride to Siasconset seemed over in minutes.

With a half-assed salute and a wave, we jumped into the shallow surf and headed for the trail leading to my house. I still urgently needed to speak to Rowan and figure out what the hell was going on. If she had been kidnapped along with Harrison, how the fuck had she ended up back at his other house? And who did she kill?

"Okay, boys and girls, get some ammo and get back in the car. We need to cross the island and check on Harrison's wife, Si, and Agent Anderson."

"Already done, boss," Wolf replied as he holstered his pistol and headed toward my new front door.

CHAPTER 61

Courville Estate

Si Wilson recognized the woman standing at the door as his neighbor Elise Courville, Senator Harrison's wife. Her face was bruised and her blouse ripped.

"Hello," she managed as if in great pain.

"Hello, Mrs. Harrison. I'm Josiah Wilson. I live just over there." Si pointed.

"Yes, I know who you are. I know your parents too, though not well."

"Rowan and I—that is, Agent Anderson and I—are here to keep you safe until my boss arrives with more security people."

"Thank you, Josiah. That makes me feel better. How much danger is there?"

"Um, I really don't know," he said. Never moving from the open doorway, Si looked around for Rowan Anderson, averting his eyes from the two bodies on the floor. He didn't know what had happened. *Had the Secret Service agent stopped those terrorists from raping the senator's wife?*

The sound of footsteps on the stairs broke through Si's trance of fear and uncertainty. Anderson appeared with a couple of blankets to cover the corpses.

Much better, Si thought to himself.

"Si, I'm going to sit with Mrs. Harrison. Why don't you close the front door, take this, and walk around inside the place—make sure it's safe and secure."

The agent held out a Glock by the barrel, allowing Si to grab it by the grip. He pulled the slide back to inspect the magazine for ammo. Displaying the basics he'd learned from Nat and Team Rhino was a confidence boost. The pistol felt good in his hand.

Satisfied, he nodded. Si Wilson was ready to begin his patrol. He decided to start with the grand living room, its magnificent Atlantic vista much like the view from his own house—or it would be, he assumed, were it not still the middle of the night.

Surveillance would do little to keep any bad guys out, he knew, but he had his orders. He was checking the window locks when he saw a flash of movement on the bluff. Possibly someone who'd earlier walked down to the beach to look for traces of the ferry explosion now all over the local newsgroups.

Whoever it was didn't seem to be heading this way, but Nat had told him that writing down observations was important. Si reached into his pocket for his phone and its Notes app, only to find that he'd drained the battery.

He'd report the sighting to Anderson instead.

Si found the Secret Service agent and Senator Harrison's wife deep in what seemed to be a hushed but serious conversation.

The two women appeared pissed off at each other; both were gesturing intensely with their hands.

"See anything?" Anderson asked as Si approached. "Are we good?"

"A guy walking up the bluff, but nothing else," Si said. "All the windows are locked. I still need to check the back door and the garage."

Without waiting for an answer, he walked back through the living room, stepping over the blanketed bodies, and entered the kitchen, where he spied Anderson's cell phone lying next to a charger. He plugged in his own phone, then continued to the mudroom. *All secure.* He marched to the rear of the house and reached for the backdoor knob.

He had just touched the handle when he heard the distinct sound of gunfire and shattering glass.

CHAPTER 62

I turned the Defender off Cliff Road and into the driveway of Elise Courville's house. Like every other 10,000-square-foot place on the island, it stood big, gray, and empty.

No sign of Josiah, the senator's widow, or Rowan.

By the time JP's voice registered from the rear passenger seat, he had already squeezed off two rounds. The gunshots had been painfully loud inside the car.

"Two o'clock, one KIA, hopefully," he shouted as he ran from my vehicle toward the house next door.

Fuck, I'd turned down the wrong driveway. JP had just stitched somebody in Courville's yard. Meg was hot on his heels, while Wolf and Oliver sprinted toward the front porch.

I hit Reverse and punched the gas, burning rubber all the way to the Courville place. I didn't hear any more shooting, which was always a good thing.

Meg was pointing her weapon toward the body on the ground, which lay next to a semiautomatic rifle that looked

Russian-made. JP kneeled next to the body, searching it with his hands. Oliver and Wolf had already gone inside.

I trotted to the dead guy—his head was a mess—as JP stood up.

"Shit, dude—that's pretty gross. But a head shot from a moving vehicle twenty-five yards away ain't hard, *said no one ever*." I gave him a nod and winked at Meg.

"Offhand, too, Nat," JP added. "Just throwing that out there."

JP wasn't being conceited. He'd been scanning from the vehicle, spotted an immediate threat, and instinctively reduced it. I really did have to give him extra credit for the offhand shot with an MP5 at that distance. I'd buy him a case of beer for that one.

"Seriously, though," JP continued, "nothing on this guy at all except for the SKS here. All tricked out with a big-ass scope and bipod and shit. He was here to do some killing, that's for sure—the widow, I'm guessing. Looks like he got a sympathetic round off on contact, but he was a dead man shooting."

"How the fuck did he get here?" I asked. "You guys wanna bag everything up and take a quick snoop around, see what you can see?"

When I turned around, there she was. Special Agent in Charge Rowan Anderson.

She was standing in the doorway, talking to Wolf and Oliver, then raising one eyebrow at me as I approached. Even with ripped clothes and mud-streaked hair, she looked amazing. And she was still a pro. No smile, no pause in the action.

I took that as my cue. I walked straight into the house,

moving past a pile of what I assumed to be dead guys under blankets near the doorway. I pieced together the scene pretty quickly.

Elise Courville's clothes were ripped, her hair was disheveled, and someone had recently hit her in the face. She looked frightened; not quite in shock, but definitely on her heels. She had the beginnings of a good-sized bruise on her cheek.

I agreed with JP's assessment: The dead guy had been about to take a shot at the widow Harrison when his head exploded. The assassin's bullet had instead launched through the top of the window and into the ceiling. That could have been ugly — really ugly.

I didn't wait for an introduction before asking Courville a crucial question: "Where the hell is your security detail?"

Rowan Anderson answered for her, and she was none too friendly about it.

"Nat, she doesn't *have* a detail. She refused it, in writing. Her father is the French ambassador — remember?"

True as all that might be, rejecting security was never a good idea for the wife of an aspiring presidential candidate. Amateur Night once again.

"Roger that, but this place is completely compromised. I want you to take over as her detail. I'll call my guys and get her transportation off the island."

"What do you mean, *my guys*? Since when are you in charge of my orders? What the hell is going on, Nat?"

I didn't have time to explain or debate. Rocket's Red Glare was in effect and I was going to run with it.

"Rowan," I said, more sternly than I intended. "You know who I work for. Right now, it's my show. The airport isn't safe.

ROCKET'S RED GLARE

Downtown is locked up. So I'm making the call that we head to the south side of the island and set up camp while we work extraction. I'll get us aircraft. And if not, we will find a boat. Meg and JP are doing a quick recon outside before we move out."

Fuck, why does this always happen? I meet someone. She's hot and I like her. I hoped she wasn't too mad at me, but lives were on the line.

Back to reality, Nat.

She must have bought my plan because, to her credit, all Rowan asked for was a gun.

I offered her my Sig Sauer. She pulled the slide to make sure there was a round in the chamber, stuffed it into her belt, and stepped off in the direction of her principal.

To Elise Courville, I calmly said, "I need you to come with us. We will be leaving this island for a secure government site. Agent Anderson will help you gather some of your belongings, but you will not be coming back here anytime soon."

She nodded at me, then looked inquisitively at Rowan—almost as if requesting permission. At a nod from the agent, Senator Harrison's widow stood up, and the two women moved past me.

I waved Team Rhino, including Si, into the house. I said, "Gather 'round, boys and girls. I want to orient you to our position."

Elise Courville's home was better furnished than most, but in one respect it was appointed identically to every other house on Nantucket. After a three-second scan, I located the tool I needed: a large framed nautical chart of the island. For some reason everyone up here thinks of themselves as playing the lead in *The Rime of the Ancient Mariner*, even if they can't tell a buoy from a tugboat.

I laid the frame on the counter.

"Thankfully, it's real easy. We are about here and need to move due south a few miles to the treacherous beachhead at a town called Madaket."

We all looked at Si. It took him a second to realize that I had stopped talking, and he looked up to find all five of us smiling at him. By now everyone knew the story about the submerged Porsche.

With a sheepish grin he muttered, "Good one," and looked back at the map.

If we'd had more time and didn't have to worry about terrorists jamming us up, we would have had a field day at his expense. But we had a plane to catch.

"Wolf, see what the senator's wife has in the garage. I'm sure it's a nice ride, but all we care is that the engine starts. Then find something to cloud the headlights so we can blackout-drive. We can't take any chances. The route is straight, but we need to stay close. I'll take Rowan, the widow, and JP with me in my car. The rest of you are with Wolf. I'll stop about fifty yards short of the beach, so you can clear the LZ. Questions?"

"None, boss," Team Rhino said in unison.

"Cool—we leave in five."

I told Si to grab a beach bag and search the house for anything of interest: phones, laptops, and the like. As he scurried away, I heard footsteps on the stairs and watched Rowan and Elise Courville descending, each carrying several Louis Vuitton bags filled with God knows what.

JP reached out for the bags and motioned the pair to follow him to my truck. He gave me a *WTF* look. Clearly we'd both been tempted to make a smart-ass comment, but figured they probably weren't in the mood for fun. All I could do was shrug my shoulders and grin.

The impromptu bag of goodies that Si had packed, by contrast, was a pleasant surprise: It overflowed with iPads and other gadgets. I gave him an approving nod and smiled as he followed Oliver to the garage.

"See you on the high ground," I said as I turned off the house lights.

CHAPTER 63

Madaket, Nantucket

During the ten-minute drive south toward the beach, I dialed Tristan on the mobile and told him we needed immediate extraction. Then I told him where we'd be waiting. This was going to be a shit show of an operation, but surprise was on our side.

I coasted to a stop along the road about fifty yards from the sand. Oliver walked up to my window for last-minute instructions. Not that he needed them. He knew what must be done way before I began to dream up this plan.

"Good call on everything, Nat. But one thing: I sure the fuck am not doing that human-lighthouse thing. That ship sailed a long time ago."

I couldn't disagree.

"Si," we both said at the same time. And then, "Jinx."

It was an unenviable job, but tough shit, someone had to do it. After we cleared the immediate landing zone of any bad guys, whoever had drawn the short straw would wait on the beach with a flashlight until we heard the rotors of the approaching helicopters. Then that unlucky bastard would turn on his flashlight and wave it in a circle over his head until the birds landed, all while being sandblasted with millions of sharp grains of sand.

My phone buzzed. After the proper authentication, the voice on the other end confirmed our location as best we could identify it. As he ran down the details of the sophisticated LZ marking plan, he told me *About twenty minutes from the west,* which in my mind meant the exfil was coming from Long Island or Connecticut. I assumed it would be flown by Team Falcon, but now that we'd launched Rocket's Red Glare, it was anybody's guess.

I could be on my deathbed and still recognize the approach of a Chinook. The lumbering, tandem-rotor helicopter was unmistakable both in sight and sound. Even in limited visibility, even blindfolded, anyone from the special-operations community could differentiate it from any other aircraft.

All kinds of helicopters are available on the commercial market, but the Chinook was reserved for military use. The fact that one was about to pick us up from a preppy island in the North Atlantic was a fact for *Ripley's Believe It or Not.*

How had Tristan managed to get his hands on the fucking thing?

I could make out Oliver's silhouette, and he turned toward me in a way that made me certain he was having the same realization about the Chinook. *Welcome to Rocket's Red Glare.*

Two additional Little Birds, similar to the ones we'd used in the search for Senator Harrison, were escorting the behemoth toward our location. Poor Si was about to get a baptism by sand that he'd never forget.

The rest of Team Rhino were positioned next to my truck,

kneeling in a line, left hand holding the left shoulder of the person in front of them. I watched the Little Birds break formation while the Chinook flared, did a one-eighty, and hovered about twenty feet above the sand.

The pilot skillfully eased the bird down to the makeshift landing zone.

I waited until the rear wheels of the aircraft settled on the soft sand before I started our movement toward the ramp and into the belly of the beast.

I did a quick head count—Team Rhino including Si, plus Rowan and Elise Courville—then tapped my head and gave the crew chief a thumbs-up. He confirmed my hand signal with a nod and a thumbs-up of his own as the MH-47 lifted off to the west just as quickly as it had arrived.

The feeling of leaving a battlefield is almost impossible to describe. *Relief* is an understatement. At least for me, it was as if every sense and emotion vacated my body at the same time, ninety mph to zero in seconds. Fear, lifted. Adrenaline, faded. Cottonmouth, gone. The last forty-eight hours had been a bear, and I was feeling certain that this would be our tempo for the foreseeable future.

The rhythm of the aircraft flying west over the ocean was almost enough to put me fast asleep. Fighting the urge, I shook my head and rubbed my eyes, only to notice that everyone else had already conked out on the hard floor of the Chinook.

Everyone, that is, except Rowan.

As much as I wanted to talk to her, conversation was impossible inside the noisy helicopter. I welled up with empathy as she sat expressionless. She looked to be in a state of near-shock. I'd seen those thousand-yard stares too many times on too many people, and it never got any easier.

I couldn't read her thoughts, and I didn't know her well enough to guess, but experience told me she was probably feeling incredibly sad and scared. And survivor's guilt must be close to the top of the shitty list of trauma reactions.

Her principal had died on her watch.

The gods of the Secret Service were about to decide Rowan Anderson's fate.

CHAPTER 64

Outside New London, Connecticut

As the bird landed and taxied along some auxiliary runway, I peeked through the portholes to suss out where the hell we were.

Typically, the crew chief gave the person in charge of the passengers a headset to speak with the pilots, but not this time. I looked around at the two crew chiefs standing near the ramp at the aft end of the Chinook.

Both had dark-tinted eyeshades pulled down from their helmets, as well as stupid-looking cartoon-printed face shields covering their mouth and nose—one was The Punisher and the other was an evil clown face. Each wore the typical olive-green flight suit, with a drop holster strapped to their right thighs. They looked all business and ready for a fight. Their aggressive and menacing body language was too cool for school. I immediately disliked them.

No way were these CSTC guys. I'd have given anything to

see members of our Falcon, Eagle, or Hawk teams. Instead I was stuck with these two wannabe super alphas. Undoubtedly good at their jobs, but train-wreck personalities.

As the ramp lowered, I saw a couple of black Suburbans parked on the tarmac in front of a hangar. A few people in suits huddled together, waiting for the blades to stop. It wasn't exactly the same feeling I'd gotten on Route Packers back in Iraq, but I had enough of a sixth sense to know that shit was about to go sideways.

We each grabbed one of the many ridiculous Louis Vuitton bags and headed off the ramp toward the gaggle of suits. As I passed Mr. Evil Clown Face, I nodded, smiled, mouthed *Fuck you*, and walked off the Chinook.

I should have been happy, but I wasn't.

I should have been grateful that we were off the island and out of harm's way, but I wasn't.

I should have been excited that the authorities showed up to help us, but I knew that wasn't the case.

Everything about this welcoming committee was wrong, and it pissed me off. I wasn't going to put up with their shit for one second. I could feel the rage starting to boil and my fists beginning to clench. I was gaining emotional momentum as the physical gap between us rapidly closed.

I chose my target—the tallest suit in the group. In about twenty seconds, he was going to start having a very bad day. As I dropped the bag I was carrying, I thought I heard someone calling my name, but it didn't register at first. Then I heard it again a little louder. Who the fuck would call me *Mr. Phillips,* anyway?

It was attorney Samuel Starnes, who was standing among the suits and once again doing his job. I caught his eye and knew that he knew. My guardian angel had just spared Tall Suit from a righteous ass-kicking. I regained my composure in a couple of steps and offered my hand instead.

One of the group started giving us the down and dirty. Sam Starnes announced that we were all heading back to Maryland and said something about a debrief back at the clubhouse tomorrow.

The suits surrounded Rowan Anderson. I could hear them pelting her with questions, rapid-fire, giving her the business. Their tone wasn't super-heated, but I could tell they were ganging up on her and that lit my fuse again.

When one of the tools extended his hand to Rowan, she handed him her pistol. *My* pistol.

"Hey, asshole, that's mine!" I yelled as the guy gave me an *eat shit* grin.

They all stopped and looked at me as I stepped off. The guy knew I was right, and tried hard to save face in front of his buddies.

"Just give me the fucking gun, dude," I said. It was a classic Fed ball-sniffing move, but I won. He handed me the Sig and I instinctively checked the chamber, made sure the pistol was on safe and turned away.

"Would you hold this for a second, Oliver?" I smiled politely at my friend. Then in one motion I did a one-eighty toward the Fed, cocking my right fist as I spun. Two of his partners tried to step in, but I was faster.

The Fed thought I was going for his face and raised his hands to block me, but I lowered my shoulder and went for the cross-check instead. The Hanson Brothers from *Slap Shot* would have approved.

I drove my left shoulder into his solar plexus and carried him about two feet into the side of the Suburban. I don't know which was louder—the thud of his body hitting the vehicle's reinforced door or the half-cry, half-moan from this oaf—but it caught everyone off guard. To my chagrin, the momentary Shock and Awe stunned his buddies for only about a second. The next thing I knew, I was at the bottom of a 500-pound human dogpile. But unlike the Team Rhino pile on at the Wilsons' party, there was no laughing this time.

Samuel Starnes, Esquire, certainly wasn't. "Enough of this shit," he spat. "I don't have the time."

Starnes was clearly the kind of guy who moved mountains with a look, relegated people to the gulag with a blink, or forced capitulation with a stare. And if he looked at his watch, you were fucked.

It was clear that ignoring his command would be a costly mistake. One by one, we sheepishly extricated ourselves and retreated to our neutral corners.

Rowan gave me a look somewhere between incredulity and sorrow. Before I could explain myself to her, Starnes started barking out orders.

"Gentlemen, please help these Secret Service agents with the luggage so they can be on their way. Mrs. Harrison, if you would be so kind as to hop in this vehicle, these agents will take you to Washington, where your father is waiting. Agent Anderson, you will join them and return to your superiors. They are expecting you. Is that understood?"

It was more of an order than a question. But as before, it was obvious that when Sam Starnes was talking, you just shut your piehole and did whatever the man said.

In a nanosecond, the bags were stowed in the back of the Suburban and the suits were buckled in. Rowan climbed into the back. Though she gave me not so much as a backward glance, the asshole I'd cross-checked sneered at me as he closed his door and they sped away.

Starnes saw him do it. "Arrogant pricks," he said. "Thirty pounds ago, I would have done what you did—given him what he deserved."

CHAPTER 65

CSTC Headquarters, Maryland

I phoned the Wilsons and let them know their son was safe and that we'd get him home as soon as we could.

This wasn't the way I'd been planning to show Si Wilson around CSTC, but it was good to have the newest member of Team Rhino with us. The shit show—no better word for it—on the island had been surreal. Everything was still a little fuzzy. My pistol and my Rolex were the only personal pieces of gear I had on me. No clothes but the smelly rags on my body, no change of socks, no toothbrush.

Tristan, of course, was one step ahead, and the team houses were stocked with clean clothes and an ample supply of whiskey. While the others drifted off to get hot showers and fresh duds, I sat down on Tristan's back porch and, over a steaming cup of coffee, filled him in on what I knew.

"You did well, Nat. Impossible challenge right out of the gate, and you guys did a great job. Starnes and Congressman

Jennings are very pleased. They know the deal and wanted me to pass on their thanks."

Tristan knew what I knew: Team Rhino was ready to go.

"Everyone did their job. No one hesitated for a second. But Tristan, it was fucking nuts. IEDs, in America? Who kidnaps and tortures, let alone kills, a sitting US senator?"

I was still in a bit of disbelief. Tristan let me talk it through for a while before bringing me back to the next phase of the plan.

"Team Rhino stays put here in Maryland," he said. "Plow through the hotwash, connect the dots, and come up with our next course of action. This review is just the beginning, and ODS is ready to run this thing to ground."

"Yeah, we're good, man, but just one quick question: What the fuck is ODS?"

Tristan laughed "Sorry, Nat, while you were vacationing in Nantucket, they decided that the official cover for Rocket's Red Glare will be to call it the Office of Domestic Strategy. That's who you work for now."

It made sense to me in a roundabout way. A paramilitary organization designed to operate outside the spotlight of the national mission should be made to sound as generic as possible. The initials *ODS* brought to mind one of those ubiquitous government departments that could just as easily be rebuilding the railroads. Whatever it took to keep wandering oversight away from yours truly.

I shook Tristan's hand and was starting to step off the porch when I turned and asked if there was any word on Rowan Anderson.

"Best I can tell is that she's being benched, pending the outcome of the investigation. Basically, no gun and no fun for a while, Nat. I gotta be honest, I don't see how this works out for her. The president wants a pound of flesh—and not only from whatever group is behind the plot against Senator Harrison. Someone on her team has to pay. Wish I had better news to tell you, amigo."

CHAPTER 66

CSTC Team Rhino Command Post

Navigating in the shadows of the federal government was a new play for all of us—exposure to an entirely different fight. But if I'm being honest here, I was troubled by the nagging thought that so far it felt like just another deployment, another mission against bad guys. I had no choice but to break it down, figure out where to go from here.

In this early phase of Rocket's Red Glare, severe compartmentalization was required. CSTC typically enlisted the aid of another team's intel officer and sometimes outside agencies. Going forward, nobody needed to know anybody else's business unless invited. By design, we did not want any overlap between operational teams.

I called a Team Rhino meeting, including Si and three other team members: medic Rudy Martin, back from his trauma-medicine symposium in Dallas, plus Stu Arden and James Teagan, aka Jimmy T.

Jimmy was our Boston guy. His family ties to the city went back to 1860, when Thomas Teagan arrived from Belfast, Ireland and began to grow a family—and an empire. Even in the new millennium, they routinely sent funds home to help families affected by The Troubles. While not quite as powerful as Whitey Bulger, the Teagans had considerable influence when it came to running Irish interests in Boston. Everyone knew that if you fucked around with the Teagans, you were either mental or had a death wish.

Stu Arden was our team commo chief and a virtuoso of all things electronic. He came from Wyoming ranchers, and was "good timber." Whenever he had downtime, you'd find Stu in Jackson Hole, looking for cowboy stuff to do on the family ranch.

Team Rhino and I talked late into the night, reviewing everything that had happened from when JP, Wolf, Oliver, and Meg landed on Nantucket up through my cup of coffee with Tristan. The process was beyond painful: necessary, but miserable.

For every pro, there were at least a couple of cons. We took every one of our actions, scrutinized and pulverized and spit them out like spoiled milk. I was starting to think I had fucked up more shit than was acceptable. Thankfully, when all was said and done, there was agreement that the wins far exceeded the losses.

Once we had exhausted the review of our techniques, tactics, and procedures, we shifted our focus to the forensics of all the intelligence we had gathered and observed so far.

It was Meg's turn at the head of the class. The bulk of the analysis would fall to her.

"Okay, Meg, where do we start and what do you need?"

"Here's where I think we get the most juice the quickest: I need to find the outside connection between all the dead people and the mainland. Nantucket is an island, so we need to find an intersection between there and someplace not surrounded by water. There has to be something, even a small thread gets us out the gate."

She tapped a pen on the table. "Why Harrison?" she asked, "and what's special about Nantucket? How did they get IEDs onto the island? Who were the kill teams? And who would have the ability—using what kind of explosives—to blow up and sink a hundred-ton ferry?"

While we theorized answers to her questions, Meg drew the highlights of the battle on a big whiteboard, creating a brilliant system of interconnected circles and squares of intelligence until they filled the board.

"I also need help with the phones and computers. I can't sweep them all myself—it would take weeks. If we can paint a picture of how they communicated and controlled the actions, we can undoubtedly answer the most pressing question: *Who the fuck did this?*"

Stu would take the lead on the electronics sweep, while Si and Wolf would assist.

Like Oliver with guns, Stu just "got" communications. There was no doubt he could quarterback the dive into the sizable boxes of cell phones and laptops we had recovered from the island.

I assigned Jimmy T. and JP to the man-tracking tasks. Rudy, our team medic, would handle the medical-examiner duties. Better him than me: We would soon have the rush autopsy results and enough pictures of dead people to give us all nightmares for the next few weeks.

"One thing that bothers me is the Russian boat," Meg declared with a sigh. "At the time, we obviously couldn't split the force, and I personally didn't find anything on board that could have tied that ship to anything that happened on the island. But I keep thinking there has to be a connection. Did you guys get that sense too? Or am I completely out to lunch?"

"I'd say we start by having another little chat with that bad boy's owner," JP said.

I nodded. "Makes sense to me, JP. Meg, any ideas?"

"Yeah, I'd go with that, but I honestly have no idea where to begin the search." Meg looked at me. "We lost track of the first yacht as soon as we climbed back aboard the Little Birds. He could be in Greenland, for all I know. Maybe while Stu and Wolf dig into the electronics, Si can help me review the satellite imagery from the night of the attack and see if I can find her."

"How long would that take?"

"Maybe a day or so. Give me some time to do some coding. It's not really like fast-forwarding a video. You have to do some reprogramming to guess next locations, then reenter the data. It's complicated—but not impossible. I'll get on it ASAP."

"Okay then, Meg. Let me know what else you need. We'll get it done. *Slow is smooth, and smooth is fast,* right?" Her smile quickly turned into a yawn. We'd been at it for a good long while.

I was about to tell everyone to take a break when Si stood up in the back of the room, put his right hand over his heart, and, in a surprisingly booming voice, said, "Excuse me, Nat, but are you going to call in the wolf?"

I gave Si a *WTF* look and rubbed my eyes. Then I turned to Oliver, who was flashing a *Who, me?* expression.

"I'm guessing we have you to thank for this?" I asked him with a half smile. "Come on, man—it's late."

"Si, what did I tell you earlier?" Oliver prompted.

Si cleared his throat and said, "Well, you told me that if they couldn't figure out the Russian yacht, that I was supposed to stand up and shout, *Nat, are you going to call in the wolf?* And then I was also supposed to say, *That's all you had to say.*"

Si's face turned bright red and he sank back down into his seat. The poor kid had no idea what rite of passage he had just gone through, but we all thought it was funny as hell.

Regaining my composure, I said to Oliver, "Enlighten us, please, Mr. Smith."

"Thought you'd never ask, boss." Oliver stood and strode to the front of the conference room, where he grabbed the pointer and positioned himself beside the map of the Eastern Seaboard that we had used for the debrief. He tapped the pointer's tip somewhere on the southeast coast of Florida.

"Well, Nat, besides being just another pretty face, you all know how much I dig the ocean, right? I love boats, especially the big ones. So when we were clearing the cabins, I noticed that the name of the yacht was embroidered on just about everything, especially in the galley. Didn't anyone else see this shit?"

Clearly our silence confirmed his suspicion.

"Shocking. Anyhoo, the *Oryol* is the name of this stinkpot. She's registered to some no-name LLC headquartered in George Town, Bahamas, and it's docked down in Si's hometown of Palm Beach. The owner shouldn't be too difficult to track down. That concludes my presentation, sir!"

Oliver paused for a bit of showboating, going through the first few motions of the Manual of Arms rifle drill as if he was on parade, substituting the pointer for a rifle. After a moment, he dropped the bit and continued.

"I was curious—so sue me," he said, back on task. "So I looked up the boat online; there's a website that tracks these big yachts. It took about two seconds. Si asked me what I thought about the boat, so I told him to hang loose and see what we found out during the hotwash. He said you all would figure it out, but I said you wouldn't, so we made a bet. When I won, Baby Rhino over here had to do his routine. Plus he also owes me fifty bucks, of course. Pay up, Si. I know where you live."

Meg rolled her eyes and smiled at Si. "Sucker's bet, Josiah. Don't worry—we've all lost to the mighty Oliver Smith at one time or another. Just don't do it twice."

With this settled, we knew where to start: We would send a couple of recon teams to Florida to see what they could find. I needed Oliver to stay with me for a meeting in DC, but Meg, Jimmy T., Si, and Rudy could go get their ninja on.

The thrill of the hunt came roaring back to life. I figured we would need about a week to plan and rehearse the recon mission. Once we knocked the rust off, however, it would be Game On.

"Si, let Al and Connie know you're going to Palm Beach!"

I had promised the Wilsons I'd get Si "home" soon. Wasn't Palm Beach their home just as much as Nantucket?

CHAPTER 67

Rowan Anderson's apartment
Washington, DC

Agent Rowan Anderson had been forced to surrender her passport and was confined to her apartment overlooking the Georgetown campus. Technically, she wasn't under arrest—yet—but "pending investigation."

For most federal law-enforcement officers, that status killed careers and shattered lives. Pensions and 401(k)s were reduced to rubble. No chance of retirement to a house in the suburbs, working a cushy consulting job.

But Special Agent in Charge Rowan Anderson of the United States Secret Service was far from the typical professional. She was a traitor.

Though the idea of spending a good bit of the rest of her life in a concrete box in Colorado made her shudder, she had more pressing concerns. She was less afraid of life in the United States

Penitentiary Administrative Maximum (ADX) Florence facility—the same supermax facility where Robert Hanssen served a life sentence for espionage and conspiracy and Ted Kaczynski for fatal bombings—than she was of dying at the hands of Haracat al Marrak or one of his followers. Would they stab her, shoot her, lop off her head with a rusty scimitar? Her fear-fueled misery was making her physically sick. Once again she ran to the bathroom and vomited.

Rowan Anderson felt no guilt and no remorse over Coleman Harrison. *But had she bitten off too much?* Wiping her face with a damp towel, she looked in the mirror and felt fresh tears building. She just wanted to survive another day.

The man in Paris had fucked her over. He'd ended communications. That could mean only one thing: She was expendable—especially now that she was the subject of a "pending investigation." It was entirely possible that she'd already been replaced by others within her own agency, ready on his command to pull the trigger on the president.

And since she couldn't move it anywhere, the five million tax-free dollars parked in her Swiss bank account might as well be sitting in a box on the moon. The Feds were surely tracking all her assets, looking for the smoking gun.

She willed her mind to a brighter place, to the glimmers of hope she'd felt when she first met Nat Phillips.

She liked Nat. He was a good guy. The kiss they'd shared that night at his house in Nantucket had stirred more passion and desire than she'd felt in years, maybe ever. She had been so close to the happily-ever-after chapter of her life when the entire plan went to shit.

Rowan's phone buzzed and she glanced at the screen. Nat again—for about the tenth time. He always left sweet, positive messages filled with both concern and earnest enthusiasm. She just couldn't bring herself to answer his calls.

In a parallel universe, she'd tell him everything that had happened. She could make up some fantastic story of blackmail, or a spectacularly botched deep-cover black op, and he would not only understand, but fix it.

Nat was definitely a fixer. In that distant galaxy far, far away, he would do his thing and work his magic, and then she could start again.

She stared out the window at the Georgetown campus. She'd always loved running through the main quadrangle. The energy of the students and the beauty of the Georgian-style architecture was invigorating. Happier times.

Though Rowan hadn't been to Mass in years, she still stopped by the Dahlgren Chapel of the Sacred Heart whenever she could. Even a few minutes inside the university's spiritual heart made her feel good. The brick masonry structure was quiet and welcoming—a place where she always felt safe, grounded, secure.

Standing in her apartment and looking at the campus, her thoughts raced with the beginnings of a plan.

The chapel was safe. The church was safe. She could go there and be protected—just as Noriega had with US troops closing in on him in Panama: He had rushed to the Papal Nuncio, Archbishop Laboa, for protection. In fact, Noriega had been preparing to request political asylum in some other country when the Delta Force guys broke him by blasting AC/DC anthems for seventy-two hours nonstop.

The Apostolic Nunciature in DC was the diplomatic mission

to the Holy See. It was a total Hail Mary, but if she could get there, maybe she could buy herself some time. Rowan Anderson was not about to be broken by some thugs.

She began to feel a little better. She glanced at the Glock 17 on the kitchen counter. That made her feel safe too. She picked it up and sat in her overstuffed chair facing the window. Looking out at the campus lights, she made a pledge to her future: *I will escape to some place where Haracat al Marrak dares not follow me.*

She felt herself getting sleepy. Her gaze was locked, trance-like, on Healy Hall's 200-foot-high clock tower. When she could no longer fight the urge to close her eyes, she let herself drift off into the darkness.

★ ★ ★

At three in the morning, Rowan woke up, still facing the clock tower. It was all the sign she needed to get herself back on the offensive. Rowan Anderson was not going to Colorado for the rest of her life; she was going to kill the president and collect her reward.

She grabbed her phone and sent a text message: URGENT. COME SEE ME ASAP.

CHAPTER 68

Embassy Row
Washington, DC

Special Agent in Charge Rowan Anderson wasn't the only one mulling over the Nantucket debacle. In the early hours of the morning, Elise Courville was awake in a bedroom somewhere on Embassy Row.

"She looks like a zombie," Courville had heard her father whispering to his private physician about his daughter's state.

What would Charles Courville, Ambassador of France to the United States, say if he learned that his daughter played a key part in multiple schemes? Turning Agent Rowan Anderson against her country; plotting to abduct and kill her philandering husband; and the ultimate double cross: killing the President of the United States.

Courville's relationship with Anderson was complicated at best. She had to admit that Anderson was smart, but Courville had seen the surprise in the agent's face when she'd held the gun against her.

Haracat al Marrak had stopped making contact. He'd never sent a message confirming the mission's completion on the island, nor had he sent any messages via their contingency method of communication. None of his network gave any sign of acknowledgment. This could mean only one thing: Elise Courville was a marked woman. Like the zombie her father described, she was the walking dead.

There was no place to hide from a man as ruthless as al Marrak. He could kill senators. He could kill presidents. And he could definitely kill the daughter of the French ambassador.

A man had come to her home with a rifle and fired inside it. At first she'd been sure he was aiming for Rowan Anderson, but now she wasn't at all certain.

While they'd been upstairs at her house, packing those Louis Vuitton bags, Anderson had laid out the terms of their newfound alliance of necessity: *We're the only ones who know the name of the man in Paris. We have to stick together.*

At 3 a.m., Elise Courville's phone vibrated on her bedside table. She was instantly alert. Could it be Haracat al Marrak? Had he finally sent the message she'd been waiting for?

"*Merde,*" she muttered, venting her disappointment before hurriedly typing her reply:

WILL BE THERE AT 7 A.M.

CHAPTER 69

Rowan Anderson's apartment
Washington, DC

"You look like hell," Elise Courville said as she walked into Rowan Anderson's apartment and handed her a large cup of coffee from a local café.

"Nice of you to say. You look like shit today too, lady. Thanks for the coffee." Anderson took a long sip of the hot brew, and seemed immediately energized by the caffeine boost.

After an awkward moment, Courville closed her eyes as if holding back tears. "Please tell me you've got something? The stress feels lethal."

Anderson put her coffee down. Then she walked to Courville and gently grabbed both her arms around the biceps, squaring her body so they stood face-to-face. "Look at me, Elise, and listen carefully. I need you to get in touch with the man in Paris."

"Are you insane? Reaching out to him means signing a death warrant—certainly for me, but probably for both of us." She slipped out of Anderson's grasp and started pacing the apartment. "We are dead women."

"Listen for a minute, Elise. Yes, we are dead women. But not yet. If he had wanted us planted in the dirt, we'd be there already. He knows how scared we are. He also knows that fear keeps us quiet. I am sure—somehow, somewhere—that his people have eyes on us. Maybe not twenty-four-seven, but he has to know we've both been brought to DC, and under what circumstances. So forget that for a moment. What he isn't expecting is for us to fight back."

Elise Courville was trying to follow Anderson's logic, but the dots weren't connecting. "So you're saying we have some kind of play here?"

"He doesn't negotiate. Trust me—I figured that out a while ago. But he also doesn't do anything half-assed, or by the seat of his pants. Right now he's trying to resurrect some sort of plan, but he's running short on time—and short on human assets. He can't afford to construct a whole new infrastructure of players to do this thing. The two of us, we're all he has. And that's why we are going to give him the solution he so desperately needs. Even if it's coming from two walking-dead women."

Courville made no attempt to conceal her astonishment as Anderson kept spinning what sounded like the longest of long shots.

"I do have a plan, and it's a plan he will like. A big bang for his buck, if you will. But Elise, you're the one who's going to have to sell it to him. The Secret Service is all over me, so my maneuverability is limited. But nobody's looking at the grieving widow Harrison."

"Except him, of course."

"Except him, of course—yes," Anderson conceded. She paused for what seemed like an extra beat before asking, "Now, do you want to hear the plan or not?"

Elise Courville closed her eyes again. It was the only way to make the world stop spinning, make the haze go away so she could think straight.

She reopened her eyes to the sight of Rowan Anderson, standing tall and sipping her coffee. She looked confident and totally in control.

Control was a quality that Elise Courville had never possessed. One that she needed now more than ever.

"Okay, Rowan. Tell me how we're going to get out of this."

"Trust me, Elise—it's going to work."

There in her Georgetown apartment, Secret Service Special Agent in Charge Rowan Anderson briefed Senator Coleman Harrison's bereaved widow on exactly how they would kill the President of the United States.

CHAPTER 70

CSTC Headquarters, Maryland

The upcoming classified meeting with the Office of Domestic Strategy was weighing on our minds, so Oliver and I met to prepare with Tristan and his wife, Alison, co-owners of CSTC.

The Nantucket event had put the cart before the horse. It was now forcing us to scramble to define the Rocket's Red Glare charter and all the necessary legalities for such an entity. As CSTC was the plank holder of the whole shebang, we were expected to build on the boilerplate of the CSTC charter, incorporating everything we had learned from recent experience. The goal was not only to describe how we could be utilized in future domestic conflicts, but to set forth a clear understanding of parameters for completing the mission we were already engaged in.

Ali Dent quietly took notes for most of the morning, asking for clarity from time to time. Tristan's wife was like the coach who is always two touchdowns ahead of the game.

"Did any of you ever read 'The Man Who Would Be King'?" she asked us after a while.

"I think I saw a movie based on it once," Tristan muttered sheepishly.

"Oh, yeah—Sean Connery and Michael Caine," I chimed in. "Awesome flick!"

Oliver shook his head and laughed. "I think you're missing the point, guys. Ali's not talking about the 1970s adventure film. She means the original source—the Rudyard Kipling story from like a century earlier, about British soldiers who decide to make themselves Afghan kings. Ali, please elaborate."

"Thank you, Oliver. At least *one* of you uses his noggin for more than a hat rack! Yes, I meant the Kipling story. But for you knuckleheads, I guess the movie is close enough. The whole point is that while the enthusiasm may be admirable and the mission may be worthy, it's still always a dangerous proposition to give anyone the keys to the kingdom—especially folks skilled with guns and explosives. We've got to be hot-wired tight so that we don't talk ourselves into acting like those men who would be kings, and get ourselves in deep shit thinking we are gods. That's all I'm saying."

Man, that stung worse than the hotwash. Alison Dent was exactly right, of course. I tried to think of a calm and collected professional response.

Tristan cleared his throat and looked at me. "Nat, I think this is where you're supposed to say something."

I frowned at him. "Thanks for selling me out, pal. I know what I want to say, but I don't know if I should say it. So that's why I'm sitting here waiting for you, the owner of CSTC, to answer the co-owner—who is, in fact, by law, your wife."

"Oliver? Please just shoot me, right here behind the ear." Ali held two fingers up to her head like a pistol and pulled the air trigger.

"I'm only kidding," I reassured Ali. "Honestly, you've just voiced my biggest fear. I've seen the Good Ol' Boys Club go bad in a hurry. I didn't want oversight while we were in Nantucket during the fight, and I don't really want it now, but I do realize we're going to need it at some point. What I don't have is a well-thought-out answer. I could bullshit you, but that's all it would be. Can I let it marinate and talk to my team and get back to you?"

"Of course, Nat—I didn't expect an answer today. We need all of you and CSTC to be bulletproof, protected. We're embarking on unknown territory, and we're sure to encounter plenty of complexities that we haven't even considered. So for a start, let's begin by tackling this one: *How do we guard against getting too big for our operational britches?*"

Now that I had my assignment, Tristan ended the meeting:

"Class dismissed."

CHAPTER 71

Paris, France

Haracat al Marrak was not surprised that the American whore had made contact following the protocol he designed. He was neither angry nor relieved. In fact, he was more amused than anything.

While it was true that his access to funds was almost unlimited, it was also true that he did not have access to an unlimited number of people. His benefactor was very generous, to be sure, but also seemed to be injecting himself more deeply into the operations than al Marrak would have liked.

The capture, torture, and execution of Senator Coleman Harrison had been a victory: The viral video was worth well more than he had paid for the entire operation. Donations pouring in to his worldwide networks had increased tenfold. (Believers were always more generous when they got proof that their money was advancing the cause.) This influx of cash, however, was being allocated to a single objective: the assassination of the United States President.

No other organization on the planet would dare attempt such an audacious act. Groups in Saudi Arabia and Yemen talked a big game, but chattering like old men was all they did. The groups in the Maghreb were no better. They picked easy targets—low-hanging fruit—and called themselves martyrs. But anyone could blow up a school or a bus or a church and then run away; it was hardly the will of Allah.

It didn't bother al Marrak that he had recently changed his mind about the fate of the infidels. *Inshallah,* he thought. *Allah's will.* What did bother him was his reliance on the Russian. The two sons were of no consequence, but he had to treat the elder Russian with respect. As long as the old man was alive, nobody could replicate what the Russian's network could do, and the plan in progress depended on his expertise. The old man would die one day, hopefully sooner rather than later. But until then, Haracat al Marrak would stuff his frustration deep inside and humble himself enough to make the call to Moscow.

The French ambassador's daughter had informed al Marrak that the new administration would be in a state of transition—sworn enemies taking the place of other sworn enemies—for months. During that time, the Americans would be the most vulnerable. It would be the perfect time to create the most chaos and watch the supposed *free world* implode.

Chopping off the head of the Great Satan was the only way to show the world the spiritual degeneracy of the American pig dogs. But time was not on his side. The elections would be held in November—hardly enough time to recruit, train, and organize a cell capable of such a spectacular operation.

Al Marrak encrypted his instructions and began the process of communicating with the Americans. Then he closed his eyes and thought about how he had planned to kill them both. The thought of watching their eyes go wide with fear as they begged for mercy was pure ecstasy. That day would come, but for now the whores were an asset.

CHAPTER 72

CSTC Sensitive Compartmented Information Facility

Meg was planning the next phase of the Palm Beach operation. I wanted to get an update on our recon plan, so I headed over to the Sensitive Compartmented Information Facility (SCIF).

I tapped out my code on the keyboard, waved my badge in front of the sensor, gazed into the retina-scanning device, and heard the door unlock. I was certain the day would come when I'd open that and find gold coins and bars stacked to the ceiling. Not today, but I did see Meg's smiling face—and that was A-OK.

We spent some time discussing a couple of key points to cover with the team during the daily intel brief. Meg was on top of it as usual, and I could sense that the plan was gaining steam.

As I turned to leave, she said something that didn't quite register, so I asked her to repeat it: "What did you say?"

"Your girlfriend—she's all over the news today."

"Say again?"

"*Rowan*, Nat—*Rowan Anderson*. The French newspapers have made her a hero." She pulled up the websites of *Le Monde, La Croix,* and *Le Figaro*. All of them showed images of Rowan's government ID photo beneath bold headlines I couldn't read.

"Check it out," Meg invited me.

Where the fuck had this come from—and why now? Meg was fluent in French, so she translated as I tried to catch up. I hadn't put two and two together that Senator Harrison's widow, Elise Courville, was the daughter of the French ambassador—likely the reason the French papers ran some completely bullshit and totally inaccurate variation of *Secret Service Agent Rescues Ambassador's Daughter.* The French president praised the United States and our dedicated professionals for keeping Courville safe from terrorists. His sympathies for her husband, the late Senator Coleman Harrison, were of course extended as well.

The glowing coverage was such an unexpected turn of events that I didn't know how to feel. Clearly, I recognized this as a positive development for Rowan. And I was relieved that not one of the news reports mentioned CSTC or any of us.

"Are you going to call her?"

"I've tried a dozen times since we got back. She doesn't answer—won't return calls or messages. I can take a hint."

Meg laughed. "Nat, if I didn't know you better, I'd say your feelings are hurt."

"That was a weak showing, wasn't it?" I asked.

"You don't have to listen to me, but if you want my two pennies, I'd bet that after this breaking news, she might answer her phone. Just a hunch." She gave me a half smile as I stared dumbly, then mouthed, *Trust me—call her.*

CHAPTER 73

CSTC Headquarters

I'd rehearsed the entire conversation in my mind a hundred times. I thought I had it down pat, but as soon as Rowan Anderson answered her phone, my mind went totally blank.

Mercifully, Rowan picked up the slack. "Hey, Nat—thank you so, so much for calling. I'm so sorry for not speaking with you earlier. I just couldn't bring myself to answer. You're such a sweetheart for leaving those messages. I loved hearing every one of them. You're the best."

It was nice hearing Rowan Anderson say those words. She had the best phone voice. Things were looking up indeed.

I stammered through a *You're welcome* and made some inane comments about the weather—and, of course, asked her how things were going. Realizing I sounded like a jackass, I apologized like a madman.

"It's okay, Nat, seriously. Don't worry about me. It's all going to be alright. I promise. I want to see you again—soon."

Rowan was so positive and enthusiastic, it was almost like nothing bad had happened. Which confused me. As much as I liked her, I'd expected her to need some heavy-duty cheerleading—hell, probably some serious therapy. After all, her principal—the former senator and presidential candidate—had been killed, and killed painfully, on her watch.

"Good deal," I finally managed to say. "It sounds like you're in a good place, and I'm so glad to hear it. I saw your picture in every one of this morning's French newspapers. I can't lie, totally caught me off guard. Wow."

"You read French newspapers?" she asked with a hint of bemusement.

Shit, how to explain this one?

"*Je parle un peu*," I laughed. "I like to practice my reading comprehension when I get the chance. Today was a slow day."

"Well, that's good to know, because in the extraordinarily fantastic news department, I am now officially reassigned to the French embassy as Chief Security Liaison Officer for the Secret Service. I think it's a made-up position, but hey—I'm not about to complain. After all that shit that went down, at least they aren't going to fire me. Not *yet,* anyway. So feel free to drop by for a visit and show off your mad language skills." She laughed.

Unbeknownst to her, Rowan explained, Elise Courville's dad had pulled some behind-the-scenes strings. Ambassador Charles Courville, a well-connected power broker, had gently persuaded the administration not to punish Rowan, but instead to promote his prominent daughter's protector. Apparently he had made a very compelling argument.

The message to the secretary of state was crystal clear: The French government was calling in a marker from its dear friend and ally. Denial of this favor would have long-lasting repercussions within the diplomatic community. *Gentle like a sledgehammer,* I supposed.

"That's pretty fucking amazing, Rowan. You should buy a lottery ticket."

So that was how Rowan Anderson went from zero to hero overnight. I knew shit like this happened all the time in DC, but not usually at this warp speed. It was a clever move to drop the news articles before the announcement, too. Bodies hit the floor and heads exploded at Homeland Security headquarters when that bomb dropped. A little leverage with a side of humble pie for dessert.

She was on her way to the office to reclaim her credentials and her gun, Rowan told me, but she promised to stay in touch. She and Elise Courville were heading out of town on some embassy business, but we would get together soon to celebrate.

"No worries, Ro," I said. "I'm heading south for a few days. Are you free later this week?"

"When you say *south,* do you mean like Argentina, or like Atlanta? Or is this another official Nathan Phillips classified adventure?"

"How about somewhere in between, and we leave it at that?" I didn't want to be rude, but she should know better. I would set her straight at dinner; it was time to have "the talk" about what I really did. If we were to give this a chance, she had to be read in on the real deal at CSTC. Shit, she had a clearance that was higher than mine anyway.

"Okay, okay. Go do your thing, and call me later. I can't wait, Nat—I'm looking forward to picking up where we left off in Nantucket."

A former soldier who does private military contracting isn't quite who I need by my side just now, Rowan Anderson thought, *but it's worth considering how he could eventually be of use.*

Perhaps she could play both sides again. Maybe.

CHAPTER 74

CSTC Team Rhino Command Center

Team Rhino gathered for our daily intelligence update. Meg stood behind the lectern and began. "We've made some outstanding progress on our do-outs. I'll lead off and let Jimmy T. follow, then Stu will bat cleanup."

According to Meg, the 39.8-meter yacht—christened the *Oryol* after the first Russian warship, circa 1660s—had been built in 2001 by Heesen Yachts, in the Netherlands. As Oliver had previously reported, the *Oryol* was registered in George Town, Bahamas, and currently docked in Palm Beach.

Thanks to what Meg called "some crafty hacking" from inside the SCIF, she had analyzed several cutout companies before determining that the yacht belonged to Alexander Egorov, a seventy-seven-year-old Russian widower with forty-three-year-old twin sons, Pavel and Taras.

Word was, the elder Egorov had cut his teeth in the 1950s selling used AK-47s and hand grenades in Algeria. One deal led to another, one uprising to another, and one civil war to another, and within two decades Egorov had become the go-to guy for anyone wanting to start a revolution.

The twins had followed in their father's arms-dealing path, building a book of business throughout Africa and some choice hot spots in the Middle East. Governments friendly to ours were decidedly not among their clientele.

Meg's assessment: Alexander Egorov was Russia's answer to our own John Gotti. He was Teflon. Nothing stuck, ever. He hid in plain sight. Though to his credit, and unlike his degenerate sons, he stayed well below the radar.

"I cannot confirm the elder Egorov's current location. He's got places all over the world. However, it shouldn't be too difficult to find the boys, who enjoy spending time at their father's house in Palm Beach. Looks like Pavel is the guy I kicked in the nuts aboard the yacht. Pavel likes to run around Palm Beach in a pink Lamborghini Murciélago, I shit you not. His brother Taras prefers to be seen in a purple Ferrari F430. We should arrest them for that douchebaggery alone."

With that, Meg stood aside so that James Teagan could take her place at the lectern.

"So I talked to some people," Jimmy T. announced. By *some people* he meant he'd worked his family network: first cousins, second cousins, their families, and so on—basically the entire Boston Irish community, and probably some Italians too. As Jimmy liked to say with a wink, his father and brothers were in no way even remotely connected to the Irish mob—but he was pretty sure his mother was.

He'd gotten a firm ID on the dead woman we'd found

upstairs at Senator Harrison's house. She was a Harrison staffer—and the senator's mistress. Her name was Aimee Sullivan, and she'd grown up in someone's cousin's Boston neighborhood. According to Jimmy's people, she was well-known to be wicked smart, very attractive, and super ambitious. But also far more eager to sleep her way to the top than to work hard to get there.

What Jimmy T. had also turned up was the news that some low-level Ukrainian toughies had recently been hired to break into her apartment and leave a bunch of cocaine behind. He couldn't find out who had paid for the drugs, but it sure as shit wasn't Aimee Sullivan. Total setup: Nobody breaks in to someone else's place and drops off a kilo or so of coke for non-nefarious reasons. Jimmy T. assured us that his dogs were on it.

One of Jimmy's cousins, a bartender at a place near Fenway, asked one of his bartender buddies on Nantucket if he'd heard anything about Sullivan or her crew. The buddy said she'd seemed friendly enough. Looker. Came into the place once or twice a week. Good tipper.

Then one night a week or two ago, some self-important, obnoxious asshole—presumably Walt Fitzgerald—came in pissing and moaning all over his scotch.

Bartender chatted him up and the old Mick started bitching about some broad who was making his life miserable. *Ever heard of Chappaquiddick?* he'd asked the bartender menacingly. It wasn't much, Jimmy conceded, but it was a pretty fucked-up thing to say.

Apart from the background on Sullivan and Fitzgerald, Jimmy hadn't heard much else. There was a lot of chatter about who could have blown up the ferry, but nobody knew anything about who had actually done it. Seven out of ten informants theorized it was Al-Qaeda.

Last but not least, Jimmy's crew said some high-level sit-downs with various bosses were said to be going down soon. There was a lot of noise about whether the Russians or the Chinese had been involved in the hit. Oh, and he had another cousin in the Boston Police Department sniffing around the organized-crime unit for more details; the cousin would let Jimmy know what she found out.

"That's all I could get so far, Nat, but they'll keep me posted."

"Please thank your mom for me," I laughed. "Next time see if your dad and brothers will get off the couch and give her a hand—it'll speed things up."

"Of course, Nat. My mom loves you. You know that."

Jimmy gave me a wink as he sat down. I turned to Stu Arden. "Okay, Stu, what's up?"

"Nerd version or what?"

"I'll take Door Number Two—the less-nerdy version, if that's at all possible." I loved Stu, but his briefs were unintelligible when he went into full-blown Nerd Mode. Stu was in fact the humblest man I knew—shirt-off-his-back kind of guy, no question—and he was aces at commo, but he could put Adderall addicts to sleep when he got going on a technical discussion.

"Got it, Nat. I'll try to keep it simple, but some of this shit is so complex that even I got confused." He smiled at us, hoping we got his sarcasm. "I of course figured it out, but you guys are all screwed."

Despite lacking the password to unlock even one of the phones we'd brought from Nantucket, Stu told us, he'd been able to rip the contents off every single device. *Holy shit—we have that kind of capability?*

"It was interesting to me that there were so many burner phones in the pile found in Elise Courville's house. Probably seven or eight, if I recall. Five hadn't even been activated yet. No prints on any of them. Could be the ambassador used them as an easy security protocol when his daughter was traveling, in case she had to call her old man to discuss something important. I've heard the Speaker of the House does something similar with his kids, just to be on the safe side."

Stu's briefing continued: "You also picked a burner off the dead sniper, and there was one more at Harrison's house among all the rest of the shit. While the numbers didn't match for outgoing calls, the country code did: France. Makes sense given the circumstances with Courville and her dad, but it's not clear why the intruder—and someone else at Harrison's—was in communication with somebody in France. Could be coincidental...but I doubt it. Pretty clear that some bad guys here were talking to another bad guy in France.

"I've got a friend over at the NSA helping me work through some of the other protocols, and I'm pretty sure we can get more—just takes some time. He's got all the gear from the yacht, plus the bag of computers that Si picked up at Courville's, so once we connect, I'm sure more details will come out. It's not a lot, but it's a start."

We had a hell of a lot more info than we did before.

CHAPTER 75

Moscow, Russia

The cold air blowing off the Moskva River made Alexander Egorov feel momentarily refreshed.

For sixty-three of his seventy-seven years, he had worked for himself. He'd been fourteen years old when his parents were taken from him during the famine of the 1940s, making young Alexander head of the house and de facto parent to his three-year-old sister. Raising her was a task that Egorov promised himself he would not fail at.

What started as petty theft for survival evolved with the times until Egorov was regarded as one of the world's most powerful arms dealers. Weakness in his business was certain to get you killed. For five decades, Alexander Egorov had literally and figuratively dodged bullets, because he was tough and he had the will to survive.

Three hours earlier, his doctor at the JSC Medicina Clinic had delivered the news with a stony expression: Brain cancer.

Inoperable. Six months—*maybe*. Egorov had laughed in the doctor's face.

He did not fear death. He had always prayed that his would be a fast one—a bullet to the head that he never saw coming. So far, this prayer had not been answered. Despite all the decidedly bad things that happened in his line of work, he took very good care of his family and those close to him. As the cold wind blew, he smiled as he thought more of all the good he had done.

He could only imagine what his idiot sons would do once he was gone. As much as they disappointed him with their flashy lifestyles and their crass behavior, he loved them. They were smart and ambitious, but all too weak. This entire generation of Russians was weak.

Egorov turned to look at Natasha, his nurse, and Joseph, his chief of security. Even former soldiers like Joseph had soft hands. The two of them tugged on the collars of their overcoats, trying hard to hide their misery, both from the cold and the morning's news. As long as Egorov wanted to stand outside, they would be forced to do the same.

He nodded toward the back door of his mansion. His compound in Rublyovka—western Moscow's most prestigious residential district—shared Ostozhenka Street with the president and prime minister, as well as many Kremlin high officials and party members.

When Egorov was forced to come to the city, he lived here, in his luxurious seven-bedroom mansion. Had they been allowed to visit, photographers from the decorating magazines would have loved to shoot his French-style kitchen, his bedrooms modeled on a Swiss chalet, his bathhouse and indoor pool. Auto aficionados would appreciate his underground garage equipped with Range Rovers for his security detail, the Bentley Arnage, and the obligatory Rolls-Royce Phantom, all jet black—and all armored, of course.

But no photographer would ever see the inside of any of his homes. Not while he was still alive.

As he made his way back inside, Egorov looked around his grounds, observing the dozen armed guards, the attack dogs, the cameras. Although he never took anything for granted, he was content that for the moment he was safe.

As the core members of his personal detail happily shed their heavy coats and enjoyed the warmer indoor temperatures, Joseph's Iridium satellite phone chirped. The security chief carried several communications devices, all encrypted and capable of worldwide service. This particular phone was used by only one client.

Egorov heard the chirp, let out an audible sigh, and prepared to speak with the asshole in Paris.

"I am listening," Alexander Egorov said evenly as he answered the phone. The conversation was short. Thankfully, the Algerian was not prone to small talk: He simply told his arms supplier which materials would be needed for the next phase of their operation.

The delicate but destructive explosive device was an interesting ask. Not unheard-of, but peculiar: It didn't fit the pattern of the man's customary purchases, which tended to be the garden-variety weapons and explosives that one would expect from a passionate but inexperienced terrorist. This new request was akin to leaving high school for a PhD program. It took the optics to an entirely different level.

Egorov lived by the simple rule that his clients' goals were not his business. He simply made transactions. He sold goods, not services. Remaining willfully ignorant of his clients' objectives allowed him to sidestep pesky questions of morality. It also guaranteed that he could never be forced to reveal what he honestly didn't know.

That said, he wasn't naïve, of course. His own intelligence network was vast, and the dots between the exploded Nantucket ferry and the murdered United States senator were not hard to connect.

That his son Pavel had been off the island's coast was not only reckless, but at cross-purposes with Alexander's desire to remain detached. Egorov would try once again to beat it into his sons' thick skulls that they must stay away from the scene of the crime — or the war, as the case may be.

Have I underestimated my client? Egorov wondered for a moment. But he trusted his gut: This idea had been generated by a third party. Haracat al Marrak was as passionate about his cause as the next guy, but in the end he was an imbecile.

Egorov made a mental note to speak to his niece and ask her what she knew.

Another attack in the US? Perhaps it would be necessary to leave the States altogether for a while. The boys could retreat to the house in Argentina, or the one in Montenegro. *Anywhere else,* he would insist when he arrived in Florida to tell them the news.

"They will be ready in a week," he told the Algerian, and pushed the Disconnect button. Handing the phone back to Joseph, he told the former Spetsnaz officer the message to be delivered to Pavel and Taras.

"In light of today's excitement," he said, "I should like to take a swim." Down the winding stairwell, Egorov arrived in the natatorium and began to change for his daily exercise.

"Alexander, do you think this is wise?" asked Natasha in her compassionate-nurse tone. "Perhaps you would care to rest."

Egorov smiled, acknowledging her concern. "Thank you, my pet, but I have work to do. I will sleep when I am dead." He laughed. "But since I am not dead yet, come swim with me."

CHAPTER 76

The mountains of North Carolina

Around the mahogany table in the secret war room in the mountains of North Carolina, the assembled principals covered the full agenda, then did it again.

Oversight of the Office of Domestic Strategy fell to five people: attorney Sam Starnes; Representative Martin Jennings, chairman of the House Armed Services Committee; Representative Carter Dempsey from Michigan; Senator Tabitha Doyle of Florida; and Senator John Henry Schaffer of Virginia.

With his trademark expert efficiency and natural authority, Sam Starnes ran the meeting to chart the way forward from the Coleman Harrison murder.

I surveyed the assembled leadership. They all were sharp. Senator Doyle definitely knew her stuff. She was fluent in counterterrorism and discussed intelligence issues as easily as she might order a gin and tonic.

Senator Schaffer was a stickler for details. He was an elderly

Virginian who wore a bow tie, spoke with a distinctive Southern accent, and made clear that his word was his bond. Whereas he was prone to question just about everything—a no-before-yes man—he was by his own admission committed to pulling terrorists "out from the attic and under the rug."

Congressman Jennings I knew from Team Rhino's recent mission in Iraq. He was solid and needed no further study.

Congressman Dempsey was the puzzle of the five. An Independent from Michigan, he bounced between issues as the wind blew. He talked way too much for my taste and seemed to agree with almost everything anybody said. He struck me as the weakest link.

Tristan and Ali Dent also had seats at the table. From the CSTC vantage point, I was impressed to witness a side of Tristan and Ali that I hadn't seen before. Their insightful questions and thoughtful answers demonstrated to everyone present that they were as well versed in constitutional law as they were in the nuances of running the newest clandestine organization in the United States of America.

Alongside them were Dallas Fletcher and Morgan Porter, CEO and COO, respectively, of Black Star Services.

Black Star was the conjoined security twin with CSTC for Rocket's Red Glare. They had in fact been the ones behind our exfil aircraft from Nantucket—call it a no-notice dry run—and had set up the delivery of our recon team with a cover: Florida Moving and Storage. It was understood that our Eagle, Hawk, and Falcon teams would fly our assault missions, while Black Star would do all the rest. I hadn't worked with them much yet, but they had delivered twice so far—and that was good enough for me.

ROCKET'S RED GLARE

Air Force Academy roommates Dallas Fletcher and Morgan Porter, by their own admission, had not been "stellar" officers during their respective military careers. Fletcher had been an Air Force logistician during Desert Storm. His claim to fame, he wryly stated, was that in the months leading up to the war he sent more pallets of MREs to Kuwait for the troops than McDonald's served Big Macs in Texas. A year of loading food, uniforms, and even body bags into large-bodied aircraft led him to the conclusion that he had made a really big mistake with his life. When he saw the planes hit the towers he called his old roommate. Something had to be done. Porter, a former C-5 Galaxy pilot, had left military life for a job with FedEx, flying heavy cargo around the world.

What they'd both realized after 9/11 was that there was absolutely no way on God's green Earth that the United States Air Force—let alone the rest of the Department of Defense—would be able to transport the millions of tons of equipment and soldiers necessary to fight a high-intensity war in the Middle East.

Like so many great ideas, theirs had been hatched over a couple of beers. After sketching a plan on a cocktail napkin at a bar in DC, they called some retired pilot buddies and figured out a way to lease a couple of heavy cargo platforms. Then they went to the Pentagon, hats in hand.

They called their new company White Star Aviation for the white stars of the American flag. White Star's first hauling assignments were humble—cargo that didn't quite make the initial load plan, the military's "leftovers." By delivering their goods on time, on target, and most importantly, under budget, White Star Aviation boasted a fleet of shiny new airplanes by 2005, burning holes daily in the clouds between Dover and

Dubai. As Fletcher and Porter created more and more business opportunities for themselves, they doubled down and opened a sister company called Black Star Services.

Black Star had a singular focus: US special operations. WE FLY NOBODY NOWHERE was their motto, and they performed it brilliantly. Siphoning platforms and networks from White Star, they quickly began ferrying special operators and their toys to nasty places around the globe.

Land, sea, or air capabilities—Black Star had them all, every one untraceable and ultimately deniable. If Uncle Sam needed to move a SEAL team to a nowhere spot in South America without leaving a signature, Black Star was the ticket. They would fly into some obscure airfield with one tail number and mysteriously depart with another. Not only did Black Star service the secret side of the government, but cutout companies used them to gain more distance from the Agency. The value of flying *nobody nowhere* was staggering.

★ ★ ★

Oliver Smith and I were up next.

We delivered a summary of the significant events of the previous few days, from my arrival on Nantucket to the movements of our reconnaissance team currently in Palm Beach, Florida. We wrapped up with a condensed after-action report.

An inquisition followed. They were all fair points, but they also revealed that none of the questioners had ever lived through an in-extremis situation. Rounds of inquiries opened with *Could you have* or *Why didn't you* or my favorite, from Carter Dempsey: *If it was me, I would've* yadda yadda.

ROCKET'S RED GLARE

Dempsey's salvo got my temper flaring. I paused, careful to choose the right words before responding.

Luckily, Tabitha Doyle beat me to it. "Carter, your vast experience in tactical operations like the one just described by our Mr. Phillips here would, of course, give you the confidence and certainly the authority to challenge the leadership decisions made under fire by the man who was, in fact, on the ground." The senator from Florida was practically spitting venom.

"Listen carefully, Carter," she continued. If her eyes could shoot fire, Dempsey would have been ashes. "We may have some worthy perspectives to offer, but I assure you that nobody gives a damn about what you *would've* done. If we are going to demand excellence, then we all need to *demonstrate* excellence—and by that I mean our courtesy and our professionalism. Mr. Phillips is a tough man who can quite clearly handle himself in a room full of politicians and bureaucrats. He signed up for that. What he *didn't* sign up for was empty rhetoric."

She stared at the Michigan congressman, her eyes flashing but her voice level: "In short, please do not ask any more stupid fucking questions. We don't have the time."

Gracefully, Senator Doyle pivoted to me: "Mr. Phillips, I am very much interested in what you and Mr. Smith think is going on here."

Her face was all business, but I caught the wink. She was on the team, signaling me to relax and speak from experience.

"Yes, Senator Doyle—thank you, ma'am. At the moment, the Russians are our only lead, but it doesn't make sense that they'd try something so brazen as to kidnap, torture, and execute a sitting US senator. That's begging for retaliation on an unfathomable scale. A nation-state gives us an easy target. Al-Qaeda makes more sense to me, but as far as we can tell, there has been no claim from them, not even following the video broadcast. Anybody with a mask and a black flag could have done that. It seems almost more of a staged play than a planned operation."

"Mr. Phillips, what makes you say that?" Congressman Dempsey asked. My girl Tabitha gave him a look but nodded in my direction for me to continue.

"The assault and kidnapping were professional. These guys sank a fucking ferry. They coordinated a spectacular diversion while killing ninety-nine percent of a Secret Service detail who do this shit for a living. Add in the calls to France and the fact that the dead sniper was a Latino, and we're facing a kaleidoscope of fragmented explanations."

Pencils scribbled across notebooks as I continued.

"Nothing is obvious about any of this, especially when the personal aspects are factored in. It was known that Harrison was cheating on his wife, who was living apart from him on another part of the island. We've also uncovered fishy behavior among Harrison's staff leading up to the night of the attack. There's a drug piece related to the mistress, but it makes no sense — obviously a sloppy frame job. Best scenario points to a group that put a lot of balls in the air — maybe one too many."

"Another cell or organization?" Jennings speculated. "Maybe one we haven't yet heard of?"

The courtly Senator Schaffer spoke up for the first time, sounding skeptical: "It seems to me that it would be a very tall order for a brand-new terrorist cell to execute such a complex operation with seemingly no mistakes...no fog of war...no Murphy's Law effects."

"Well, John, I agree with you on almost every point. But we also have to consider the possibility that these people had access to inside information."

Jennings looked at his watch, then made eye contact with Doyle. "Why don't we take a quick break to stretch our legs—perhaps get a drink from the bar—before we continue?"

An agreement was reached.

"When we reconvene, Tabitha will close us out with an update from her position and some guidance for us all to move forward."

CHAPTER 77

Palm Beach, Florida

The Wilson home on South Ocean Boulevard was receiving a delivery on a hefty pallet draped with a giant tarp.

In the driveway, a woman in aviator glasses, coveralls, and a ball cap directed two muscled deliverymen to maneuver the large pallet off the truck and into the Wilsons' four-car garage.

Passersby might imagine the delivery was a sculpture or some artwork or some crazy piece of exotic furniture the Wilsons wanted to shield from prying eyes. That sort of secrecy was pretty typical behavior for the families who lived on Palm Beach Island.

Once the pallet was securely settled in one bay of the garage, the stout men closed the garage door, retrieved the clipboard with the signed receipt from the son of the property owner, and pulled away in the big box truck marked *Florida Moving and Storage*.

While Meg and Si unpacked and inventoried the contents of

the large pallet, Jimmy T. and Rudy headed due west to exchange the *big box of fun*, as Meg called the truck, for an old 5 series BMW. Ordinarily a nondescript Chrysler or even a minivan would work for a recon and surveillance operation, but in a place like Palm Beach, a bland American model would draw more attention than a sporty European sedan.

The Russians had never seen Rudy or Jimmy T., so it was decided that the two of them would operate wherever they could get clear "eyes on" either of the objectives. After they got the BMW, they'd drive around the island for a cursory look at the Egorov place and the yacht *Oryol* in the boat basin, then link up with Meg and Si after sunset.

Si Wilson's house provided a slight hiding-in-plain-sight advantage, but even with Meg and Si operating as a buddy team focused on video and electronic surveillance of the Egorov house, the weak link was still Meg: Pavel Egorov certainly wouldn't have forgotten the woman who had rappelled onto his yacht from a helicopter in the middle of the ocean and kicked him in the nuts. But the decision was made that as the chief intelligence officer for Team Rhino, Meg needed to be there for the inaugural reconnaissance mission of an official Rocket's Red Glare operation.

"Okay, Si, time for us to make some money," Meg said. "You know how to throw a paper airplane?"

Si gave her a slight scowl. "Just how pampered a life do you think I've led? Believe it or not, Meg, I once even played in a mud puddle."

"I didn't mean it that way," Meg said. "I am asking so you'll understand the motion I need you to replicate so you can launch our drone."

"Okay, okay," Si chuckled. "When the time comes, I'll show you what I've got."

The tall hedges around the Wilson property gave them plenty of free space to play sneaky Pete, but they waited until Meg determined that it was dark enough to fly the drone without any interference from neighbors.

With perfect form, Si launched the drone, then sat next to Meg as she remotely controlled the aircraft.

"Look at the clarity of that camera feed!" Si exclaimed as the small TV screen came alive in bright green.

Meg maneuvered the aircraft out to sea, then had it make an easy 180-degree turn back toward the house. She gently nudged the toggle guiding the nose of the plane to the south and watched as it slowly traced the breaking waves along the beach.

Si saw the lifeguard stands and the Worth Avenue clock tower, then the breaker walls protecting the mansions along Ocean Avenue. He knew most of the houses, or at least the names of the owners, and he called off each one as Meg steered the drone farther south.

"Holy shit—wow," Meg commented as the drone flew past the impressive buildings. "Did you see that place?"

"Yeah—it's crazy money, Meg," Si laughed. "No bullshit, some of the owners spend barely a few days in those places—not months or even weeks. These are their third or fourth homes. Like I said, crazy."

"Speaking of *crazy*, looks like the Egorov boys are home tonight." The unmistakable silhouettes of a Lamborghini and a Ferrari loomed in the half-moon driveway of their estate. "Let's do a flyby and see what's what."

CHAPTER 78

Governor Larson HQ, Colorado

The view of Cheyenne Mountain was breathtaking as night began to fall. To Governor Theresa Larson, the sun's slow descent highlighted both the beauty and the might of the Rocky Mountains—not to mention the beauty and might of the United States.

"Will you be joining us, Theresa?"

The governor sipped her Grey Goose as she turned from the window of her suite at the Broadmoor to face her husband, Mark.

"I momentarily lost myself in the beauty of the mountains," she lied. "My apologies, Mark, everyone."

Theresa Larson's adoring campaign staff was gathered around. The assassination of Senator Coleman Harrison was a tragedy, but it also left little doubt that their candidate would be firmly on the road to Pennsylvania Avenue, delivering the reassuring message that America needed and wanted.

The system, as every campaigning politician in history

categorically stated, *was broken*. Well, the same was true of her marriage.

Her husband, Mark Larson, had no official role in her campaign. She put up with him. She had to. That was the agreement. But she also knew that deals were made to be broken. Maybe one day soon, if the stars aligned, she would set the record straight.

She was well aware of the rumors, and she hated her staff for spreading them. Some said Mark's domineering attitude revealed his anger at her success. Others said that theirs was a marriage of convenience, that he was obviously having an affair because they never displayed any affection in public. Yet another theory was that she tolerated Mark because she was mildly depressed. Depending on who was around and how much alcohol was being consumed, the staffers occasionally delighted in even more scandalous Page Six–level gossip.

By January, they would all be vying for jobs in the Larson administration, where Theresa would be commander in chief. Mark could enjoy the life of the First Gentleman, treat his staff like shit, and be an asshole to whomever he pleased.

While Mark took a phone call, Larson glanced around the room, reminding herself why she hated each of them so much. The guy on the couch was obnoxious. The woman in the blue skirt was a liar. The tall one was an ass-kisser. And that gem of an aide of Mark's—Cindy something—was just fucking worthless. For all Larson knew, Mark could very well be doing her.

No matter how often she tried to give her staff the benefit of the doubt, she realized the real reason why she hated them: *Every single one of these pretentious, blood-sucking leeches thought she was just as afraid of her husband as they clearly were.*

The truth was that Theresa was not the least bit afraid of Mark Larson.

"Mark, would you let the briefer know we're ready for the intelligence update?" the governor commanded.

The video conference with Langley was about to begin. Larson nodded to her chief of staff, who ushered those without proper security credentials out of the room.

As the briefer appeared on the giant plasma screen in front of Theresa Larson's eyes, all her problems with Mark and the others drifted away.

This was her arena and she was at home.

CHAPTER 79

Egorov Gulfstream

The Gulfstream cruised effortlessly above the clouds at 39,000 feet and about 480 knots.

Natasha slept soundly on the couch while Alexander Egorov nodded absently to whoever was on the other end of the phone. Joseph had excused himself to the aft of the plane when the secure phone line rang, allowing his boss to speak in private.

After a minute or two, Egorov ended the call and signaled for Joseph to return. Joseph picked up where they had left off—going over the current contracts to be discussed with Pavel and Taras—but as he ran through the details of the used AK-47s and archaic tracked vehicles they'd sold to some revolutionaries in the Maghreb, Joseph could see that, despite the projected revenues, his boss was distracted.

"Sir?" he asked politely.

Alexander Egorov closed the folder, looked his protégé in the eye, and asked evenly, "Who the fuck were those people who boarded my yacht off the coast of Nantucket?"

Joseph was ready for the question, having received the latest bit of intelligence from his sources while the G5 engines whined before takeoff.

"They are members of an organization called Chesapeake Security and Training Company. This company employs former military and has contracts for hire all over the world, but lately a lot of PSD protection in Iraq and Afghanistan. Prior to the event on your yacht, the unit in question was involved in a significant engagement in Iraq, where they killed several supposed terrorists and saved an American patrol outside Baghdad. The team was then rotated home, but it's unclear how or why they wound up on Nantucket Island at the same time as your yacht. They have obviously since been caught up in the events that unfolded."

"Your assessment, Joseph?"

"Formidable. They have deep resources and clearly first-class talent. My sources couldn't gather any details beyond what I've told you, but we know this group retreated behind the fences of their facility in Maryland. We've done only passive reconnaissance on the property, but it appears to be professionally staffed and very secure.

"The main entrance to the compound looks the same as any other estate in the area: a large, wrought-iron gate, hung between two brick façades on either side of the driveway. Thick woods provide natural concealment and limit visibility to about ten yards. It is surrounded by almost ten thousand acres of nature sanctuary, affording additional privacy.

"Expertly concealed around the foliage of the entrance are a series of high-resolution infrared cameras that record everything that passes the gate, day or night. The driveway has a pronounced serpentine drift, preventing anyone from driving faster than a crawl. A variety of early-detection devices throughout the property are reinforced by armed patrols constantly monitoring the compound's security.

"About a quarter mile inside, a twelve-foot-high chain-link fence topped by razor wire protects the inner perimeter, along with a manned guardhouse and attack dogs."

Joseph handed his principal a thick folder containing his notes, a few photos, and all the open-source documents about CSTC his team could gather. The day after the storming of the yacht off Nantucket, Joseph had told his Russian-mobster contacts that any information they provided about the event would be well rewarded.

It wasn't long before a dock worker in Charlestown, Massachusetts, mentioned that some Irish guys had been asking about Russian and Chinese crime syndicates, and poking around about the ferry explosion.

The guys asking questions worked for the Teagan family. Plenty of Boston families had Irish names, and then there were the true Irish—the believers. The Teagans were the latter. It didn't take too long to find out that one son, James, had left the family business for the greener pastures of the American army. And that James had been an Army Ranger, had deployed to the Middle East multiple times, and was now employed by a private military contractor on the Eastern Shore of Maryland.

Egorov listened intently as his security officer finished the briefing.

"This is all very helpful, Joseph, but I have one more request. I'm afraid I need you to deliver it by the time we land."

Joseph nodded, his mind racing: *What order was he about to receive?* (These were never really "requests.")

"I want the names and photos of everyone who was on my yacht, starting with their leader."

Joseph did some mental calculations. They were four hours from Palm Beach. The names alone would be difficult enough to locate, but people in the spook world were notoriously camera-shy, so it was entirely possible that no images existed. He would have to shake the tree hard.

"Sir, I will do my best and get this started, but I can't lie to you: This task will be challenging. May I ask why the rush for photographs?"

Their eyes locked, steel to steel and no emotion.

"Because right now they are surveilling my fucking house."

CHAPTER 80

The mountains of North Carolina

"Folks," Senator Tabitha Doyle began as she stood at the head of the mahogany table after a brief break. "From here on, we are all in this together, right?"

The gravity of the moment was not lost on any of us. We all nodded our assent.

"At some point, each of us will be forced to break an oath and share information that we have sworn not to share. For me, that time is now."

She paused before revealing her secret.

"We have a source in Taiwan who suggests that for some time a Chinese agent has had access to the inner sanctum of our Justice Department. This source has recently mentioned details about Senator Harrison's abduction and torture that are not widely known, nor have they been made public. Although Rocket's Red Glare is brand-new, it may already have weaknesses. What do we do next?"

I realized that everyone in the room was looking at me to answer Doyle's question. What came naturally to me was to ask one in return: "How reliable is the source?"

"Our Ground Branch friends have found his intelligence to be actionable."

"Senator, is there any chance this guy is probing to see what we confirm for him? I've heard all the *Manchurian Candidate* rumors since I was an Army private. What makes this one so credible?"

"I say this with great caution, but given his past, and the quality of the information he has previously delivered, I believe we should consider this source reliable. Could he play us? Certainly. There is a spy somewhere close to us. I don't suspect that Rocket's Red Glare is compromised per se, but I believe they may be stumbling toward us."

I looked at Oliver. He nodded, confirming that he already knew what I was thinking.

"Then let's roll up the twins in Florida. Right now. Do not pass *Go*. Oliver and I will alert the rest of the team, and we will snatch those two idiots where they sleep. Then we'll find out exactly who, what, when, where, and how this mole knows what he knows. Case closed. That's my suggestion."

"Mr. Phillips," Congressman Dempsey said, "please forgive me, but I thought you said you didn't believe the Russians were behind this attack? Why would these two know anything about the mole who may have infiltrated our Justice Department, or even Rocket's Red Glare?"

"I was going to ask the same question," Doyle said matter-of-factly.

"Yes, ma'am, it's a fair question. Deception is one act that terrorists do well. Rarely do events occur at face value, or at legitimately random times," I said. "The enemy's consistent calculus: Maximize damage while efficiently using a limited amount of time. Sending the good guys in the wrong direction allows more time to accomplish their real objective.

"In this scenario, I would say that although the Russians may not have orchestrated it, and probably have fantastic deniability, the Egorovs' business is arms dealing. They sure as shit had something to do with the arms and ammo the bad guys used. If you want to find dirty people, don't hang out with clean people. Those two fuckers are as dirty as they come. They'll know something."

"How soon can you execute?" asked Congressman Jennings.

"Plan on our takedown in thirty-six hours, like 0300 the day after tomorrow." I looked at the principals of Black Star Services, Dallas Fletcher and Morgan Porter. "Can you guys get us in that soon?" Realizing I had put them on the spot in front of everyone, I mouthed a weak *Sorry*.

"Do you want a window seat or an aisle?" Fletcher laughed. "Nat, the answer is yes. Morgan and I will get the assets organized and brief you as soon as I get off the phone with our planners. Too easy."

"Well, folks, it seems that we now have our first sanctioned Rocket's Red Glare mission," Sam Starnes said. "The president will be briefed as soon as we conclude. Before you get busy, I want to remind you that while you're cleared to use what force you need, be safe, be smart, and don't get caught."

With that, Tabitha Doyle raised her glass, saying, "God bless you and God bless America."

CHAPTER 81

Egorov compound
Palm Beach, Florida

"The beauty of this device is its simplicity," Pavel Egorov explained. "A child could work it."

Pavel was giving his demonstration to his twin brother, Taras, as well as to Rowan Anderson and Elise Courville.

Courville had been able to secure a French embassy jet for this trip to Florida, ostensibly to take a meeting on behalf of her ambassador father, though the assumption that the new widow would also take time out to do some retail therapy didn't hurt. The women would be able to transport the materials back to Washington, DC, as easily as they could bring a purse purchased on Worth Avenue without fear of TSA or customs. And Anderson's badge and pistol would be quite enough to send anyone who did get too close in the other direction.

Now the four co-conspirators were gathered around a large

heavy wooden table in a fortified room—essentially a bomb shelter.

While Alexander Egorov was a master of the arms trade, both his sons were savants with explosives. They partied too much and spent outrageous sums of money pushing the limits of their father's patience. But if a customer ever needed something exotic in the explosives department, the Egorov boys were as good as could be found anywhere in the world.

For the past year, they had given both product and advice to the customer in Boston. The Serbian was good, but they were better. Most of the bomb building and design work had been done offshore, but this latest order was homemade in Florida.

"Only three things you need," Taras Egorov explained. "One, the bomb sheet. Two, the miniature initiating device. And three, your cell phone. Let me show you how it works."

He pulled from a heavy cardboard sleeve what appeared to be a three-by-four-foot sheet of green Christmas wrapping paper. At the southeast corner of the sheet were several items that resembled sticks of chewing gum.

Pavel Egorov pointed to the sticks, which were all wrapped—not with aluminum foil, but a neutral-looking cover. "This is the igniter that is built into the device. We color-coded everything, so there is no mistake about what goes with what. This green wrapper is matched with the green initiating device my brother is holding. The parts can be easily adapted for camouflage purposes."

Taras Egorov reached inside a box the size of a pack of cigarettes and held up what looked like a green coin, no bigger than a half dollar. "This is the initiating device. Again, it is color-coded to its matching explosive sheet so you don't get mixed up.

The industrial-grade adhesive can be applied to almost any surface, wet or dry."

"What's the range between the two?" Rowan Anderson asked as she nodded her head in appreciation.

"Fifty feet, maximum," Taras said. "It has worked at fifty-two, but there are too many variables. At forty-five feet or less, it has never failed."

"So all I need to do is set up the device where I need it and then plant the initiator about forty feet away?"

"Set it and forget it," Pavel Egorov laughed. "Once you dial the number, the detonation is almost instantaneous."

"Using heavy shears," added Taras, "you can cut this sheet to whatever size you need. A three-inch square will vaporize a human body. A foot square will cripple and demolish an armored military vehicle, and this whole sheet with make a three-story building crumble." His face was expressionless. "It's good work, and our client said this is what you wanted. Yes?"

Anderson looked at Elise Courville, then back at the twins. "Oh, yes—this is precisely what we wanted. I promise you it will be put to good use."

CHAPTER 82

Egorov Compound
Palm Beach, Florida

Alexander Egorov's entourage pulled through the iron security gate and parked in the half-moon circle at the front of the mansion.

"What the fuck is going on here?" Egorov roared, the veins in his neck thick as ropes as he entered the house to find his sons sipping red wine with two women as some old jazz musician played a tune on his clarinet. Joseph and Natasha followed close behind Alexander.

At the sound of the old man's voice, Taras Egorov spilled his wine and Pavel Egorov tried and failed to lower the volume of the music.

Joseph turned off the stereo while Natasha hovered around Egorov, who rebuffed her attentions.

Snorting like a bull, Egorov spat orders at the unwanted

guests. "Get the fuck out of *my* house and never come back. As you stand here, I will kill you personally."

The women avoided eye contact with the old man as they scrambled to obey his command and make their way outside.

"Papa, I'm sorry," Pavel groveled, "but I don't understand your anger. We just finished the deal you told us to do, and the money has been transferred to our account in Geneva. What have we done to upset you?"

It now made sense. This was the traitor he had heard whispers about: the federal agent, Rowan Anderson. She was here to purchase the product. The other woman must be her accomplice. He'd seen her somewhere before.

"Stop," Egorov barked at the women. "Sit!" He turned to Pavel. "I expected you to conclude the transaction, and I expected the money to be wired. What I did not expect was to find the two of you sitting around listening to music and trying to get in the pants of these whores. Especially when it has come to my attention that a federal fucking agency has had surveillance on you for at least twenty-four hours. And not one of you had any idea." He slapped the wineglass out of his son's hand.

"Alexander, enough!" Natasha begged. "You must calm down."

Egorov smiled at his nurse as if to humor her, then glanced at Joseph in a way he knew his security chief would understand. Then he walked to the bar and poured himself a tumbler of fine whiskey.

Joseph moved quickly to his briefcase and retrieved a thick folder. He marched across the living room and handed the document file to Pavel, who was now sitting next to Anderson on an exquisitely upholstered couch. The accomplice sat in a chair opposite. Egorov recognized her now: The French ambassador's daughter—the one whose husband had just been murdered. *Interesting.*

Pavel opened the folder and flipped through identification photos. "Who are these people, Papa? The spies?"

Anderson spoke up. "I know who they are. And I know they are planning to come here tonight or tomorrow."

"How do you know this information?" Egorov demanded.

"They were on Nantucket with us, but unaware of my role. The leader is Nat Phillips. He told me he's 'heading south for a few days.' Now you show up with his picture? Doesn't take a genius to connect the dots."

Anderson pointed to a photo of a young man's student ID in the folder. "I don't have the address, but I know this one's family has a house here in Palm Beach."

Egorov's eyes darted from the traitor to Joseph, who was already dialing his phone and swiftly making his way to another room. After thirty seconds of uncomfortable silence, Joseph returned and whispered into his principal's ear.

Another thirty seconds passed before Alexander Egorov made his decision.

"Bring one to me," he ordered Joseph. "You know what must be done."

Joseph bowed his head and left the room to assemble the tools and talent needed for this delicate mission.

Egorov turned to the women. "How soon can you be gone?" he asked politely. "I assume you have a way out of here—compliments of the embassy, perhaps?"

"Yes, we do," the accomplice answered quickly. "Departure happens within minutes of my call."

ROCKET'S RED GLARE

"Our business is concluded. However you use my product is not my concern." He looked at each of the women. "It is true you know who I am, but I remind you that we know who you are. There is no place on earth where I cannot find you. Now leave."

CHAPTER 83

Asheville, North Carolina

Oliver and I had made some half-assed plans before, but this was by far the most half-assed one we had ever conceived. We would take off from Asheville Regional, then land at Palm Beach International around midnight. Meg's team would pick us up in a dark corner of the base operations parking lot.

Meg and Si would stay at the Wilsons' and fly the drone as overwatch for the assault. Oliver, Jimmy T., Rudy, and I would stage as close to the Russian compound as we could get.

If we made it inside without compromise, we figured, the grab itself should take no more than ten minutes, tops. Oliver and Teagan would go for one of the twins, while Rudy and I would tag the other.

Once we called *Jackpot,* Wolf and his crew would arrive in, as Meg called it, the *big box of fun.* At that early hour, we should be able to drive into the Everglades undetected, then call for our exfiltration all the way back to Easton, Maryland. If shit went south, Fletcher and Porter's Black Star Services was supposed to have a dedicated bird circling off the Florida coast for an immediate medevac.

Once in Easton, we'd go to work on the twins and politely ask them to give up the mole. If that didn't do the trick, we'd switch to more, uh, persuasive methods.

Oliver and I knew the plan was shitty and there were lots of ways it could go sideways, but we agreed that surprise was on our side and that made up for a lot. We had suppressed weapons in case we met armed resistance, but the whole idea of the snatch mission was to take the targets alive, using dart guns loaded with enough sedative to knock out a friggin' elephant. The op would be smooth and silent.

By the time we were in the air heading south, Wolf, JP, and Stu were in Daytona Beach, loading another Florida Moving and Storage truck. Meg, Jimmy T., Si, and Rudy seemed hyped about the snatch mission. I think we all were excited to be back in the saddle. Hopefully there would be no fireworks tonight.

I told Meg I would call her when we were about ten minutes from wheels down.

CHAPTER 84

Alexander Egorov swallowed the last of his whiskey, his eyes burning.

"When Joseph returns," Egorov told his sons after the traitor and her accomplice had departed with their product packages, "we will be leaving. Joseph and Natasha will close this house for a while—maybe forever. Bad people will come, so we must be prepared. They are most formidable."

Pavel and Taras knew enough not to question his plan. *But leave the house permanently?* That was a drastic move. One vault in the garage held $10 million in cash alone. Another contained thousands of ounces of gold. And then there was the art. But Joseph was a master when it came to deception: He would make all of it disappear without a trace.

Egorov asked Natasha for another drink, studying his sons while he waited. Of course he loved them both, more than anything—when he wasn't pissed off at them, which was often. He didn't think he'd spoiled them after their mother died, but they were soft, probably because of him. He definitely hadn't been spoiled when *his* mother died. But none of that family history mattered now: He was hard and going to die; they were soft and going to live.

An electronic signal from the front gate broke the silence in the room.

The cargo is about to arrive, the arms dealer thought to himself.

Natasha handed Egorov a fresh glass as Joseph and two of his men entered. They placed a limp body on the floor, its head covered with a black hood, its hands and feet bound.

Egorov took a sip as he surveyed the cargo, then nodded at Joseph to remove the covering.

Joseph pulled the hood off. It was a woman. "This one is Meg Fuller," Joseph reported, "the intelligence officer for the group."

"And the others?"

"Taken care of, Mr. Egorov—as you ordered."

CHAPTER 85

Embassy jet

As the Dassault Falcon 2000 climbed to altitude, Rowan Anderson looked around the cabin of the French-made business jet.

It had been so easy for them to fly to Florida unnoticed, and now to fly back with three cardboard sleeves of state-of-the-art explosives.

The pilots had their orders. Now that the connection to Alexander Egorov had been made, everything would happen at warp speed. Had Nat and his people seen Elise or her? They were on their ninth life, the grains of sand running quickly through the hourglass. Anderson shook her head in disgust. *How could I have been so complacent?*

"What do you need me to do?" Elise Courville asked nervously.

"We need to be ready to execute this plan fucking soon,

while we can still move without restrictions. If the Russians talk, they could connect us."

"I could contact him," Courville said.

"Absolutely not. He would sell us out in two seconds." Anderson thought for a moment, then asked, "Elise, you have access to a car with diplomatic plates, right?"

Courville nodded.

"Excellent. I need to borrow it for a couple of days."

Rowan Anderson smiled. It was time to kill the president.

CHAPTER 86

Palm Beach International Airport

The pilot gave me the *Prepare for landing* alert, so I punched in Meg's number and let it ring. Nothing. Fucking cell phones on planes. I hung up and tried again. *Shit*.

Oliver pulled his phone and dialed Teagan: *Nothing*. Rudy: *Voicemail*. Si: *Same*. I was getting worried. Nobody was answering. What the fuck? There was no one else to call. How could all their phones be out of range or turned off when they knew we would be calling?

I dialed Si again. He answered on the third ring.

"Si? What's going on?"

"They took her, Nat—they've got Meg." Si sounded punch-drunk, slurring his words. "They shot me and they took Meg." He was on the verge of tears, almost hyperventilating.

Fucking Russians. I knew it was those fuckers.

"Si, calm down, man," I said slowly but firmly. "It's okay. Take a breath. Just tell me where you're shot and how much you're bleeding." I looked at Oliver and shook my head.

"Not bleeding. I was tranked."

CHAPTER 87

"Come on, man—we're in a hurry!" I yelled at the pilot, knowing that every second we weren't attacking, they were inflicting more pain on Meg. I couldn't let my mind go there. All I knew was that people were going to die violently in the very near future. Oliver and I were out of our seats and standing at the galley door.

"I'm sorry, sir, but I have to hold here 'til this other plane gets around us. He's almost done."

A minute later we were parked at the base ops and sprinting to the parking lot. I told Oliver to find us a ride while I ducked into the shadows to call the rest of the team. Stu answered on the first ring and I gave him the shitty news about Meg's abduction. *We have a THUNDER mission,* I told him, *and I need your team to meet us on the target.* The plan was as simple as we could make it on the fly, I explained: no intel, almost no situational awareness—nothing at all but guesswork.

I could feel his anger rising. "Fuck, Nat—we're still about fifteen minutes out."

"That's okay, Stu. We just got here. Oliver is getting us a ride — we'll be on the north side of the gate along the road. Si is staying put at his place in case Jimmy and Rudy show up. You and JP will go with Oliver. Wolf will be with me, and we will launch as soon as you get here. We are all cleared hot. Want to keep it as quiet as we can, but understand that I need someone alive."

"Roger that, Nat. We will leave one." He hung up just as Oliver rolled up to my position in our new assault vehicle.

"Nice ride," I said, as I closed the door to the 4Runner.

"It was either this or the Bentley."

"I'd have gone with the Bentley, but that's just me." I screwed the suppressor on my Sig as Oliver put the SUV in gear.

"Hey, man," he fired back, "have you ever seen desperadoes in a $350,000 car? I haven't. We're fucking desperadoes, and this is what we are driving to do our desperado shit."

Oliver was as calm and casual going to a gunfight as he would be heading to a Waffle House for midnight chow. It helped. We'd done this a thousand times, but never in either of our careers had we planned a rescue mission for one of our own. And of course it being Meg was a kick in the nuts.

Oliver must have sensed my emotion, because he told me to cool it.

Yes, Sensei.

We reviewed the plan. Wolf and I would breach the Egorovs' door and flow into the first floor. Oliver and his team would pass through and clear the upstairs. We'd meet in the garage. Too easy — but we'd have to pray we had enough ammo to get it all done.

CHAPTER 88

Rowan Anderson's apartment
Washington, DC

Rowan Anderson parked Elise Courville's Peugeot in the handicapped spot in the lot at her apartment building. Between the diplomatic plates and her USSS credentialed parking pass on the dashboard, no eager-beaver DC cop was going to mess with her tonight.

She was almost sucked into a delightful fantasy of her future life in Morocco—enjoying her money under an assumed name as well as the non-extradition status offered to expats in the kingdom—when she saw the mark. One wavy red line between the *M* and the *L* on the west side of the mailbox was the signal that he'd called a meeting.

Wearing a Glock on her hip loaded with seventeen Black Talon rounds would give her the confidence she needed to walk alone through DC's Oak Hill Cemetery at that hour. She hid the explosives under her bed and put a fresh magazine in the Glock.

The protocol was simple. Make entry and move to the first marker. Wait for exactly five minutes, then move to a second marker and wait for the same amount of time. These two vantage points allowed him to ensure she was not followed. After two minutes, she would move to a lone bench on the east side of the farthest gravesite and wait. He would make his approach when he felt comfortable. Then he would kill her or he wouldn't.

Anderson strained her eyes and ears for a sign of his presence. Her eyes never stopped scanning. She felt him before she heard him, sensed crosshairs or some infrared laser centered on her head.

"If your cover's not blown by now, it will be soon," he said in his lightly accented English.

"How do you know?" she whispered, thankful that he'd chosen to let her live. She could hear his security detail taking near-silent breaths.

"It is not your concern, Ms. Anderson. The mission has changed. Your new targets are in the folder, along with your exfiltration plan. Take care of this local business and I will get you to Paris on Saturday."

She sucked in a deep breath as she contemplated his directions.

He stood abruptly and faced her. "You'll have your chance to kill the president when I say so. But for now, we take care of loose ends. Don't be a loose end, Ms. Anderson."

She watched him casually walk away, feeling the invisible laser withdrawn from her head. She realized that she was still holding her breath.

Ming Yu made people do that.

CHAPTER 89

Egorov Compound
Palm Beach, Florida

Oliver drove the 4Runner over the Royal Park drawbridge and onto Palm Beach Island. The place was beautiful to the point of intimidation. If I thought Nantucket reeked of money, this place was positively stinking.

Multimillion-dollar yachts as far as I could see in every direction. Manicured hedges, exotic plants decorating the streets. Even the well-groomed palm trees that lined the roads projected an attitude of perfection.

The directions Si gave us were easy enough: *Drive east 'til you hit the Atlantic, then turn right. About a quarter mile later, watch for a mansion with a turret; it'll have crossed lances above its front door.*

Finding the place wasn't difficult at all. The real challenge was that there was nowhere to park, hence no place to stage the assault. We were screwed before we even started.

"What the fuck," Oliver whispered as the 4Runner rolled

past the Russians' place. "Nowhere to dump this thing, of course."

Clearly Oliver was feeling a little put-upon, but I had a solution.

"Hey, man, check it out up there on the right." I could see some construction ahead—a perfect place to park without upsetting the natural order of Palm Beach.

I fantasized a reason for the construction: *If the hedge-fund manager's wife hadn't nagged him to tear down their 13,000-square-foot "starter mansion," we would have been looking for a place to park all night. Thankfully he capitulated, and their mid-century classic is now a large pile of rubble. Good for his wife, probably good for him, but definitely lucky for us.*

Oliver was right—the Bentley would have been out of place in this mud. We were about 400 meters past the Russians, so we grabbed our gear and started jogging toward the target. Thankfully no traffic and no dog walkers.

I said, "It's gonna work, man. Let's push past the driveway and grab those guys on the fly."

Wolf drove the Florida Moving and Storage truck about a hundred meters north of the compound and coasted to our position. I stepped up on the sideboard to update him.

"Look at these two monkeys we found swinging from the trees a little while ago." Wolf smiled as he pointed to the rear seat of the truck, where Jimmy T. and Rudy sat shaking their heads.

"Fuck, Nat—I'm sorry," said Jimmy. "After you called the first time, we went down to the marina to give the boat one more look. Bad reception. Missed your calls. Si filled us in, so we ran over here and got picked up by these assholes about half a mile from here. We're ready."

"No sweat, man. You two stay with the truck 'til we breach. Once we're inside, you guys figure out how to open the front gate, then bring this thing around back. With any luck we'll have someone to toss in, and we can bail.

"Team Eagle is on station off the coast for a medevac if we need one. Same plan as before: Once we meet the objective, we get the hell out of Dodge and head west to the sugarcane fields. At that point we'll ditch the truck and call in the helo. Cool?"

Everyone nodded.

"Okay, Wolfgang, you're with me. Boys, we need one alive. Let's get it done."

Since Jimmy and Rudy had been on recon, neither had body armor. I knew both would have gone on the assault without their plates, but there was no reason to risk it.

We assumed the Russians had early-warning devices around the place, but we had to press on.

Oliver gave me the thumbs-up and the fun began. The lights inside the mansion were on, but nobody was visible. Wolf and I were over the fence and on our way to the breach point at a gallop. I bounded up the front steps and immediately put two rounds into the dead bolt, then two more into the doorknob, rolling away for Wolf to kick it open.

Wolf hit the door with the bottom of his boot as hard as any NFL kicker. It was perfectly choreographed—except that neither of us realized exterior doors in Florida open to the outside, not the inside. The shock of his foot making contact with what was clearly a very solid piece of some exotic South American hardwood stopped Wolf dead in his tracks. He fell backward like a bag of cement. If anyone had been sleeping, they weren't now.

"That was graceful," I chuckled. "Wonder if they heard that? Ready now?"

Wolf was back on his feet in two seconds, saying, "Yeah, fuck me. Note to self, right?"

I grabbed the doorknob and yanked. Mercifully the 9mm rounds had done the trick and the door opened on my first pull. As I followed Wolf inside, I saw the blur of Oliver's team closing the distance in a hurry. I hustled to clear entry so they could pass through.

"Clear!" Wolf called.

"Stairs eleven o'clock, deep," I relayed to Oliver as they blew by in a sprint. I heard the sound of a car engine turning over and figured the twins must have opened the front gate.

So far, so good. Wolf led us into an adjacent room and immediately fired two suppressed shots from his HK. I stepped over the body of a dead Russian with his AK still on Safe. Muffled sounds came from upstairs, but I couldn't tell what was going on. I had to believe it was good news.

I entered the hallway and noted two doorways on the left. At the end of the hallway was a large window, illuminated from outside by the high beams of our moving truck. Knowing Wolf was behind me, I followed my gun into the first room. Nothing.

Wolf led us to the next door and held up a hand in the *Halt* position.

I saw what he saw: The door was ajar. I squeezed his shoulder and had my suppressor over his right shoulder and into the room way before my body.

The sound of the AK was deafening from two feet away.

Egorov's guy had flattened himself against the wall just inside the door of what appeared to be an office. Unfortunately for him, by the time he recognized the suppressor he had three bullets ripping through his face, neck, and chest, and had collapsed in a heap.

More sounds from upstairs; several loud thuds on the floor. I guessed Oliver was doing okay. Wolf and I moved through the kitchen and finished up in a great room across from where we started.

Wolf spied the door to what looked like either a vault or a bomb shelter, so I stacked right on his hip. He twisted the knob and we prepared to drive our barrels in first, only to find another door—a heavy-duty bastard—six inches deeper. Whether it protected a vault or a safe, we weren't getting in there without dynamite or a torch.

"Keep an eye on it," I told Wolf.

"Why," he deadpanned, "is it going to run away?"

I gave him the finger, then yelled upstairs, "First floor clear!"

"Collecting intelligence, then coming down," Oliver called from above.

CHAPTER 90

I made my way to the large window at the front of the house, surprised to find Rudy and a Russian rolling around in the driveway in some kind of grappling match. I trotted out the door and toward the scuffle.

Jimmy T. was trying to get a shot in, but the two combatants were way too close to each other. Every time he tried, either Rudy or the Russian rolled the other one in or out of the way.

This must be the intel officer—the guy we needed alive. "We want this one, Jimmy," I said as Jimmy lowered his Beretta and gave me a *Now what?* look.

"Okay, stop this shit. Let him go, Rudy—I said *Stop!*"

Rudy relaxed his grip and the Russian immediately mounted him in a classic jujitsu position, preparing to take a swing. His problem was that when he wound up for the haymaker, his arm landed perfectly in my grip.

I yanked back hard with my right hand, making the Russian fall backward off Rudy's chest. He tried to roll out of my grasp, but I let myself fall directly on his back with all my weight.

Before he could move, I hopped up and drove my right knee into his rib cage as hard as I could. He cried out in pain as I wrenched his right arm behind his back, twisting his wrist in the opposite direction.

"Something's gonna break, motherfucker. Where is she?"

"I don't know," he wheezed.

"Bullshit! Where is she?" I applied more leverage to his upper arm and less to his wrist. "Your fucking shoulder is about to dislocate, and I will gladly do the other one if you don't tell me where the fuck she is."

"Mr. Egorov...plane...talk to you—" was all he could manage through the pain.

They'd already flown Meg out of here? Fuck. She could be anywhere by now.

Jimmy T. broke my concentration. "Check this out, Nat." He had walked over to the garage and scoped out the only bay whose door was open. "The guy was in here when we pulled up."

While Rudy and Oliver held our prisoner motionless, I walked over to the garage and stopped in my tracks. In one bay were perhaps twenty-five heavy plastic Pelican cases, each stuffed to the gills with cash. I'd guess half a million per case.

In another bay stood a dozen or so pieces of expensive-looking art, all in various stages of being crated for transport. And in the third bay I saw stacks of hundred-dollar bills, each the size of a hay bale, shrink-wrapped and piled five high and five deep. Millions of dollars without breaking a sweat. These fuckers were ready to vamoose tonight. *Had they known we were coming? How could they? No way—no fucking way.*

I turned back to the intel guy and pointed the Sig at his face. "Who are you? What's in the vault? Lie to me and I'll kill you."

He said his name was Joseph and what I assumed was a Russian last name that I immediately forgot. *Mr. Egorov has a nurse named Natasha,* Joseph chattered. *She's hiding in the bomb shelter but I don't know the entry code.*

"Tell her to open the door and come out right now."

"I have no way to contact her," Joseph stated flatly.

I walked to the stack of art and pulled out a nifty oil painting of what appeared to be some noble Russian fighting someone not so noble in the middle of a snowstorm. The horses were snorting in the cold air and the hero had a big-ass sword and was about to lop off the head of the less-noble guy. Looking at Joseph, I drove my foot right through the center of the canvas.

"I hope that one was priceless. Listen, bud, get her out here right fucking now or I'll do this all night long. First the art, then the cash, and I'll finish by torching the house. Your choice."

I purposely gave Joseph only a second to answer. "No? Okay."

He was still looking in horror at the painting I had just destroyed when I pulled out my Gerber, flipped open the blade, and turned to another artwork, this one of a Russian warship firing its many cannons at some unfortunate adversary. Ruining antiquities wasn't my MO, but in this case I had to. Plus, these had probably been stolen anyway.

"I do like this one," I said, "though that water sure looks cold." It took me about five seconds to cut the painting from its frame and start rolling it up.

The next painting was a portrait of a beautiful czaress — or is it *czarina*? I hoped Joseph would cave before I had to disfigure her face. I raised my knife like a slasher.

"Stop!" he cried. He asked for his phone, punched a few buttons, then reported that he had unlocked the vault door.

I looked over at Rudy. "Hey, Bullwinkle. Take Boris here and go find Natasha. We need to get out of this place like five minutes ago."

Rudy lifted Joseph to his feet and pressed the Russian to lead the way to the bomb shelter, where they freed the nurse Natasha.

I looked around. Six enemy dead, no friendly casualties, and a fortune in cash and artworks in the garage.

The security team left behind to guard the property hadn't put up much of a fight. Joseph had sold out Natasha in about two seconds—almost as if he'd expected all this to unfold precisely the way it did.

Rudy and Jimmy flex-cuffed Joseph and Natasha with their hands behind their backs and marched them to the truck.

"Let's get out of here before a cop drives by," Rudy said.

"My medicine kit," Natasha hissed. "I am nurse—I must have medicine kit." She pointed at one of the bags on the garage floor.

Rudy picked up the aid bag, quickly looked through the contents, and tossed it to JP in the back of the truck.

★ ★ ★

I was about to call Tristan and initiate the exfil when my phone rang.

I answered. "Alexander Egorov, I presume?"

"Nat, it's me."

The sound of Meg's voice sent my heart into my throat. "What have they done to you?"

"I'm fine. But he wants to talk to you."

CHAPTER 91

Port of Baltimore

We had fifty million dollars' worth of Egorov's stuff. Of course he wanted Joseph and Natasha released, and the cash and the art delivered to a place of his choosing. If I complied and played nice, he would release our girl.

The message from Egorov was simple and to the point:

Bring me my money in a moving truck. Come alone. I will watch you until I am satisfied that you are not being followed too closely by your friends in Chesapeake Security. I will call you from a number you won't bother to trace and tell you where to park. You stand in front of truck, and I bring Ms. Fuller to you. We make the trade, and we are done. Once I leave, you call your friends and have them pick you up. Simple.

I had to hand it to the guy—he was thorough when it came to instructions. But I was going to find out what he really wanted from me—clearly it was something besides delivering his dough.

In ten minutes, we had loaded everything and everybody

into the 4Runner and the Florida Moving and Storage box of fun.

The Black Star folks had their own cleaning crew wheels up before we finished packing. The cops hadn't posted yet, so we would leave it to the cleaning crew to deal with the dead bodies and remove any prints, shell casings, or other items that might connect us with the assault.

We picked up Si from his house and headed west to the sugarcane fields. Stu had the pilots dialed in on his Iridium, and within five minutes we heard the blades cutting through the sky and assumed the PZ posture. At touchdown, Oliver, JP, and Jimmy loaded the two Russian passengers into the Bell 429, which left seconds later.

The second exfil was slightly trickier in that the heavy load going out with me and the rest of Team Rhino would require a much larger helicopter. The Black Star guys had a heavy-lift, modified Chinook available, but it would need to change crews and refuel somewhere in the Carolinas before it could get to us. We picked an alternate PZ north of Lake Okeechobee and waited there for our exfil.

Every one of us was thinking the same thing, but knew enough not to bring it up. We'd had a gunfight, with no friendly casualties. We'd killed some bad guys and captured two high-value targets. We'd changed the plan on the fly and had met no resistance from the boss. Our first package was en route to home base and the last moving piece of our puzzle was inbound in an hour. Achieving these markers defied staggering odds.

My only mission now was to bring Meg home safe and sound.

CHAPTER 92

Easton Airport

We landed at Easton Airport on Maryland's Eastern Shore. From there I would go on to the Marine Terminal in Dundalk, Maryland—the Port of Baltimore's largest cargo facility. The driving distance was sixty miles, but in a loaded, twenty-six-foot moving truck, it felt far longer.

Driving a box truck full of illegally gotten booty into a deserted container yard in the middle of the night posed serious risks. Yet, for Meg's sake, here I was.

Egorov was no amateur and had undoubtedly done this a time or two.

Did I trust him? Hell no.

Was I playing it straight? Almost.

Oliver's team was tracking me and would dutifully stay just far enough away for Egorov's comfort but close enough to assault if the deal went off the rails.

All the contact we'd had so far had been professional. No

needless chatter, just simple instructions as I passed each poorly lit checkpoint until I reached Egorov's chosen gate, which was indeed unlocked. The exchange location was a good one. The stacks of shipping containers provided very good cover and concealment from prying eyes—as well as from potential snipers in a hide site.

I cut the lights and maneuvered the truck to face the gate the way Egorov had specified.

As my eyes adjusted to the dark, I checked the chamber of my Sig and slipped it in my belt. Then I climbed from the cab, keys in the ignition as directed. If anyone got frisky, I'd readily put two hollow-points right between their running lights and another one in the chest to fuck up their hydraulics.

I heard the car rolling across the gravel before I saw the outline of the Lincoln, headlights off, circling the open area between the containers. The driver parked the car in the same direction as the truck. Smart enough. *Who wants to do a three-point turn during a gunfight?*

The rear passenger door opened and an older man stepped out. The pictures I had seen of the stout seventy-something didn't do him justice: Even in the dark, he had a presence that no doubt stopped people in their tracks.

Without taking his eyes off me, Egorov extended his hand inside the Town Car and helped Meg step out. My heart beat faster at the sight of her face. She was stunning. I had never recognized it before, but Meg Fuller was beautiful.

During the drive here, I had rehearsed my next movements in my mind a million times over. My hands felt good and loose, and I said a silent prayer that God would guide me to be faster than my opponents.

Meg looked at me and then at Egorov. He released her with a nod that seemed almost paternal, and she half-trotted the ten yards between us. I held my breath. If anything was going to go south, it would be in the next few seconds.

My eyes told her to stand behind me for cover. *Let's finish this thing.* I smiled when I heard her whisper, "Thank you, Nat."

"Mr. Phillips, may I?" Egorov showed me that his hands were empty, gesturing that he would like to move closer to me. Trusting soul. He knew I was carrying.

I shook my head. "That's close enough. Who else is in there with you?"

"My driver and my two sons. Pavel and Taras are here to drive the truck. They have no more business here. May they leave?"

The request didn't surprise me. I told him they were free to go—slowly, so I could watch them. After a few words from Egorov in Russian, out popped the two sons from the back of the car. I was sorry that I wouldn't get a chance to hurt the accomplices to Meg's kidnapping personally, but a deal was a deal.

Avoiding eye contact, the pair followed my instructions and climbed into the moving truck. Five seconds later, the truck started to roll forward on its way toward the unlocked gate.

"So why me, Egorov? What do you want?"

He glanced at my right hand ready for action, then slowly raised his hands to his waist as if asking for quiet before he spoke.

"Hear me out, please. I have a favor to ask, and I believe that you are the only one who can help me." The deliberate pattern of his speech indicated his sincerity.

"Why should I believe you?"

"Listen to him, Nat." Meg whispered from behind my right shoulder.

Okay—I'll listen to the bastard.

"What could I possibly do for you that you can't do yourself?" I asked Egorov.

"Protect my niece."

His what? Who?

"You're a fucking billionaire arms dealer. You deal with armies and revolutionaries, and—oh yeah—terrorist tough guys every single fucking day of your shady life. Get one of them to do it. Come on, man—this is bullshit."

I was aggravated, but I couldn't deny the guy was emitting an earnest vibe.

"I am dying, Mr. Phillips. There is no one I can trust."

Now he was royally pissing me off.

"He's telling the truth, Nat," Meg said quietly from behind me. "I'll fill you in when we get out of here. This is a big one, Natty."

Egorov was watching me closely.

"I see you understand the value of a brilliant woman. I feel the same way about my niece. Having her by my side all these years has brought me much success. She has a genius intellect, second to none, and she figured out something that she shouldn't have. Now she is in danger. That is it. I am asking that you listen to her. She helps you, and you help her stay safe."

"But why me?" I asked again, trying to buy time to process the absurdity of this entire fucking conversation. "You must have contacts we can't even dream of tapping into. What about your boy Joseph, your security chief?"

"Because you have an interest in this, Mr. Phillips. Believe me—you do."

Without taking his eyes off me, Egorov reached slowly inside his coat pocket and pulled out an envelope.

"Here is all the information I have about the man who orchestrated and controlled the events in your Nantucket. He is an Algerian named Haracat al Marrak. He is in Paris."

"What's that got to do with your niece?"

"Because while al Marrak believably plays an Arab terrorist, he is not one—he is an idiot. But *a useful idiot,* as I believe you Americans say. He is run by the Chinese, a fact that my niece figured out. They have people everywhere. That is all I know. The rest you will have to hear directly from her."

What the fuck?

"You don't trust me, and you probably want to kill me. This I understand and respect. But what I have told you is true. I will be dead within weeks—maybe a few months, if I am not killed first. That is why I need someone outside the apparatus, if you will, to protect my niece. I have accounts all over the world. If you help my niece, Joseph has been authorized to grant you access to a sizable amount for your troubles. I am as protective of my family as you clearly are of yours." He glanced at Meg, then back at me.

The bastard was right about that.

The sound of the gunshot was deafening. I recognized the flash at twelve o'clock, five meters, the thunderous sound of instant death. The blast came from Alexander Egorov's driver. Must have been at least a .45. A chunk of Egorov's neck and a piece of his jaw flew before my eyes as I watched his body collapse in a heap.

My Sig was out and squeezing rounds at the driver's window as the car—fucking bulletproof—lurched forward, fishtailing as it gained speed. I changed magazines.

"You okay, Meg?" I asked as I spun around.

I didn't see her at first. She was lying on the ground, her left arm pressing against her right shoulder. Her eyes were wide as silver dollars, and her lips were quivering from the shock of rapid blood loss.

Fuck—the bullet must have hit an artery.

I hit the push-to-talk button on my vest. "Oliver, Meg's down. Gunshot wound right shoulder. She's going into shock. Need a medevac!"

"I'm one minute away, boss."

"You're gonna be okay, Meg. Hang in there, baby—I've got you." I grabbed a bandanna from my pocket, balled it up, and pressed it to the wound.

I kept my eyes locked on hers as she looked up at me, struggling to stay conscious.

"Good news, Meg: It's through and through. Just hang tight. You're gonna be good. Quick ride on the Little Bird to get you patched up."

I spoke in a soothing tone even as my concerns mounted. Despite my battlefield first aid, she was losing a lot of blood.

When I heard the buzz of the Little Bird, I checked my watch. We were minutes from downtown Baltimore and a trauma center where Meg could be stabilized. The Golden Hour was on our side.

CHAPTER 93

Baltimore Washington International Airport

The driver of the Town Car eased onto the Baltimore Beltway, then headed south on I-97 toward BWI Airport. There he would board an American Airlines flight to Dallas, then connect through Customs with a perfect passport and clean credentials for the fifteen-hour flight to Seoul, South Korea. His last leg would be a Cathay Pacific flight to Hong Kong.

He would meet his contact at the airport and be taken directly to a safe house owned by the Commissioner's Office of China's Foreign Ministry in Hong Kong. There he would shower, change into fresh clothing, eat a large breakfast prepared by a private chef, then share everything he could remember about his last five years with Alexander Egorov, beginning with his assassination.

CHAPTER 94

Pavel Egorov rubbed his eyes and wished he had some coke. Now that they had collected the cash, he needed something to keep him going. The crash was coming fast and he was about to drop dead asleep. His brother, too. They had pulled into a deserted rest stop to wake themselves up.

"Another hour, man, and we are home free. In Philadelphia, we can sleep and chill till Papa comes. Have a smoke, it'll help," Taras said cheerfully, passing a lit Marlboro to his brother.

Pavel smiled and took the cigarette. The tobacco tasted good. He floated a blue smoke ring magically toward the windshield.

CHAPTER 95

The driver of the Town Car lit a cigarette and inhaled deeply as he drove down I-97 toward BWI.

He would miss American tobacco. *The price I pay,* he smiled to himself.

With his free hand, he withdrew a clamshell phone and dialed the number. The phone connected on the first ring. He punched in the five-digit code.

One-tenth of a second later, a fireball ignited from Natasha's medical kit in the cargo hold of the moving truck.

He couldn't see the Egorov brothers, but he was certain they'd been instantly incinerated, along with their millions of dollars' worth of cash and works of art.

Too bad.

CHAPTER 96

Rowan Anderson's apartment
Washington, DC

Rowan Anderson was drinking vodka and reviewing her kill list.

Elise Courville would be the easiest.

Anderson didn't know who this *Natasha* person was, but tough luck for her. It wasn't Anderson's problem that her boss believed Natasha was working for the KGB.

Killing the man in Paris would be a little more challenging, but she looked forward to making him die a painful death. After all the shit she had endured because of this asshole, payback would be a bitch.

The idea of killing Nathan Phillips was a different story. A mental tiger trap. She poured herself another vodka and looked out at the Georgetown night. *If I don't kill Nat Phillips, Ming Yu will snipe me at 1,000 yards or put a .22 bullet in my head or kill me some other shitty way.*

If she was to have any chance of surviving, she would have to kill Nat, then make her way to Dulles Airport and out of the country.

Killing Elise Courville would start the clock ticking fast.

Anderson intended to use Courville's Peugeot as the murder weapon. Maybe she could turn the French sports car into an Al-Qaeda–style VBIED. Every news agency would blame the militant organization first. Or she could plant an explosive, return the car to the French embassy, then detonate it remotely when Courville was behind the wheel.

That plan needed some work. The French press had made Anderson a hero for "rescuing" the ambassador's daughter, but the old man and every frog in Europe would ask why the Chief Security Liaison Officer for the Secret Service had failed to protect Elise Courville from a terrorist hit.

This Natasha would have to be a one-two punch, so to speak. Same day, within hours or even minutes. Anderson would make it quick—a bullet to the head or back or whatever target the Russian woman presented. Rowan knew the safe house where Natasha was hidden, and she knew its access codes. Hell, she could go over there and kill her right now.

That would leave a very small window in which to kill Nat Phillips. Not knowing his current location was especially problematic. He might still be in Florida. With any luck, she could make it look like she had tried but failed as the clock ran down.

Sirens of some distant DC police chase sounded an exclamation point.

Rowan Anderson drained the vodka, pleased with herself. She had her plan.

CHAPTER 97

R Adams Cowley Shock Trauma Center
Baltimore, Maryland

CSTC pilots Felix Green and Tommy Lopez had the Little Bird touching down on the roof at the R Adams Cowley Shock Trauma Center exactly eight minutes after they picked up the package.

Felix had called ahead to the hospital while Rudy worked on Meg inside the tiny space behind the pilots and Oliver and I rode the assaulter benches affixed to the port and starboard skids. Felix had given the dispatcher the patient's vitals, as well as the code that an unnamed government agency was making the delivery. The latter officially qualified the patient as a *Jane Doe*.

It was a through and through, I repeated to myself. *She's going to be fine. Just need to plug the holes and keep her calm.*

A five-person trauma team was waiting on the roof to rush Meg inside the building and into surgery.

I called Tristan. He'd been following the action from the SCIF in Easton and knew everything I knew—and then some.

"So they found the Egorov twins—what's left of them, anyway—at a rest stop in Aberdeen, Maryland. They are two crispy critters, and the truck was baked pretty good."

"It wasn't my money," I reflected, "so oh well. Bomb, maybe? Remote-detonated, of course. Could have been called in from Virginia—or from anywhere, really. But by who?"

"Not sure," Tristan said evenly. "Could be the Russian mob, could be the KGB—no idea."

"I've had no time to look at the information in that envelope Egorov handed me," I said. "But every one of these events has to be connected."

"Talk it through, Nat."

"All three Egorovs got stung on the same night, in two different places. Meg took one in the shoulder. Bad shooting or bad luck? I'm thinking bad shooting. The driver didn't anticipate me returning fire."

Tristan murmured encouragingly to keep me on track.

"For whatever reason, he had to kill Egorov—and the sons, too. Did he see Egorov pass me the envelope? If he figures out Meg is alive, he'll make another try at her. Suggest we get a protective detail up here ASAP."

"Roger that, Nat." Tristan being Tristan, he got to worrying about everybody else, starting with me. "You doing okay, buddy? Meg's going to be fine. Sam Starnes will be up soon to make sure the hospital plays nice."

"Okay, Tristan—cool. Oliver and I will take turns until they get here. I'm going to stick around 'til we get news on Meg."

CHAPTER 98

Anacostia, Washington, DC

The neighborhood around 14th Street referred to as *Little Kabul* was long forgotten by the city. Even in daylight, the best DC cops were never in a hurry to respond to calls about the drug dealers, winos, pimps, gangbangers, or other degenerates who roamed the streets at will.

It was a dangerous place to live. It was a perfect place for a safe house.

When Natasha arrived that morning, Yuri had complimented her on her efforts to help apprehend the enemy, Alexander Egorov.

While she waited to be recalled to Moscow for her next assignment, KGB agent Natasha took refuge in the ground-floor apartment. The bars over the windows provided security from a street-level break-in. The front door was made of reinforced steel, with a dead bolt and hinges that had been drilled into several inches of solid cement.

Egorov had used and abused his power and privilege to gain

unfathomable wealth. Many had suffered because of him. His corruption was witnessed at the highest levels of government; once enough evidence had been gathered against him, the security services would take action.

Several years ago, Yuri had explained that perhaps a nurse could be assigned to treat a mysterious ailment diagnosed by doctors—actually fellow agents—who would show Egorov phony X-rays to persuade him he had inoperable cancer.

Natasha was indeed a trained nurse, but the crippling symptoms of Alexander Egorov's "illness" were induced by the chemicals she administered as his daily "medicine." Stay close—*stay closer*—Yuri demanded, instructing her to feed him information about Egorov's business associates and travels while treating him—as well as sharing the arms dealer's bed. Through Natasha's sacrifice, she was told, she would uncover information beneficial to the state.

Natasha's thoughts were interrupted by the coded knock on the door. She looked at her watch. Yuri had said he would bring food and wine in celebration of her first successful operation. She tapped her response code—one-two-three-one-two, in rapid succession—on the inside of the door and waited for the confirmation.

The dead bolt slipped easily, but as she turned the doorknob the steel door slammed into her face, knocking her back several steps. Slightly dazed, she blinked her eyes to focus. Before she could, the first 9mm bullet entered her left eye and exited just behind her left ear. The second bullet hit her in the throat center mass, and the third turned her heart to Jell-O.

CHAPTER 99

The hit took less than five seconds.

Rowan Anderson walked back to the Peugeot with the diplomatic license plates and hoped that whoever was watching would remember the car more than its driver.

Anyone bothering to look at the driver would have seen only someone — could have been a man or a woman, no idea — in a black ball cap, a long black coat, and dark sunglasses, with a scarf covering most of the person's face.

Besides, on the off chance that some toothless crackhead did remember the car's make and model, or even its tag number, who the fuck were they going to tell anyway?

Anderson made her way back to I-295 and blended seamlessly into traffic. Someone would find Natasha at some point and call the cops. Maybe. It really didn't matter, since she would be long gone.

Twenty minutes later Rowan was southbound on the George Washington Memorial Parkway, passing Ronald Reagan National

Airport. She reached into her go bag for another burner phone to make a call.

"It's me. We've been summoned."

"When? Where?" Elise Courville asked, her voice trembling. "What does he want?"

"I got an encrypted message a little while ago. I'm out in your car, just driving. I don't know if he's here himself or if it's one of his goons, it just said to meet him tonight at nine somewhere over on Capitol Hill. He'll send the location when we get close.

"Listen, Elise—just relax. We haven't done anything wrong, and if that shithead tries to say we have, I'll kill him myself right there." Rowan said all this with the calm confidence she knew Courville needed to hear.

"But how can he be here? We said we weren't going to contact him—did you?"

"No Elise, I didn't contact him. Look, for all we know he just wants an update. Which we do have, and it's a good plan. Now don't get carried away—it'll be okay."

"If you say so. I was supposed to have dinner with my father. Should I just tell him that you and I are getting together for a drink?"

"Hmm—don't do that, Elise. My boss will fry my ass if we're seen doing social stuff outside normal work hours. We're too close. Tell your father we're going to see Nathan Phillips—that he wanted to check in and see how you and I were doing. Totally believable, and nobody's the wiser."

"What an odd suggestion. Why would you say that, Rowan?"

"I don't know. I've just been thinking about him lately, and it's plausible without being contrived—know what I mean?"

Anderson had been caught off guard by the pushback, but Courville would do as she was told. *Hopefully.* Anderson thought back to the moment at Courville's home, when she had momentarily feared that Elise really was going to pull the trigger of the Glock pointed at her head. *You never know with people when they get in power mode.* She had to hand it to Ming: He was the master when it came to deception and subterfuge.

"You like him, don't you?" Courville teased.

"Yeah—he's okay," Anderson said truthfully. "But right now, man, we need to get through the night and finish this soon. I'll pick you up around the corner at eight thirty." She hung up without giving Courville an opportunity to ask more questions.

Now it was Rowan Anderson's turn to be nervous: She had to make a date with Nat Phillips.

CHAPTER 100

Shock Trauma Center
Baltimore, Maryland

Meg was undergoing reconstructive shoulder surgery, and that would take some time.

Once a doctor stepped out of the OR with a positive progress report, I said an extra prayer of thanks and went back to examining the contents of Alexander Egorov's envelope.

I had studied some detailed target folders in the past. This information—starting with a brief biography of Haracat al Marrak, along with photos and strip maps of his Paris hideout—was pretty damn good. Certainly actionable.

Egorov had been the supplier for all the weapons and explosives used in the attacks on Nantucket. The boys had delivered everything, personally, by towing submersibles filled with the illicit goods below their yacht. If the Coast Guard—or anyone, for that matter—had decided to drop by for a look, the submersibles would have dived to the ocean floor until the coast was clear for recovery.

ROCKET'S RED GLARE

It was a just-about-foolproof plan. I was frustrated with myself that I hadn't considered options this ingenious.

The deliveries were wide-ranging: several explosive devices to a guy in Boston, and then some major hardware to a dead drop off the Nantucket coast.

Too bad Egorov went into the dirt before sharing more of his treasure chest of good information about a lot of bad people. Still, he had promised that his niece, whoever she was, would help us in return for our protection.

A lot of variables there, including the obvious one that any niece of Egorov's might well be as shady as her uncle. *But if we can get some love from her, who knows?* I made a mental note to dig in once Meg was awake.

We would have to send a recon team to Paris to get eyes on al Marrak quickly. Assuming the intelligence checked out, we would have to roll him up immediately and get the hell out of there.

Governments don't like dirty laundry, so kidnapping a foreign national in a sovereign nation would be sticky business on a good day, especially if the local intelligence agencies were likewise looking to nab him.

Getting in country, putting a hood over al Marrak's head, and stuffing him in the trunk of a car was not rocket science. The trick would be getting him out of Paris before anybody noticed. Some kind of jet under a fake company name would be ideal. If Black Star had some covered aircraft nearby, we could load him onto a civilian plane and head toward Africa. I knew we had some boats in the Red Sea we could use as a rendition site.

Planes, trains, and automobiles—the movies always make it

look so easy. But when you're hunting humans, they have a pretty loud say in where, when, and especially *if* they will get caught. The smart move was to get the target folder over to CSTC, where the others could start making a real plan.

My body had no idea what time it was. All I knew was that I was smoked—and so was Oliver. He started to snore, so I gave him a nudge and woke him from his catnap.

"Any word?" asked Oliver even before his eyes opened.

"Not yet, but no news is good news. Let's get some coffee, little fella." I stood and stretched while Oliver rubbed the sleep from his eyes. I may have been the senior guy, but Oliver was the one who held all of us together. He was a stud with the skill, knowledge, wisdom, and personality to push all of us across the goal line when we needed it.

A hardworking nurse at the station saw us lumbering toward her and read our minds.

"There is a river of coffee for you two down that hall to the right."

I thanked her and was almost run over by Si and Wolf as I turned the corner.

"Nat!" There was no mistaking how happy the team was to be back together.

"Holy shit, you guys made it here from the Eastern Shore?" I barked, doling out massive bear hugs all around.

"How's Meg doing?" they asked in unison.

It was good to pass on positive news for a change. "She's gonna be okay. They have to reconstruct her wing, but after some physical therapy, she'll be back with us, alive and kicking."

I saw their relief immediately. I also noticed how Wolf had

zeroed in on the pretty blond nurse at the desk and was about to work his magic.

"Easy there, Don Juan." I joked. "Don't get too comfortable—there's been a slight change of plans for the day."

Everyone looked at me quizzically.

I led the charge to the hospital canteen. We filled our coffee cups, then found a secluded table.

"So here's the deal. I'll give you the download from the shipping yard later, but basically before Egorov bit it, he gave me this target folder of the guy who masterminded the Harrison kidnapping and murder. He's an Algerian asshole named Haracat al Marrak. He is hanging out in Paris, and we are going to go fuck him up."

Everyone's head bobbed north and south. Even Si had a smile at the prospect of another mission. I explained that I wanted them to head back over the Chesapeake Bay Bridge and make a real plan—or at least one a little more sensible than the gibberish I'd conceived in my sleep-deprived brain.

"What about you?" Oliver chided me. "You need some rest, daddy-o."

"I want to be here when Meg wakes up. I'll meet you in Easton after that. *Capisce?*"

I walked everyone out to the lobby and was waving goodbye when my phone rang.

Rowan Anderson. What a nice surprise.

CHAPTER 101

Columbia, Maryland

The simple message—*Jane Doe, Shock Trauma, 2345, ICU*—was all the information he needed.

No reason to rush. He could be in downtown Baltimore in about forty-five minutes. His experience taught him to wait for the right moment, when guards and nurses were less inclined to wander and certainly less interested in examining his bona fides too closely.

"Dr. Curtis Lee, attending physician" had graduated from Johns Hopkins University School of Medicine but never practiced. Still, he had credentials for almost every major hospital from Philly to Richmond.

Medicine was his niche in the Ministry of State Security. Virtually anyone in the medical system—diplomats, politicians, entertainers, and especially enemies of the state—was his to observe.

Or, as in this case, exterminate.

Dr. Lee had been recruited as a young student in Beijing. He then began his cycle of intimidation among the thousands of Chinese medical students in the mid-Atlantic region.

All he had to do was mention the words *state security,* or offer someone the choice between keeping their badge or having immeasurable pain inflicted on a loved one, and he was in business. He had access to the world's best forgers and counterfeiters, any one of whom could deliver a brand-new access badge with his legitimate photo overnight.

Dr. Lee gathered his props for the drive to Baltimore, making certain that the small glass vial was securely packaged in its crushproof box. The toxic contents of the vial could stop the heart even through mere dermal contact. Once he had injected Jane Doe with the venom from the Inland Taipan—the world's deadliest snake—a cure would be impossible.

It would not take long for Dr. Lee to find his target.

CHAPTER 102

Washington, DC

"Nat, we've got to plan a long weekend together," Rowan Anderson said over the phone, sprinkling in some sexual undercurrent just to keep him dreamy. "There's an amazing place outside Charlottesville. It's got huge soaking tubs, and four-poster beds so big you have to climb into them."

"Oh, yeah? That sounds pretty great right about now, Rowan. I'd love to see you."

She believed him, carrying on the heavy flirting that would help her gauge whether he was in love, or at least in lust, maybe even just crushing on her.

Despite Anderson's many debriefings, the CSTC business remained a mystery to her. It was also clearly one that had spooked Ming Yu enough that he wanted Nat dead.

"How about a late-night cocktail—tonight? We can get bombed and watch the sunrise."

"I am so sorry, Rowan, but I can't. I'm in the middle of something, and then I might have to head out of town again. Won't know 'til later."

Rowan detected a little pain in his voice as he sighed.

"I hope you're okay, Nat," she said truthfully. "You sound beat."

Nat was enough of a pro that he definitely wasn't sharing his current whereabouts, nor the status of his trip south, but she decided to lob a long shot. Any information he provided might help her box his location.

Then Rowan Anderson got the break she'd been waiting for: the sound of a hospital loudspeaker blaring. The message—something about a delay in the shuttle to the parking garage—was beside the point. Now that she knew Nat was at a hospital, maybe she could persuade him to tell her which one. Even better if she could discover why he was there.

"Are you in the hospital, Nat? Buddy, what's going on? I'm worried about you. Where the hell are you?" Rowan said rapid-fire, giving it as much fake concern as she could muster.

"Yeah, I'm at Shock Trauma in Baltimore. We were in a little scrape last night, and Meg got banged up."

"I'm sorry, Nat. Is Meg okay?" Anderson's luck was improving by the minute.

She could take care of Elise Courville in DC, drive straight to Baltimore, hit Nat, then fly out of BWI.

"Hoping so. I'm hanging out while she's in surgery."

"Oh, Nat. I am so sorry for you and Meg. I know how much she means to you. I'd love to come see you for a bit. Even for a cup of coffee."

Anderson hoped the emotional tapestry she was weaving was enough to ensnare Nat.

"That would be great. Hate to take you out of your way, but some company would be awesome."

"Can't wait, Nat—see you tonight. I'll take good care of you, I promise."

★ ★ ★

Circumstances now dictated that Rowan Anderson send an SOS to Ming Yu. She parked Elise Courville's car on a side street in DC and, following the emergency protocol, sent Ming an encrypted message.

The reply was simple: 3D, SHOCK TRAUMA GARAGE, SE CORNER, BLACK CAMRY, PHILLIPS, 2400, E&E.

Those were her orders: *Kill Phillips in the garage. At midnight, escape and evade in the black Camry.*

CHAPTER 103

Amtrak Maintenance Facility, Washington, DC

The massive Amtrak Maintenance Facility loomed from across Route 50, marked by the WELCOME sign.

Elise Courville had swallowed Rowan Anderson's explanation for their trip to the train yard—that the man in Paris "wants us to tell his guy how we're going to do it. That's all."

The train yard, Anderson explained, was the safest place for them to meet because it ran 24/7. Someone was always nearby, she said—leaving out the detail that the Brentwood neighborhood, where gunfire was a part of daily life, was perennially named DC's most dangerous.

The rail yard provided perfect cover for Anderson's lethal intent, though navigating their way through the extensive construction on the facility's north side proved difficult.

They crept along until the Peugeot found the gate in the chain-link fence surrounding the construction site.

Anderson was in hunter mode, her killing senses on high

alert. This was a perfect spot to end the life of Elise Courville—ambassador's daughter, senator's wife, terrorist co-conspirator.

If Anderson felt any emotion about what she was going to do, she didn't show it. Somehow she had always managed to talk Courville down from the ledge of her perpetual anxiety. She would lend the frightened woman her welcome strength and support this one final time.

"The message said the gate would be unlocked—just pull on the padlock and it'll open. We can drive in and he'll come to us. Would you get the gate, Elise?"

"They always want to meet in the nastiest places," Courville half joked as she got out of the car.

Anderson kept her eyes on the woman as she screwed the suppressor onto her pistol. When the other woman tugged on the lock with no success, she mouthed, *It's locked.* Then, true to form, Elise Courville turned to Rowan Anderson for guidance.

Anderson opened her window and told her to try again.

Courville tugged on the padlock a few more times, then shook her head in frustration.

"Come here and let me see if I can call him," Anderson said, holding up her cell phone in her left hand.

Courville trudged over to the driver's side and put her hands on the roof of the Peugeot, leaning toward Anderson's open window.

Anderson looked up and noticed that her target was scanning the rail yard for potential threats. "You're learning," Anderson told her protégée. "But it's a little too late for that."

Rowan Anderson squeezed three rounds into Elise Courville's chest, then put the car in Reverse and backed up a few feet, turning the wheel to the left to avoid running over the dead woman.

She leaned over to the passenger side and lifted Courville's Birkin bag from the floorboard. Being the kind of person who might fly to Monte Carlo on a whim, Rowan knew, Courville carried her passport everywhere she went.

Anderson used a handkerchief to open the bag and pull out the passport. Then she opened the door of the Peugeot and walked over to the body. Elise Courville's lifeless eyes stared into the darkness, and the bullets had made a mess of her chest. Gingerly, Anderson lifted the lapel of her coat and slid the passport into an interior pocket, making it a simple matter for the DC cops to determine the identity of the deceased.

Careful to avoid any blood, Anderson swept her foot side to side so as to erase her footprints. They might get one, and they might even identify her as its owner. But by then she would be living under non-extradition status in Morocco.

Rowan checked her watch. A particular sequence of events now needed to happen in order for her to make her escape. First, someone must find Elise Courville's corpse. Second, they'd have to find Nat's body and the gun, too.

She practiced her breathing during the hour-long drive north on the Capital Beltway and eventually I-95. *It was just work,* she told herself.

The bad music on the radio bothered her more than what she had just done to Elise Courville, a woman with whom she had laughed and cried on several occasions. Yet she had killed her without blinking an eye.

But Nat Phillips? Totally different. The connection Rowan Anderson felt to him was primal...instinctive...unfamiliar yet hypnotic. And now she was about to destroy perhaps the only bit of goodness she had ever experienced in her life.

CHAPTER 104

Hospital parking garage
Baltimore, Maryland

Just as Ming Yu's message had specified, Rowan Anderson found the black Camry on the third level of the hospital parking garage in an unlit parking spot that even the best infrared camera could not easily watch.

It was part of her strategy for Elise Courville's Peugeot to be recorded entering the garage. Her own identity was easily concealed beneath the same black hat, scarf, and coat she'd worn at her job in Anacostia earlier.

The conditions were perfect. All she had to do was wait until midnight.

Anderson called Nat and put on her best needy voice. "Hey, Nat, it's me. I'm here. Can you come over and walk with me? It's really fucking sketchy and there are some weirdos in this garage."

"On my way," Nat replied. "Sit tight in the car 'til I get there."

CHAPTER 105

ICU
Baltimore, Maryland

I was in a good mood.

The surgeon had emerged from the OR with a glowing report of complete success. Not only had the shoulder reconstruction been virtually flawless, but Meg's vitals were the strongest the surgeon had ever seen post-op. Between her physical conditioning and positive attitude, he was extremely optimistic that Meg would be back in action in six to ten weeks. She could call these next two months a vacation and never miss a beat.

They let me watch her sleeping peacefully for a few minutes. She was heavily sedated, of course, and they would keep her under for another day of rest. I couldn't wait until tomorrow, when they brought her out of it.

As beaten up as she was, Meg always had my back and supported me even when she may have disagreed. She made me laugh. She knew how to push my buttons when I needed them pushed.

Rowan's call brought me back to the present. I was looking forward to seeing her. Rowan was awesome. I could totally see a long game with her. Maybe after the trip to Paris, we could go away together and see what happened. For now, it would be great just to spend a few hours together. It was a good day—and about to get better.

I waited 'til I was outside the hospital to check my Sig P225. I had two magazines on my belt plus the one in the well. I unbuttoned my jacket for an easier draw if I needed it. So far, I hadn't seen a single person on the ground floor as I waited for the elevator.

I hit the button and headed to the third floor. There wasn't a soul around—not that I minded. When Rowan said she needed a chaperone, it had put me in a good mood. She could easily have walked over by herself. I knew she knew how to handle a gun. Rocket's Red Glare didn't quite give me carte blanche to go around town whacking bad guys, but it also didn't tell me not to.

It was pretty dark, but I could see Rowan looking for something in the trunk of her car—leaning over in a very seductive way, though that might've just been my own wishful thinking. She must have heard me, as she turned away from the car without closing the trunk. Not quite like the reunited-love scenes in movies, but we did walk a little faster toward each other as we went in for a hug.

Her ball cap fell off as I wrapped my arms around her and lifted her off the ground. I felt her hair against my face. She laughed and our lips connected. We got lost in each other for a few seconds. I was exactly where I needed to be.

"Man, I needed that," I laughed. "Thanks for coming, Ro. You look amazing." She held on for an extra beat.

"Well, it takes two to tango, mister." She laughed back at me, composing herself. "Let me grab my purse and we can get out of this dump."

She walked back to the trunk of her car and grabbed her bag. She slung it over her shoulder. She was so beautiful. It reminded me of the first time I had seen her at my house.

"Nice wheels," I said.

"Elise let me borrow it for the night."

"Well, thank her for me." I turned away from her instinctively to make sure no one had followed me. The third floor still looked deserted. "How is the widow Courville, anyway?" I laughed over my shoulder, waiting for Rowan to catch up to me.

Silence.

"She's dead, Nat."

Dead? Did I hear that right?

I started to turn toward Rowan when that familiar report registered in my mind. It felt like someone had hit me with a baseball bat just above my belt on my left hip. The fire spread immediately through my body. The second round hit me exactly where Meg had been shot. I spun around involuntarily as I fell to the ground. The pain was excruciating. I could feel the warm blood soaking my shirt. I kept blinking my eyes, trying to focus. I tried to crawl but my legs would not respond.

Where was Rowan? Why wasn't she helping me?

She was standing there watching me.

There was no white light, no chapters of my life unspooling at warp speed. There was pain and there was anger. I was helpless, lying on the floor of a shitty parking garage in fucking Baltimore bleeding out because the woman I'd thought I could make a long game with had killed me.

CHAPTER 106

Shock Trauma

It was as easy this time as it had been before. Dr. Curtis Lee arrived wearing his lab coat over his scrubs. He had a large Starbucks coffee cup in his hand and his trusty stethoscope draped around his neck. He entered through the emergency-room doors and nodded at one of the night security guards. He moved confidently down the corridor, following the signs for the elevator. He checked the directory and found the floor he needed.

Predictably, the foot traffic in the ICU was almost nonexistent. He shuffled from the elevator to the nurses' station and gave his well-rehearsed speech: "I'm an embarrassed and very tired doctor whose late wife will haunt me from the afterlife if I don't find that damn pen."

Sympathy always wins. The nurse even offered to help him with his scavenger hunt.

Maybe it was with the Jane Doe GSW? Which room, please?

He nodded and carried his coffee down the hall to Jane Doe's private room.

The lights were dim and the patient was heavily sedated. *Such a pretty girl,* he mused. Dr. Lee didn't know what she had done to necessitate a visit from him. But then, he never did.

He put the Starbucks cup on the bedside table and pulled a pair of gloves from his pocket. He pried the plastic lid off the cup and reached in to retrieve his syringe and glass vial. Then he expertly inserted the needle through the rubber seal and drew 10ccs of the toxin into the syringe.

With a gentle touch, he pulled back the covers to expose the woman's left arm. The IV was already working, so all he needed to do was insert the needle into the extension of the tube; gravity would do the rest. She stirred gently as the contents of the syringe flowed into the solution. He deposited the syringe in the hazardous materials tamper-proof box, placed the vial back in his cup along with the latex gloves, and left Jane Doe to die.

As he passed the nurses' station, Dr. Lee gleefully pulled the pen from his pocket and triumphantly waved it at the kind nurse.

"It wasn't in Jane Doe's room—it was in the one across the hall," he said, thanking her and waving good night.

The elevator closed and started its descent. He was one floor down when he heard the faint sound of the Code Blue alarm blasting through the ICU. By the time Dr. Curtis Lee said good night to the ER security guard, Megan Marie Fuller had been pronounced dead.

CHAPTER 107

CSTC Headquarters, Maryland

It was a miracle I was still alive.

I was going to be sidelined for a good while, but the doctors were encouraged by my initial recovery. I was on track to be exercising in four weeks, maybe even running in six.

Rowan Anderson was the traitor. She was the spy alluded to at the briefing in North Carolina. The only survivor from Senator Coleman Harrison's protective detail. How could we all have been so stupid?

She was responsible for Meg's death. And she had almost pinned Elise Courville's murder on me, until Sam Starnes put an end to that investigation.

We were all in agreement: The first order of business was to get Haracat al Marrak out of Paris. After that I would make sure Rowan Anderson died a heinous death.

Meg's death shattered me. I felt responsible for failing her. I'd left her vulnerable to attack. I'd promised to protect her. I hadn't, and now she was dead.

As I grieved, my rage would ebb and flow. One moment I'd be melancholy, on the verge of a meltdown, the next almost giddy in the fantasy of putting a bullet through Rowan Anderson's temple. She was no longer a person to me, just a target for my hatred.

We all have those *Where were you when?* moments in life, like the Kennedy assassinations or 9/11. Tristan and I were sitting on his back porch sipping twenty-three-year-old Pappy and telling stories about Meg when one of those moments stopped me in my tracks.

Unknown Caller rang through on my work phone.

"Phillips."

There was a pause on the other end, then a voice saying, "I'm so sorry."

I felt the tears welling up, colliding with the furious sound of my heart throbbing.

For a good ten seconds, I willed the image of Meg lying in her casket to disappear. It wouldn't go away.

Tristan looked at me, perplexed, and mouthed, *What gives?*

"You're an evil fucking person, Rowan Anderson," I said in the most measured voice I could muster, "and I will kill you very soon."

"Nat, I am so sorry. You don't understand. They made me do it. You must believe me," she begged.

"Who, Rowan? Who the fuck made you shoot me and kill Meg?" I felt my emotional temperature rising sky fucking high.

"Meg?" she questioned. "I didn't kill Meg—I swear. I had to

make them think I tried to kill you, but I purposely let you live." There was panic in her voice. "I swear to you, Nat."

"You're lying and I am going to kill you," I said, my voice rising with every syllable of the threat before I hung up.

Tristan figured it out pretty quickly and just nodded as I tried to breathe. He opened the bottle and poured three fingers into my glass. It was a nice burn as the bourbon hit the back of my throat.

The phone rang again. *Unknown Caller.*

The fucking nerve.

"Don't ever fucking call me again."

"Mr. Phillips?"

A woman's voice. But not Rowan Anderson's. The voice sounded authoritative. Senator Tabitha Doyle, maybe? I went into recovery mode.

"I am so sorry, ma'am," I said humbly into the receiver. "I thought it was somebody else calling. Who is this, please?"

"Mr. Phillips, my name is Theresa Larson. I believe my uncle Alexander told you I would be in touch. We have much to discuss."

ABOUT THE AUTHORS

James Patterson is one of the best-known and biggest-selling writers of all time. Among his creations are some of the world's most popular series, including Alex Cross, the Women's Murder Club, Michael Bennett and the Private novels. He has written many other number one bestsellers including collaborations with President Bill Clinton, Dolly Parton and Michael Crichton, stand-alone thrillers and non-fiction. James has donated millions in grants to independent bookshops and has been the most borrowed adult author in UK libraries for the past fourteen years in a row. He lives in Florida with his family.

Matt Eversmann retired from the United States Army after twenty years of service. *Rocket's Red Glare* is his first novel with James Patterson. They've written several nonfiction books together, including the No. 1 *New York Times* bestseller *Walk in My Combat Boots*.

Also By James Patterson

ALEX CROSS NOVELS

Along Came a Spider • Kiss the Girls • Jack and Jill • Cat and Mouse • Pop Goes the Weasel • Roses are Red • Violets are Blue • Four Blind Mice • The Big Bad Wolf • London Bridges • Mary, Mary • Cross • Double Cross • Cross Country • Alex Cross's Trial (with Richard DiLallo) • I, Alex Cross • Cross Fire • Kill Alex Cross • Merry Christmas, Alex Cross • Alex Cross, Run • Cross My Heart • Hope to Die • Cross Justice • Cross the Line • The People vs. Alex Cross • Target: Alex Cross • Criss Cross • Deadly Cross • Fear No Evil • Triple Cross • Alex Cross Must Die • The House of Cross • Return of the Spider

THE WOMEN'S MURDER CLUB SERIES

1st to Die (with Andrew Gross) • 2nd Chance (with Andrew Gross) • 3rd Degree (with Andrew Gross) • 4th of July (with Maxine Paetro) • The 5th Horseman (with Maxine Paetro) • The 6th Target (with Maxine Paetro) • 7th Heaven (with Maxine Paetro) • 8th Confession (with Maxine Paetro) • 9th Judgement (with Maxine Paetro) • 10th Anniversary (with Maxine Paetro) • 11th Hour (with Maxine Paetro) • 12th of Never (with Maxine Paetro) • Unlucky 13 (with Maxine Paetro) • 14th Deadly Sin (with Maxine Paetro) • 15th Affair (with Maxine Paetro) • 16th Seduction (with Maxine Paetro) • 17th Suspect (with Maxine Paetro) • 18th Abduction (with Maxine Paetro) • 19th Christmas (with Maxine Paetro) • 20th Victim (with Maxine Paetro) • 21st Birthday (with Maxine Paetro) • 22 Seconds (with Maxine Paetro) • 23rd Midnight (with Maxine Paetro) • The 24th Hour (with Maxine Paetro) • 25 Alive (with Maxine Paetro)

DETECTIVE MICHAEL BENNETT SERIES

Step on a Crack (with Michael Ledwidge) • Run for Your Life (with Michael Ledwidge) • Worst Case (with Michael Ledwidge) • Tick Tock (with Michael Ledwidge) • I, Michael Bennett (with Michael Ledwidge) • Gone (with Michael Ledwidge) • Burn (with Michael Ledwidge) • Alert (with Michael Ledwidge) • Bullseye (with Michael Ledwidge) • Haunted (with James O. Born) • Ambush (with James O. Born) • Blindside (with James O. Born) • The Russian (with James O. Born) • Shattered (with James O. Born) • Obsessed (with James O. Born) • Crosshairs (with James O. Born) • Paranoia (with James O. Born)

PRIVATE NOVELS

Private (*with Maxine Paetro*) • Private London (*with Mark Pearson*) • Private Games (*with Mark Sullivan*) • Private: No. 1 Suspect (*with Maxine Paetro*) • Private Berlin (*with Mark Sullivan*) • Private Down Under (*with Michael White*) • Private L.A. (*with Mark Sullivan*) • Private India (*with Ashwin Sanghi*) • Private Vegas (*with Maxine Paetro*) • Private Sydney (*with Kathryn Fox*) • Private Paris (*with Mark Sullivan*) • The Games (*with Mark Sullivan*) • Private Delhi (*with Ashwin Sanghi*) • Private Princess (*with Rees Jones*) • Private Moscow (*with Adam Hamdy*) • Private Rogue (*with Adam Hamdy*) • Private Beijing (*with Adam Hamdy*) • Private Rome (*with Adam Hamdy*) • Private Monaco (*with Adam Hamdy*) • Private Dublin (*with Adam Hamdy*)

NYPD RED SERIES

NYPD Red (*with Marshall Karp*) • NYPD Red 2 (*with Marshall Karp*) • NYPD Red 3 (*with Marshall Karp*) • NYPD Red 4 (*with Marshall Karp*) • NYPD Red 5 (*with Marshall Karp*) • NYPD Red 6 (*with Marshall Karp*)

DETECTIVE HARRIET BLUE SERIES

Never Never (*with Candice Fox*) • Fifty Fifty (*with Candice Fox*) • Liar Liar (*with Candice Fox*) • Hush Hush (*with Candice Fox*)

INSTINCT SERIES

Instinct (*with Howard Roughan, previously published as* Murder Games) • Killer Instinct (*with Howard Roughan*) • Steal (*with Howard Roughan*)

THE BLACK BOOK SERIES

The Black Book (*with David Ellis*) • The Red Book (*with David Ellis*) • Escape (*with David Ellis*)

TEXAS RANGER SERIES

Texas Ranger (*with Andrew Bourelle*) • Texas Outlaw (*with Andrew Bourelle*) • The Texas Murders (*with Andrew Bourelle*)

STAND-ALONE THRILLERS

The Thomas Berryman Number • Hide and Seek • Black Market • The Midnight Club • Honeymoon (*with Howard Roughan*) • Sail (*with Howard

Roughan) • Swimsuit (*with Maxine Paetro*) • Don't Blink (*with Howard Roughan*) • Postcard Killers (*with Liza Marklund*) • Toys (*with Neil McMahon*) • Now You See Her (*with Michael Ledwidge*) • Kill Me If You Can (*with Marshall Karp*) • Guilty Wives (*with David Ellis*) • Zoo (*with Michael Ledwidge*) • Second Honeymoon (*with Howard Roughan*) • Mistress (*with David Ellis*) • Invisible (*with David Ellis*) • Truth or Die (*with Howard Roughan*) • Murder House (*with David Ellis*) • The Store (*with Richard DiLallo*) • The President is Missing (*with Bill Clinton*) • Revenge (*with Andrew Holmes*) • Juror No. 3 (*with Nancy Allen*) • The First Lady (*with Brendan DuBois*) • The Chef (*with Max DiLallo*) • Out of Sight (*with Brendan DuBois*) • Unsolved (*with David Ellis*) • The Inn (*with Candice Fox*) • Lost (*with James O. Born*) • The Summer House (*with Brendan DuBois*) • 1st Case (*with Chris Tebbetts*) • Cajun Justice (*with Tucker Axum*)• The Midwife Murders (*with Richard DiLallo*) • The Coast-to-Coast Murders (*with J.D. Barker*) • Three Women Disappear (*with Shan Serafin*) • The President's Daughter (*with Bill Clinton*) • The Shadow (*with Brian Sitts*) • The Noise (*with J.D. Barker*) • 2 Sisters Detective Agency (*with Candice Fox*) • Jailhouse Lawyer (*with Nancy Allen*) • The Horsewoman (*with Mike Lupica*) • Run Rose Run (*with Dolly Parton*) • Death of the Black Widow (*with J.D. Barker*) • The Ninth Month (*with Richard DiLallo*) • The Girl in the Castle (*with Emily Raymond*) • Blowback (*with Brendan DuBois*) • The Twelve Topsy-Turvy, Very Messy Days of Christmas (*with Tad Safran*) • The Perfect Assassin (*with Brian Sitts*) • House of Wolves (*with Mike Lupica*) • Countdown (*with Brendan DuBois*) • Cross Down (*with Brendan DuBois*) • Circle of Death (*with Brian Sitts*) • Lion & Lamb (with *Duane Swierczynski*) • 12 Months to Live (*with Mike Lupica*) • Holmes, Margaret and Poe (*with Brian Sitts*) • The No. 1 Lawyer (*with Nancy Allen*) • Eruption (*with Michael Crichton*) • The Murder Inn (*with Candice Fox*) • Confessions of the Dead (*with J.D. Barker*) • 8 Months Left (*with Mike Lupica*) • Lies He Told Me (*with David Ellis*) • Murder Island (*with Brian Sitts*) • Raised By Wolves (*with Emily Raymond*) • Holmes is Missing (*with Brian Sitts*) • 2 Sisters Murder Investigations (*with Candice Fox*) • The Imperfect Murder (*with J.D. Barker*) • The First Gentleman (*with Bill Clinton*) • Emma on Fire (*with Emily Raymond*) • Never Say Die (*with Mike Lupica*) • The President's Shadow (*with Richard DiLallo*) • The Picasso Heist (*with Howard Roughan*) • Billion-Dollar Ransom (*with Duane Swierczynski*) • The Invisible Woman (*with Susan DiLallo*)

NON-FICTION

Torn Apart (*with Hal and Cory Friedman*) • The Murder of King Tut (*with Martin Dugard*) • All-American Murder (*with Alex Abramovich and*

Mike Harvkey) • The Kennedy Curse (*with Cynthia Fagen*) • The Last Days of John Lennon (*with Casey Sherman and Dave Wedge*) • Walk in My Combat Boots (*with Matt Eversmann and Chris Mooney*) • ER Nurses (*with Matt Eversmann*) • James Patterson by James Patterson: The Stories of My Life • Diana, William and Harry (*with Chris Mooney*) • American Cops (*with Matt Eversmann*) • What Really Happens in Vegas (*with Mark Seal*) • The Secret Lives of Booksellers and Librarians (*with Matt Eversmann*) • Tiger, Tiger • American Heroes (*with Matt Eversmann*) • The #1 Dad Book • The Last Days of Marilyn Monroe (*with Imogen Edwards-Jones*) • The Idaho Murders (*with Vicky Ward*) • Disrupt Everything (*with Patrick Leddin, PhD*)

MURDER IS FOREVER TRUE CRIME

Murder, Interrupted (*with Alex Abramovich and Christopher Charles*) • Home Sweet Murder (*with Andrew Bourelle and Scott Slaven*) • Murder Beyond the Grave (*with Andrew Bourelle and Christopher Charles*) • Murder Thy Neighbour (*with Andrew Bourelle and Max DiLallo*) • Murder of Innocence (*with Max DiLallo and Andrew Bourelle*) • Till Murder Do Us Part (*with Andrew Bourelle and Max DiLallo*)

COLLECTIONS

Triple Threat (*with Max DiLallo and Andrew Bourelle*) • Kill or Be Killed (*with Maxine Paetro, Rees Jones, Shan Serafin and Emily Raymond*) • The Moores are Missing (*with Loren D. Estleman, Sam Hawken and Ed Chatterton*) • The Family Lawyer (*with Robert Rotstein, Christopher Charles and Rachel Howzell Hall*) • Murder in Paradise (*with Doug Allyn, Connor Hyde and Duane Swierczynski*) • The House Next Door (*with Susan DiLallo, Max DiLallo and Brendan DuBois*) • 13-Minute Murder (*with Shan Serafin, Christopher Farnsworth and Scott Slaven*) • The River Murders (*with James O. Born*) • The Palm Beach Murders (*with James O. Born, Duane Swierczynski and Tim Arnold*) • Paris Detective • 3 Days to Live • 23 ½ Lies (*with Maxine Paetro*)

For more information about James Patterson's novels,
visit www.penguin.co.uk.